KING OF THE SHADOW FAE

AMELIA HUTCHINS

Authored By: Amelia Hutchins

Cover Art Design: The Book Brander

Copy edited by: Melissa Burg

Edited by: Melissa Burg

Published by: Amelia Hutchins

Published in (United States of America)

10 9 8 7 6 5 4 3 2 1

Warning

This book is dark. It's sexy, hot, and intense. The author is human, just as you are. Is the book perfect? It's as perfect as I could make it. Are there mistakes? Probably, then again, even New York Times top published books have minimal mistakes because, like me, they have human editors. There are words in this book that are not in the standard dictionary because they were created to set the stage for a paranormal-urban fantasy world. Words in this novel are common in paranormal books and give better descriptions to the action in the story than other words found in standard dictionaries. They are intentional and not mistakes.

About the hero: chances are you may not fall instantly in love with him, that's because I don't write men you instantly love; you grow to love them. I don't believe in instant love. I write flawed, raw, caveman-like assholes that eventually let you see their redeeming qualities. They are aggressive assholes, one step above a caveman when we meet them. You may *not* even like him by the time you finish this book, but I promise you will love him by the end of this series.

About the heroine: There is a chance you might think she's a bit naïve or weak, but then again, who starts out as a badass? Badass women are a product of growth, and I am going to put her through hell, and you get to watch her come up swinging every time I knock her on her ass. That's just how I do things. How she reacts to the set of circumstances she is put through may not be how you as the reader, or I, as the author would react to that same situation. Everyone reacts differently to circumstances and how she responds to her challenges is how I see her as a character and as a person.

I don't write love stories: I write fast-paced, knock you on your ass, *make you sit on the edge of your seat wondering what is going to happen next* in the books. If you're looking for cookie-cutter romance, this isn't for you. If you can't handle the ride, *unbuckle your seatbelt and get out of the roller-coaster car now*. If not, you've been warned. If nothing outlined above bothers you, carry on and enjoy the ride!

FYI, this is not a romance novel. They're going to kick the shit out of each other, and if they end up together, well, that's their choice. If you are going into this blind, and you complain about abuse between two creatures that are NOT human, well, that's on you. I have done my job and given a warning.

Dedication

To the ones who didn't make it home this year. To the dreamer's that dream, but never take the leap. Trust the process, and go for it. To the stars that are trying to burn too brightly for everyone else, you're going to burn out if you don't do things for yourself. Stop being the savior, and learn to be your own hero. To you, that exhausted soul just trying to wake up and paste on a smile. Stop pretending everything is okay. It's alright to not be okay. So get off the floor, put down the vodka, and let your shine show, sparkle with your self-worth. You're loved and needed. Life sucks, but in the darkest hour and the weakest moment, those stars will shine for you. And, of course, to my haters: Hi! I see you, but you should set the book down and go. I got too much to do, and there are no fucks falling from the sky for free for me to hand out today. But maybe I'll find one if I even care to look around. If you spent half the effort you put into hating me on something positive, you'd probably be happier. And because I am that bitch, I hope you find it, but like, elsewhere.

Books by Amelia Hutchins along with reading order for series

LEGACY OF THE NINE REALMS

Flames of Chaos

Ashes of Chaos

Ruins of Chaos

Coming Soon

Crown of Chaos

Queen of Chaos

King of Chaos

Reign of Chaos

THE FAE CHRONICLES

Fighting Destiny

Taunting Destiny

Escaping Destiny

Seducing Destiny

Unraveling Destiny

Embracing Destiny

Crowning Destiny

Finished Series

THE ELITE GUARDS

A Demon's Dark Embrace

Claiming the Dragon King

The Winter Court

A Demon's Plaything

A GUARDIAN'S DIARY

Darkest Before Dawn

Death before Dawn

Midnight Rising -TBA

MONSTERS SERIES

Playing with Monsters

Sleeping with Monsters

Becoming his Monster

Revealing the Monster

Finished Series

WICKED KNIGHTS

Oh, Holy Knight

If She's Wicked

Book Three -TBA

If you're following the series for the Fae Chronicles, Elite Guards, and Monsters, reading order is as follows.

Fighting Destiny

Taunting Destiny

Escaping Destiny

Seducing Destiny

A Demon's Dark Embrace

Playing with Monsters

Unraveling Destiny

Sleeping with Monsters

Claiming the Dragon King

Oh, Holy Knight

Becoming his Monster

A Demon's Plaything

The Winter Court

If She's Wicked

Embracing Destiny

Crowning Destiny

Revealing the Monster

KING OF THE SHADOW FAE

AMELIA HUTCHINS

Chapter One

Sundays were meant for religion, families, and relaxing. Yet, here I was, on my day off, hunting a werewolf. Few women could brag that they tracked and hunted otherworld creatures or that they'd been raised with beings that belonged in fables and fairytales. I was one of the select few who earned the title of hunter. Well, huntress if you wanted to get technical.

Peering through the forest, I scanned for any signs that the werewolf had come through this section. Crumpled bushes and twigs were usually easy to spot, but this werewolf was clumsy. It didn't bother to cover its tracks, allowing me to follow the blood trail that had started in Montana. It wasn't hiding the carnage or corpses left in its wake. I was more than likely dealing with a newly bitten wolf, one abandoned by the alpha that had created it. Sad as it was, more often than not, they had to be put down.

Their first change brought on an endless hunger, and without an alpha to teach them how to stave off that need to feed, they did so gluttonously. This one, in particular, had eaten its way through a herd of cattle, five horses, and a rancher's family. This turn of events forced us to intervene, ending its life before it was featured on the front page of the town newspaper.

Stopping by a brook, I kneeled, cupping water in my hands and drinking it before splashing it on my face and wetting my hair to cool off. The spring sun was sweltering today, making my task bothersome. Refilling my empty canteen, I hooked it onto my backpack and withdrew my compass. Checking my location, I quickly marked it on my GPS, then stood, readying myself to go deeper into the woods.

A branch snapped behind me, forcing my attention toward the noise. The hair on my nape rose, and my senses heightened, knowing that I wasn't alone in the forest. Stepping into the brook, I stifled a groan as my new boots filled with water. Then, ignoring the icy nip of the snow runoff, I moved in a tight circle, pausing as a blur of motion caught my focus.

I didn't have time to think or react as the beast collided with me. The air left my lungs in a whoosh, sending pain radiating throughout me. Lifting my hands, I pushed against a set of broad shoulders as sharp, elongated teeth snapped inches from my face.

"Bad dog," I growled as my feet lifted against its chest, forcing the wolf up and shoving it away as I rolled, producing a blade seconds before it slammed into my body again. "Shit, you're heavy!" I groaned, wincing against the red-hot pain pulsing through me.

Huge, razor-sharp nails protruded from its fingers, slicing through my side. A burning sensation began where the poisonous claws had cut across my flesh. I thrust forward, and my blade found purchase in the wolf's abdomen, and it howled in agony as I crawled backward on my hands and knees, putting distance between us.

The beast's mutated face was grotesque, half human and half wolf. Unfortunately for the werewolf, the full moon was a week away, which prevented it from fully shifting. The creature screamed, then stood, vanishing into the thick brush on the other side of the brook.

"Freaking pussy," I muttered, standing up to look down at my wound that was already oozing. My phone started buzzing, and I reached into my back pocket, silencing it before trekking after my prey.

Only a few feet into the woods, I scented the blood trail. Quickly following it, I entered a rocky path, frowning at the stupidity of the wolf, until the air whizzed with power. My forehead creased with worry moments before something rammed into me.

My body slammed against the ground, and that power rushed over me. Forcing myself to roll, I glanced around the forest, finding that I was alone. What the hell was that? Swallowing the aches and pains, I got to my feet once more. My hackles rose, knowing the werewolf wasn't the only thing hunting me in the woods.

A shiver of fear trickled along my spine, and I changed courses, forcing myself to push through the pain in my side as I headed back toward my jeep.

Before I could exit the forest, I felt the air rushing around me, as if something was coming at me from all angles.

I was lifted, and a scream ripped from my throat before my body smashed against the rock wall of the valley. The heavy scent of pine trees and evergreens surrounded me. But there was something else there, too. It was dark and wicked and clung thickly in the air. Before I could get my bearings, the unseen force smacked my head against the rocks, and a yelp escaped me.

"Does the hunter not like being the prey?" a deep, seductive voice asked.

"Not entirely," I mumbled, realizing I was immobile, unable to move anything other than my lips. "Care to make it a fair fight?"

My head was slammed into the rocks again, causing a soft gasp to echo against its smooth surface. An elbow pressed against my neck, and stars danced in my eyes. One second it firmly planted me against the rocks, and the next, I was on my knees, gasping for air. Whatever the fuck was behind me, it was powerful.

The being threw my body without warning, and I shouted in rage, landing hard against more rocks. Blood poured from my forehead, and my vision swam. Nausea caused stomach acid to burn against my throat, threatening to spew from my lips. I lifted my head and withdrew a blade, searching for a target. I found nothing, not a single trace of anything or anyone within the forest.

Pushing up from the moss-covered ground, I held

my forehead, moving in a tight circle, still looking for my unseen enemy. Blood continued to trickle down my face, and I repeatedly blinked to remove the droplets from my vision.

The sound of branches crunching had me aiming and thrusting my blade toward the noise. I felt it sink into flesh as I saw the wolf, and I twisted my knife upright to ensure the wound would be deep. His claws ripped through my shoulder, and I whimpered before unseen hands pulled the beast away from me, sending it flying through the air as I searched the empty space around me. The werewolf lifted from the ground, lunging at where I teetered unevenly on my feet.

It never reached me. Instead, its body was torn apart, and a scream of horror escaped my lips as I turned, rushing away from the mangled corpse. Laughter followed my retreating form, and I lost my footing as I tried to cross the brook, splashing as I went down hard. Air left my lungs rapidly, threatening to hyperventilate my brain.

Before I could rise, a foot pressed against my back, forcing my face beneath the icy water. I screamed, sending air bubbles to the surface, but no sound escaped. My assailant lifted me by the hair, causing me to jerk my head away from the water before I was submerged once more.

I blindly grabbed for a weapon or anything to use against the creature that was prematurely trying to end my lifespan. My hand landed on a rock, and my fingers gripped the smooth, solid item before I was picked up once more. I jackknifed my body, propelling my hand through the air, colliding with something solid.

It snarled in rage, but I wasn't waiting for it to retaliate against my assault. Finding my footing on the creek bed, I bolted toward the trees. I didn't make it far before I was thrown to the ground, and I jerked wildly against the warm body holding me there.

"You're a fighter, aren't you?" the male voice purred huskily, forcing my stomach to tighten with unease. "I wonder if you got that trait from your mother or your father?" he asked, sending my thoughts swimming from the heated breath fanning my ear.

"Screw you!" I snarled, slamming my head back, hearing bone crack from the hit before I screamed in agony as something seared into my back. "Stop!" I shrieked, curling into a ball as everything inside of me demanded I give in and quit fighting.

"You make the most exquisite sounds when you're hurt, Xariana." Pain washed through me, stealing my strength as I drifted on a sea of agony. "That's it, let me in."

I slammed my mental walls shut and doubled my fight. I wasn't dying like this. I wouldn't go silently into the night while this sadistic prick got off on hurting me. I ignited my power, sending needles of red-hot pain to my assailant. He hissed, which was the only indication he'd felt my attack.

Blinking, I swallowed the bile that was trying to escape my lips. I crawled away, unable to stand as the world swam around me. My vision blurred, threatening to turn black as consciousness abandoned me. Dark, velvety laughter filled the forest, and my strength waned as twigs broke the skin on my hands and knees while I tried to retreat.

The creature yanked my hair once more, forcing me to grab onto it to prevent it from being ripped out. I touched his hands, and he hissed at the contact. Shocks rushed through me, and then something else, something foreign, collided inside of me. The being released me abruptly, but the pain in my spine continued. It was as if poison was rushing through my skin, burning the tissue in its wake.

I heard feet crunching over the vegetation of the forest floor behind me, alerting me that he was following my clumsy attempt to escape him. I'd never lost a fight, and I didn't intend on doing so today. Reaching into my waistband, I withdrew my gun and turned back toward the direction of the noise.

Nothing was visible inside the wooded area other than trees. I squeezed the trigger, firing blindly around me. A grunt sounded, and I watched as blood dripped to the ground in front of me. My eyes rounded, and then he slammed me into the dirt, hard. My head bounced, causing my teeth to clatter together. The body that landed on top of mine was solid and unmoving as an elbow pushed against my throat, preventing air from reaching my lungs.

"That wasn't nice. Now was it?" he purred angrily.

My eyes swam with stars, blinding my vision. One of the creature's hands moved to my stomach, pushing nails through the flesh on my hips. I opened my mouth to scream, but no sound escaped. His heated breath fanned my cheek, and then just as abruptly as it started, it ended.

"Run, little hunter, before I change my mind and end you here and now," it growled through a multilayered voice.

Turning onto my hands and knees, I forced my abused body off the ground, moving away from the unknown creature. Unfortunately, I didn't make it very far before the pain became too much, and my legs gave out as everything swam around me.

When I came to, I slowly blinked at the sight of my jeep. Rising again, I grabbed my head, fighting the agony and dizziness as I fished through my pocket for the keys. I opened the door and shook out of my backpack, sliding it onto the passenger seat.

Lowering the driver's visor, I stared at my battered face in the mirror. I looked like I'd fought an entire pack of wolves instead of one. Whatever attacked me, it had merely been playing with me. If it had wanted me dead, I'd have been so.

Dialing the guild's number, I struggled with the nausea swimming through me. Then, reaching down to my stomach, I lifted my shirt to look at my wound, discovering wispy black swirls of what appeared to be ink.

Starting the jeep, I leaned against the headrest, hearing my father's voice coming through the speakers.

"Xari? Is that you?" he sounded worried. I hadn't been checking in over the last week. Instead, I'd been entering my coordinates, allowing him to track my movement that way.

"Hey, old man," I muttered through the debilitating pain.

"Where the hell have you been?" he demanded, not

bothering with small talk.

"Oh, you know, around," I whispered, smiling as he swore violently.

We had an agreement, one that I'd never broken until recently. Shit had changed, though, and I'd changed, too. My father was forced to play devil's advocate between my ex, Micah, and me, and I'd lost. I didn't envy him playing referee, but in the end, I'd chosen to leave, and he had to accept that as my employer and father.

"Dammit, Kid. Get your ass back here, now. The supes are acting strange, and we've got an unprecedented number of attacks happening here. I need my fucking hunters back at base, and I need you to pull your head out of your ass for a minute and see the bigger picture."

"I'm coming, but I won't be staying. You can't ask me to stay there with Micah and—her," I muttered through clenched teeth. "I was attacked on a hunt, so I'll head in to get patched up. After that, you can assign me elsewhere."

"Xariana, I need you here. You're my fucking daughter, dammit. Get your ass home, and we'll discuss this. How badly hurt are you?" he asked, pressing the phone to his shoulder as he shouted orders to someone beside him.

"I'm not sure," I admitted. "I don't even know what the fuck attacked me, but it kicked my ass. If it intended to kill me, I'd be dead, Dad. Have Bali ready for medical to check me out, yeah?" I swallowed, putting the jeep into drive before pulling onto the road.

"He'll be ready to receive you, Kid."

I cut the call to focus on my driving. By the time I reached the city, the sun had gone down. Traffic was near zilch, and there wasn't a pedestrian in sight, which had my hackles up. I pulled in front of the guild, peering through the jeep's window, noting that the entire block was dark, as if there was a power outage. Exiting the vehicle, I moved toward the gate to slip past the wrought iron fencing, but a whoosh of otherworldly power erupted around me.

My father turned, staring at me as his mouth opened to yell out in warning. Only, it never escaped his throat. Vehicles exploded inside the gates, imploding as metal crunched and screamed in protest.

Icy fingers of dread wrapped around me, and a shiver rushed down my spine. I glanced about the courtyard, staring at the lifeless bodies littering the ground. The air grew even thicker with power, and then everything moved in slow motion.

Beings appeared from thin air, surrounding my father as a pair of startling amber eyes locked with mine. Silver hair wafted in the wind, and all sound was sucked from the world. Slowly, I started toward the creature as if drawn by an unseen thread. My hand lifted to touch the gates, but then the sounds came rushing back as another explosion ignited beyond the gate.

I watched in horror as my father vanished, and the rest of the vehicles inside the courtyard erupted. My body jerked, thrown backward by the blast before I slammed into something, and everything went dark.

Chapter Two

The sound of machines beeping brought me back to the surface. An intense ache laced through my head, and I groaned, trying to sit up as someone gently pushed me down, forcing me to remain in place. I screamed past the red-hot pain that burned through me at the wound in my side. Lifting my hands, I fought to remove the ones touching me, too sensitive to handle them on my flesh.

"Xariana, stop fighting us," Noah's stern tone brushed my mind, and I rounded my eyes on him. "We got you, Xari. You're okay," he promised.

I struggled to remember what had happened. My right side was on fire, and I could feel the fever ravishing throughout my system. The amber-colored eyes of the being that stood beside my dad flashed in my memory, and I turned to Noah, fighting the fear that threatened to swallow me whole.

"Where's my father?" I whispered past the sandpaper in my throat.

"Just worry about yourself for now. You're hurt badly," Rhys Van Helsing stated, and I swung my attention to where he sat in the darkened corner. His somber eyes held mine, and grief shown inside of them. I shook my head, preparing to argue, but he exhaled slowly. "Xavier was taken, but we don't know by whom or what they want."

Rhys was one of my father's closest friends and ran E.V.I.E., one of the organizations that often assisted us. He and my father spent a lot of time hunting or brainstorming missions. Rhys and his brother Cole were notorious badasses and ran the Van Helsing Knights. It was a group of otherworldly creatures that spent their time hunting down sex-crazed, maniac incubus demons. He was also the head of the House of Van Helsing.

"Can you explain what happened to you?" Bali asked, drawing my focus to where he stood, looking down at me. "You were in the explosion, but most of your wounds aren't from the blast, are they?"

"I was hunting," I admitted, even though I could hardly recount what had happened in the woods. It was blurry inside my mind because the memory of the vibrant amber eyes seemed to dwarf everything. "An unseen creature attacked me, but it didn't want me dead."

"You don't know what assaulted you?" he questioned.

"Something powerful," I replied. "No more drugs."

"It isn't drugs, Xari. It's the antidote for the venom.

Whatever it was, it bit you and left a nasty poison inside of you. We had to guess the kind of creature that attacked you, so you have a few antidotes in your system. The scratches on your left side looked like the claws of a werewolf, but the black markings on your right are different. You don't have a guess as to what it was?"

"I don't know," I whispered, fighting to remain awake. "It was pissed off and powerful. I couldn't fight it," I groaned as more burning started in my stomach. "It fucking burns!"

"Yeah, it's almost like the creature branded you. Look." Bali held his phone up for me to see the wispy tendrils of a dark inky substance that covered my right side. "You scream each time it moves. I've never seen anything like it before. It's as if the marks are alive inside of you."

"Get it out," I moaned, turning as more pain sliced through me.

Bali exhaled slowly, puffing out air as he put his phone back into his white overcoat and sat beside me. "Here's the thing, Xari. Every time I touch it, the mark reacts and grows. Whatever it is, it won't let any of us near it to get a sample without harming you more."

"Remove it, Bali," I demanded, lifting to peer down at my side. I noted the markings were eerily beautiful, and then it slithered within me. "What the hell?"

"You need time to recover, Xariana. You were pretty banged up when we got to you," Noah chided, ignoring the panic that threatened to engulf me.

"I have to leave this bed," I grunted, forcing my legs over the edge.

"As much as we don't mind the sight of your naked behind, Anderson, you should rest. First, you were hurt before the attack on the guild. Then, you were thrown back by the explosion that killed several hunters tonight." My eyes snapped to Cole Van Helsing's, narrowing at his words.

"Who died?" I whispered, hating the pain that twisted my heart, sinking into my stomach. His silky dark head shook slowly, indicating he didn't want to disclose the deceased. "Tell me, now," I ordered.

"We lost a lot of people," Noah stated, sitting beside me to grab my hand. "Over twenty hunters and many are still fighting for their lives."

"I need to get out of here," I whimpered, standing and turning to face Noah. "Get me the names of those who died and their next of kin. We need to offer their families a place to go where they can grieve in peace."

"I have handled it, Xari. You need to get back into bed, now," he argued.

"No," I firmly asserted. "I'm fine. I'm a little woozy, but otherwise, I am okay. I have to figure out what happened here and who attacked us. We have to get my father back."

"I've got people out looking for him," Rhys stated, nodding at Cole, who backed him up. "You ought to take it easy. We have no idea what the hell that is on your side. In all of my time alive, I've never felt anything like that before. What did you experience when it appeared?"

"Pain," I spat out, groaning as my fingers slid over the inky black markings. It didn't react to my touch, causing Bali to snort.

"Touch it again," he ordered.

I did, tracing the markings lightly, with no reaction at all. Bali's fingers brushed over it, and I gritted my teeth before a scream of pain exited my throat.

"You guys see that?" he asked softly, removing his hand as I replaced it with mine.

"It's almost like a warning to stop touching her," Rhys grunted. "Tell me what transpired on your hunt."

"I was tracking a werewolf, but something else was stalking me. It easily overpowered me. It felt like the creature was toying with me, wanting me to know how quickly it could have ended my life. Only, it didn't wish to kill me. If that's what it had wanted, I'd be pushing up daisies right now. It was powerful and masculine. It laughed when it hurt me, and it enjoyed me fighting against it even though I was hopeless to do so."

"How do you know it was powerful?" Cole asked softly, his blue gaze heating my insides. Of course, I shouldn't be reacting to him in my condition—freaking incubus demons.

"I could feel it in the air. Its raw power was all around me, and I could sense it in its touch and presence. Everything about it was deadly and powerful. So why didn't it kill me?" I whispered, asking what had been burning in my mind. "I think it carried me out of the woods, too. I didn't make it back to my Jeep on my own. If I did, I don't recall that happening. The creature wanted me alive, and that is terrifying considering the marking it left behind."

"You never saw it?" Cole asked skeptically.

"No," I confirmed. "I heard him, and I saw his blood on the ground when I shot him, which he let me do, showing me that he's not afraid of our bullets. Silver didn't slow him down, and neither did the iron nitrates in the metal jackets. I don't know any creature that is immune to both. He just laughed and slammed into my body again. He wasn't even fazed a little."

"I knew a couple, but they're not around anymore. Did you see anything before you lost consciousness?" Rhys asked, watching my face closely. "Is there anything else you can recall? Unfortunately, I can't find anything on the cameras to help us search for your father, Xari. I need a starting point because we all understand what happens to the people who go against the enemies that we've collected over the years."

"There were people; no, they were creatures. One had amber eyes and silver hair. He looked right at me, and then everything went haywire. I had a connection to him, Rhys. I actually felt him when we made eye contact."

"Could he be the one that assaulted you in the woods?" Noah asked softly, tightening his hand over mine.

"No. It wasn't the same sensation. The creature that attacked us here was cold and calculated. The other felt like unfiltered power released in a show of strength. It wanted me to understand it could kill me and that it enjoyed taunting me. It was playing with me, like I was its prey," I admitted. "I have never felt that fragile or powerless in my life. I've never lost a fight, and I got my ass handed to me."

"Sounds like it," Noah muttered. "The question is, why mark you and not end your life? What is it gaining by marking you?"

"It would depend on the breed of the person or creature that left it," Cole pointed out, nodding at me. "You'll need to keep a close eye on it." His gaze traveled to my side as he studied the inky substance.

"What I need to do is get back to work, and tend to the guild." I wrapped the gown around my backside and started forward, but Noah stopped me.

His soft gray eyes held mine before he spoke. "It's bad, Xari. Outside this room, it's chaos. You should prepare yourself for what you're about to walk through."

"I can handle it," I promised.

But I wasn't prepared for what was beyond the door to my room. On gurneys, people lay lifelessly staring up at the ceiling. My gaze skimmed over body after body until it landed on a familiar form. My heart dropped, and tears burned my eyes.

"No," I whispered so softly I wasn't sure it was heard over the crying of the hunters gathered in the infirmary. Micah, my ex-fiancée, sat against the wall, holding my former best friend, Meredith, in his arms. Meredith and I had grown up together, best friends since we'd met, up until she slept with Micah, days before our wedding. Tears slowly rolled down my cheeks as he lifted his head, staring directly at me.

"She died an hour ago," Noah replied, slowly urging me to keep moving as more eyes lifted to watch me. "There's nothing you can do here, Xari."

"We have to find out who did this and make them pay, Noah. They have to pay for this. It cannot go unanswered."

"We will," he promised. "Go get cleaned up and prepared to speak with the other guilds. You're in charge now, and you can't do your job in a hospital garment with blood caked to your face. So move," he urged, forcing me to walk away from the scene unfolding around us.

Chapter Three

Showered and dressed in clean sweatpants and a tank top, I stared at the swirling ink that adorned one side of my abdomen which had spread across my stomach. I'd seen nothing like it, not even close. It pulsed as if it were alive inside of my flesh. I brushed my fingers over the tendrils of the wispy black spot, watching it move toward my fingertips.

"It's attracted to your touch," Enzo snorted, leaning against the doorframe. "Interesting that someone would attack you and mark you."

"You're here?" I whispered, fighting the emotion that burned my throat and nose. "They took him, Enzo. They took my father."

Enzo and his brother Ezekiel were twin incubus demons. They co-owned a strip club, doubling as the headquarters for their order, which they ran beneath it. They were part of an old guard that had agreed to watch over portions of the world, ensuring the families and bloodlines of their offspring continued to grow. The brothers helped us hunt down the really bad guys, so out of respect, I hadn't interrogated them to learn more about their background.

Enzo smiled sadly, nodding as he closed the distance between us, pulling me in for a tight hug. I whined from the pressure, and he relinquished his hold on me. Frowning, he withdrew a vial from his pocket containing an amber liquid.

"Drink. It will heal your wounds. They may still be tender, but the tonic will assist your tissue by expediting the healing process."

I popped the cork and sniffed it, turning my nose up at the obnoxious odor released from the bottle. He winced, watching as I tipped it up, emptying it without complaint. It tasted like ass, but then so did most homebrews offered by Enzo and Ezekiel.

"Rhys filled us in on what happened, and we came the moment we heard the guild was attacked and your father was taken. I'm sorry, Xari. We should have been more watchful when the supes began acting up."

"My father mentioned that, too. Care to fill me in on why you guys think that has anything to do with what happened here?" I asked pointedly, watching Enzo's broad shoulders shrug in reply.

"Don't know what has them spooked or making them think they're invincible. I can only tell you we've been out hunting down all those that have gone rogue instead of handling our issues at home. About a week ago, the supes started attacking humans at an alarming rate. It was like they no longer feared the repercussions of their actions," he explained. "Caught some of the little bastards alive, but all they said was that judgment day was coming for those who trespassed against their own."

"What the hell does that mean?" I wondered out loud.

Shrugging again, Enzo exhaled. "No bloody clue. There's crap happening that I don't have answers to, either. One informant that you protected was allowing creatures to feed on humans inside his club openly. Your father issued a warning to the supes that this behavior wouldn't be tolerated, and normally that would have calmed them down, or at least made them hesitant to fuck around. It didn't, though, and that's when Xavier call us in to help hunt them down. It's been a shit show for two weeks, Xari."

Swallowing, I nodded my head as my thoughts went back to the infirmary, seeing someone I had once been close to lying lifeless in the arms of my ex. I didn't need that image stuck in my mind while trying to piece together what had happened.

"Did we recover the camera feeds?" I asked, knowing I had to snap out of it and get myself under control.

"Yeah, they're working on getting them cleaned up and on the monitors downstairs. We're all waiting for you," Enzo stated, smiling as his blue eyes slowly slid down to my belly. "That's a powerful mark, Xariana. I can sense it pulsing when you are close to me. Whatever placed this on you wants to feel you and to warn others away from you. It's almost like a symbol of claiming, but stronger."

"That's just what I fucking need," I complained, exhausted from hunting days on end without eating, and then being attacked had drained the remainder of my strength.

"How long were you out?" Enzo asked, noticing the sheer willpower it was taking to remain upright.

"A little over two weeks of hunting, and I did so with minimal sleep. That wolf left eleven bodies out in the open. I didn't have time to rest for long or eat while it killed without a care of being discovered."

"You end it?"

"No, but the thing that marked me ripped the werewolf in half as if it were a piece of paper," I admitted, chewing my lip while recalling the events. "It was terrifying, Enzo. I was nothing against that creature, and it wanted me to know that I was weak and feeble. It threw me around like I was a rag doll. I've never felt that kind of fear or helplessness against an enemy before."

"You're not alone," Enzo declared, and voices agreeing with his sentiment sounded from across the hall. "Your father helped a lot of people, Xari. You're an extension of him. We're here for you, to fight this battle with you."

"Thank you." I moved into the other room to discover it filled with the familiar faces of our extended family of hunters. Enzo joined his brother Ezekiel, who sat across from Rhys and Cole. Eryx, one of the Fenrir wolves from Montana, was beside him, here on behalf of Saint, his alpha, and Braelyn, Saint's mate.

Noah, Micah, Onyx, Kaderyn, and Meredith were my unit that often hunted together. Unfortunately, when Micah and I split because he slept with my best friend the night before our wedding, it caused a rift in our group.

"Micah, you shouldn't be here," I warned, fighting the urge to tell him how I felt. "You should be with Meredith."

"She's dead. There's nothing I can do for her," he shot back, pain filling his words. "I need to catch the asshole that did this."

Nodding slowly, I fought the nausea swirling through me. "I get that, but I require you to be level-headed, Micah. This will not be a quick fight. Whatever hit us, it's strong. It attacked hard and fast, and we weren't prepared. But, if you can keep it together and not allow emotions to overrun you, I will let you join us."

Not bothering to wait for his agreement, I entered the kitchen, grabbing a bottle of water. The shit Enzo had given me was making me dizzy and had my mouth tasting like ash. Downing the contents in one swig, I set it down on the counter, holding onto it for balance.

"You're wounded, Xari," Kaderyn stated, sidling next to me.

"The entire fucking guild is hurt. I am fine," I argued, turning to look into her shimmering silver gaze. "Tell me what we've learned so far. I can't go down there without knowing more details before I enter that room."

Noah cleared his throat, and I turn to see him

leaning against my fridge, holding out another bottle of water. Accepting it, I listened to him report everything I already knew. It wasn't until he looked me in the eye and shook his head that my stomach dropped to the floor.

"On the video, you flew across the street, but you never hit your Jeep. Something prevented you from impact, and then you fell to the ground," he explained, shrugging. "Either you have a guardian angel, or something didn't want that blast to kill you."

A shiver snaked down my spine as the thing on my stomach heated. I slid my hand down, brushing my fingertips across it absently. Noah nodded, as if reading my mind. No one spoke for a moment, then Eryx broke the silence.

"Braelyn and Saint will take the families of the fallen hunters," he announced softly. "The mountain is thawing, but we'd need to get them to the top using the Blackhawks. The roads won't thaw for a couple more weeks yet. They wanted you to know that if you require anything further from them, they'll come."

"No," I swallowed down the urge to ask them here, but I didn't wish for anyone else to be in the path of this mess. Not until I had a better idea of what had happened and what we were facing. "Tell Saint and Braelyn that I appreciate their help and that we'll ask those in need where they wish to be for now. The sanctuary is full already, and our oath is not only to our hunters, but their families as well. We protect our own."

"They know that, Xariana. No one is assuming you won't do your job to keep them safe. The thing is, you're right. Whatever attacked this place hit fucking hard, and they did it before anyone knew they were even here. Your father is the best hunter I have ever met, and they escaped with him without a trace. That says a lot more than the damage left behind. They snatched Xavier Anderson from the steps of his guild in broad daylight." Eryx shrugged, not needing to elaborate. He silently held my stare, fussing with the cuff of his sleeve, which revealed the hint of the tattoos that covered his arm from the wrist up.

"Kaderyn, please reach out to the families and let them know that there is a safe haven for them to seek shelter once the funeral rites have been completed. We should get started on that process. Our dead deserve tending to immediately. I have to inform the other hunter guilds about what took place here as well. Call the leaders of each guild and ask them to hold. Once we've reviewed the videos, I'll speak with them directly."

I swallowed the uneasiness that came with speaking to the other guild leaders. Admitting that my father was missing would make it all real. Right now, it merely felt like a nightmare, and I'd wake up soon and discover nothing amiss.

"Are you ready for this?" Kaderyn asked.

Noah snorted along with Jensen. "Xariana Anderson was born into this role. She's ready," he stated firmly. "If anyone can do this, it's her."

"Thank you, Noah. First, let's find out who attacked us and took my father. Then, we'll send them to Hell."

Chapter Four

The video showed exactly what I'd seen, minus the creatures, who were invisible in the video. The final explosion had thrown me backward, but as Noah stated, I never reached the Jeep, even though it held a massive dent in the driver's side door where I would have landed. We examined the door, then my wounds, and they didn't match up.

Once I explained to my extended team where I'd witnessed the beings standing, we'd created a layout and reconstructed the scene. Nothing of the incident made sense. The cars inside the gate blew up, but it looked more like one giant bomb had gone off instead of two separate explosions. After studying the charred remains, we still knew very little about what transpired.

"The scene is confusing," Enzo snorted, leaning his long muscular tattooed arms against the table. "You said there were two explosions, but only one appeared on video. Bodies littered the ground before the second, which backs up your story. So why make it appear as if there had only been one blast?"

"I don't know," I swallowed, staring at the last frame of the video. "Why save me? None of it makes sense. There have been no demands for my father's safe return, either. One would assume they'd want something in exchange for him, right? Nothing has come through."

"It's still pretty early, Xari," Ezekiel offered. "I don't think they would presume you'd be up and handling shit so soon. Normally, chaos and bedlam would ensue, and then would come the calm. But, instead, you're up and about, running on pure stubbornness. Your ass should be in bed, resting."

"We've had this conversation already. If I was my father, would you be telling me to ignore what happened, sending him to bed?" I snapped, closing my eyes at the tone I'd used. "I'm sorry, Eze. It's been a long day, and I can't rest. I'd literally lie in my room, wanting to be right here helping. This is where I am needed right now."

"Then let's deal with the leaders of the guilds and see what they know?" Enzo offered, turning to face the wall of monitors.

Swallowing the urge to run away like a scared child, I steeled my spine and squared my shoulders. The men and women that controlled the computers and electronics began bringing up images and nodding to the names on the screens.

"They're all up, Miss Anderson," Clyde stated.

"Just Xari, Clyde," I chided. "Ladies and gentlemen, I come to you with news I never wished to deliver." The hunters on the screen straightened, giving me their undivided attention. "Last night, an unknown enemy attacked the Washington guild. They hit us quickly and violently. My father was taken, and we don't know where he is or who took him. There's been no ransom or demands made of us yet. We lost a lot of brothers and sisters in the assault. For now, all guilds need to be on heightened alert until we know if this was an isolated incident."

Craig, the leader of the Ireland guild, was the first to speak, his thick Irish accent cold and unfeeling. "And who is in charge now? You? You're barely ooeht o' yooehr trainin bra. I wahn't be answerin to a cheld, Xariana."

I blinked, unprepared for his clipped response. "I fail to see where my age would make me less qualified for the position. I have been a hunter, assisting my father in the daily affairs of our guild for longer than most of you have been members. In fact, Craig McFarland, I hand-delivered your report with a recommendation to Xavier, earning you the job you now hold. You didn't seem appalled or found my age a problem when I got you elevated to lead the Ireland guild. My bra size and how long I'd been wearing the fucking thing didn't come into account at all. Explain why that is an issue now?" I snapped coldly, finding my spine.

"You're a cheld," he continued.

"I killed my first demon on my own at seven years old, Craig. Then, at seventeen, I eliminated the demon you were supposed to kill at your trial to earn your spot in the guild while you pissed your fucking pants. I was born into the guild and have a higher kill count than all the leaders of the guilds placed together. I don't say this to boast or brag. It's just a fact and a reminder of whose daughter I am. My father brought you in, Craig, and he did so because I told him you'd be a good leader."

He shook his head, smiling coldly. "I dahn't give a shet who yooehr father is. I dahn't answer to a cheld. And I sure as 'ell dahn't answer to a female wethooeht enooehgh balls ahr aoehthahrity to roehn 'er own guild, let alahne mine"

"Eryx, see that the Ireland guild is cut off from communication. Enzo," I said, sliding a snide smile at Craig while crossing my arms over my chest. "Cut their funding and weapons as well. Rhys, see that our allies within Ireland, Scotland, and the British Isles know that the Ireland hunters guild is no longer in need of assistance as they've cut off their nose to spite their face. Kill the call. Craig, good hunting," I snorted as the color drained from his face before the screen went black.

I pointedly looked at each of the other leaders before continuing. "Does anyone else have a problem with me running the guild until we retrieve my father?" My gaze landed on each leader as, one by one, they nodded in agreement that it wouldn't be an issue. "Good, then place your territories on high alert and contact the hunters outside of your respective guilds to ensure they're aware of the threat. I don't need to tell you that whoever did this to us has declared war on all guilds."

"What do we know so far, Xariana?" Blade asked, studying me through crimson eyes. He was the lead hunter in London and one of the oldest vampires we had in the guilds.

"Not much, other than they wanted to hit us hard enough that they left a mark. We have video footage we're forwarding to you. The video illustrates the power behind the assault, but it doesn't show you who attacked us. I will compile an image with our forensic artist and get that out to you and the public based on the creature I saw. He had amber eyes and silver hair. I couldn't tell you more than that or even hint at his breed. Only that he was powerful, and that he seemed able to stop time, and when it restarted, everything exploded around him."

"Bloody hell." Blade rubbed his forehead, observing me. "You saw it and survived? Yet no one else did?"

"Yeah, you'll see it all on the video." I paused, creasing my brow as I noticed the guild in Ireland kept calling. A quick glance at Forest had the calls going straight to voicemail. "I was on a hunt before the attack, and when I returned, I witnessed the attack. Something or someone prevented me from dying with the others. I should have slammed into my jeep from the explosion, but I never touched it from what we can tell in the video. The same creature or one similar to it left this on me," I stated, pulling my top up to expose the marking.

All the leaders adjusted in their chairs to look at the mark, and no one seemed to know what it was, as they all silently shook their heads. Dropping my shirt, I explained the encounter in the woods, leaving nothing

KING OF THE SHADOW FAE

out, studying their facial expressions while recounting the details. When I finished, everyone was somber and silent.

"If you recall any creature that could attack in such a fashion, I need to know. The marking isn't painful at the moment, but it reacts when anyone else tries to touch it. If it becomes an issue, I will stand down and allow Noah Jameson to assume control of the guild. I won't take a chance on something happening to any of you. Your safety and that of our guilds are first and foremost in my mind. We are still gathering the names and information on those we've lost. At the service tomorrow night, I will honor our fallen and do a last call of arms. Are there any questions?"

"Do you need us to come to Washington? You're not alone in this, Anderson. We will be on the next flight if called or needed," Blade offered, frowning, as I shook my head in reply. "Bloody hell, Xar, let us help you. When one guild weakens, we gather to show force."

"We're not weakened, Blade. We will continue hunting." I could hear the sharp inhale and gasps of the surrounding hunters at my announcement. "My father would have my ass if we stopped and allowed the Otherworld creatures to infringe on the humans. We do not stop hunting, even at our darkest hour. Those are the rules Xavier created, and we will keep this place moving along until he is returned to us. The Underworld is probably already buzzing with the news of my father's disappearance. They will seek to try us, but we will strike back."

Swallowing past the lump in my throat, I repeated

the words in which my father always ended his calls. "We are the unwanted, the unseen, that walk among the mortals. We are needed to hunt those that prey on the weaker race, enforcing the laws to protect them. We are hunters of the night and are never alone. For when we hunt, we do so as a family. They cannot break us, for we stand firmly together. Until next time ladies, and gentlemen. Safe hunting, and may the gods favor you always."

The call ended, and I silently leaned against the desk behind me. Tears pricked my eyes, burning my throat. The command room was quiet, and an unsettling foreboding was present that everyone felt. Since the beginning of the guild, it had been no one other than my father that uttered those words.

"You did great, Xari," Kaderyn whispered, breaking the silence.

"Thank you," I replied, turning to peer up at the open office door that looked out over the command room. Eventually, I would need to enter my dad's office to work. My heart pounded, and my stomach churned with uneasiness as my hand slid to my side, skimming my fingers over the mark before I turned to the men.

"Forward the videos to the other guilds, but not Ireland. They need to know what it feels like to be cut off for a few hours. Reroute their calls and those of the hunters who refused to align with the guild, choosing to hunt alone. I want those calls taken and addressed based on the nature of the offense. Nothing goes unanswered. Also, get a pulse on the news swarming in the Underworld. Reach out to our informants and find out what is being said about Xavier's disappearance.

Vet that information against what others are saying. Someone knows what happened here, and I need to know what they do. Enzo, can you get your girls working on their clientele and see if any of the high rollers in your club know anything?"

"I already asked the ladies to gather information from their patrons. You might ask Rhys to talk to his little baby mama to work her club since she's taking my business away," Enzo replied, chuckling as Rhys made a strangled noise in response. "Nymphs bring in more clients, and Nyx has refused to allow the few nymphs Remington Silversmith added to her house to outsource. After all, Remi has allowed all outcasts to join her and Nyx."

My eyebrows lifted at that news. "Remington knows she has to be declared an official house by vote, correct?"

"I don't think Remi knows the rules nor cares what they are," Rhys grunted, pushing from the desk beside me. "I will head to the Sanctuary and see what I can learn. If you need me, Xari, call. I'm only a town away and can get here quick enough to help you. Your father is my friend; know that you are among the select few I actually care about."

"Thank you," I said, allowing him to hug me quickly before the others followed suit, all heading out for the night. With a quick glance toward my father's office, I dismissed the command center staff to allow them what sleep they could get before the funeral rites began.

I didn't relax until I was inside my apartment, settling into the small desk covered in a thick layer of dust. I'd figure out who branded me and attacked us, and I would make them pay. But first, I had to figure out what the hell was covering my ribcage and why it was there. I could feel it pulsing, which strangely comforted me, even though it shouldn't. Firing up my computer, I placed my phone beside it and eyed the kitchen cupboards.

It was going to be a long night. It was my first inside the apartment that I would have shared with Micah. We hadn't been able to be within it together, and I was glad I'd chosen the smaller one, since I'd be in it alone now. I'd left the guild on the day it was to have been ours, choosing the life of a nomad hunter to escape seeing my ex with the woman I'd once considered my best friend.

I hadn't planned on coming back here, but plans changed, and shit happened.

Chapter Five

I'd searched the endless chatter from the Underworld, which was the term we used for the underground world of immortals from the Otherworld, of which our kind originated, and it made sense to refer to us as such. Like us, most beings inside this realm were half-breeds—castoffs of full-bred creatures that couldn't be bothered to accept the ones they made or created.

Scanning the last page of intel gathered, I shut down my computer and went to wash out my mug. At the sink, I rinsed it and placed it onto the drying mat, frowning at the details my father had gotten perfect.

Xavier Anderson still surprised me with how thorough he was sometimes. He'd remembered that I loved chamomile tea but needed cubed sugar to appease my sweet tooth, even before bed. He had food bought for the apartment that was fresh and quick to prepare meals. He'd even added the vitamins, along with the assortment of herbs I'd taken since I was little. Then, without warning, tears unleashed, and the uncertainty I felt at his disappearance hit me all at once.

My legs gave out, and I slid to the floor, sobbing as the knowledge that he could be dead slammed into my mind. Wrapping my arms around my middle, I cried until I couldn't anymore. Everything ached, and the stitches Bali had placed where the wolf had clawed my side itched, causing my fingers to scratch at the red, raw skin until they untied, and I pulled them out.

Pushing from the floor, I walked into the bathroom, stripping out of the top to stare at the welts left behind. My wounds were healing, but angry purple bruises covered my neck, shoulders, and middle. I was sure that if I stripped myself bare, I'd find even more bruises.

The wisps of ink seemed to slither over my side. I wanted to scream in frustration that I did not know what the hell they were. The internet had revealed nothing that looked even remotely close to the design or thin tendrils of delicate and beautiful black markings. That, too, pissed me off. It wasn't just beautiful—it was intricate and feminine.

Glancing at my tired reflection, I took in my sandy blonde hair and soft lime-green eyes. The welt on my cheek stood out starkly against my bronzed skin. I looked exhausted, and the bags beneath my eyes had bags of their own packed. Undoing the braid I'd quickly platted earlier, I freed my waist-length hair, combing through it slowly. After brushing my teeth and using the bathroom, I entered the bedroom.

On the dresser was a photo of my mother, heavily

pregnant with me, held in the arms of my father. It was the only picture I had of us together since she'd died giving birth to me. Her long blonde hair was a softer color than mine, with darker highlights mixed into it. Her emerald green eyes were darker, and her skin tone was lighter in comparison to mine.

Beside that picture sat one of me, my dad, and the entire guild on the steps of this building. Every year on the anniversary date of the opening of the guild, we'd gather and take a photo. It was the one day we didn't hunt and celebrated living.

In the snapshot, I stood between Micah and Meredith. The two people who'd betrayed me the most in my life. I'd caught them fucking on the kitchen counter beside the cake I'd been coming home to taste for our wedding. But instead of getting married, I'd packed a bag of my things and walked away from the only home I'd ever known.

Shoving away the pain of those memories, I slipped into bed, switching off the light. Within moments of lying down, I sat up, sensing that I wasn't alone in the darkened room. Turning the light on, I gazed around as the hair on my neck rose and my stomach sank with fear. I pushed the blanket off, fully intending to leave the bedroom, when something collided with me.

I opened my mouth to scream, but a hand covered it, and I growled, bucking against the weight pressing down on it. I spread my legs for balance and gasped at the pressure held against my lips. Power was rushing through the room, causing the light to flicker, adding to the horror of what was happening.

I struggled against the hold, needing to get air into my lungs. The moment my mouth was free, I gasped, taking in air and fighting to get the scream from my throat, but I was flipped over, and my face was pushed into the pillows. Fingers slid against my scalp, gripping my hair painfully as a hand skimmed over the spot on my side.

I froze in place, sensing the creature's touch as it caressed the marking. The chuckle that sounded beside my ear was silken, dark, and masculine as it pressed against my stomach. Closing my eyes, I fought against the uneasiness mingling with something sinister growing within me. Lips brushed over my shoulder, and I jerked away, only to have more pressure applied against my body.

I muffled words through the palm of a hand, but if it understood the threat, the intruder chose to ignore me. The body against mine was warm, sending heat along my bare flesh. Squeezing my eyes shut, I focused on forcing myself to project away from where I was pressed into the bed.

It took a lot of effort to slam my consciousness away from my physical body. From the corner, I looked as if I was fighting myself on the mattress, alone. There was no one inside the room with me, nothing I could sense or see.

My body went slack on the bed, and panic ripped through me until the male slammed me against the wall. I slowly blinked, realizing that he had fucking caught my projected image, which wasn't a solid form, not entirely. It was more of a ghostly form that could see, hear, and feel.

I shouldn't have been able to be touched or harmed, let alone held to the wall by an invisible creature that shouldn't have seen me in this state. Whatever the intruder was, it was freaking tall and solid. He held me firmly to the wall, and before I could manage to shove my projected form back in my listless body, something warm and soft skimmed over my throat, sniffing me.

"Do you get off on scaring the shit out of women in their bed, pussy?" I uttered through trembling lips. Masculine laughter whispered against the sensitive flesh, causing my body to tremble. "Get off of me," I demanded through clenched teeth.

"Make me, hunter. What other tricks do you have?" he asked in a multilayered voice that caused the markings on my side to slither, writhing over my skin.

"What did you do to me?" I fought to get him off of me, to no avail. He was a solid wall of muscle, one that easily subdued mine.

"I look good on you, don't you think?" he teased in a hoarse tone.

"No, I don't think it looks good," I grounded out, still struggling to free myself enough to project back into my body.

The more I struggled, the more I drained precious energy I didn't have to spare. My body sagged and gave away the precariousness of the situation. A soft cry escaped my lips as the male pressed something against my throat, forcing my head back while he did whatever the hell he was doing.

"You're weakening, aren't you?" he asked, his tone

echoing through my mind while my eyes rolled back in my head. "Bloody hell, you're a disappointment, woman."

"Fuck you," I muttered. "What are you?"

"Fuck me? What are you? You're not what you're pretending to be, are you?" he asked, and his mouth lowered, tracing heated breath along my neck. "You don't smell like one of us, and yet you have enough power to project your image, even though you weaken from it. No half-breed can do such a thing without dying. So, little one," he uttered while licking my jugular like a sick freak. "How is it that you have this ability and aren't expiring?"

"I'm a freak," I whispered, shivering as I felt fangs scrap against my pulse. "Let me go," I pleaded, uncertain of what was taking place.

I should be fighting him, and yet his touch created a soothing sensation within me. The pulsing in my side had turned into something twisted and dark. He smiled against my throat, as if he sensed the internal battle I waged, and found it amusing.

"Return my father to me," I whispered.

"And if I had him, what would you give to me in exchange for his life?" His question caused my heart to beat painfully against the cage of my ribs. "Would you trade yourself for him?"

"Never," I hissed, pushing against him, but he was immovable.

"Even if I had your father, you'd never get him back alive," he laughed coldly, sending a wave of ice rushing down my spine.

My body slowly sagged, and he made a strangled sound before stepping back, allowing me to leap into my physical form. The moment I was settled, I opened my mouth and released a blood-curdling scream. My bedroom oozed with power before it slithered to nothing more than a trickle. My door burst open, and Micah and Noah were there, searching for the threat with guns drawn and aimed at the vacant room.

"Xari?" Noah asked, needing a target.

I shook my head, unable to get my lips to work. Projecting your image took a lot of strength, and when I used my ability, it left me weakened. His wide gray eyes slid over my body, noting that I was half on and off the bed. My face was sideways, and I was rapidly inhaling air into my burning lungs.

"What the fuck happened?" Micah demanded, as even more people started filing into my apartment.

"He was here, inside my room," I whispered through the dryness of my mouth. The reality of the situation hit me, racing through my mind painfully. He'd been able to bypass the protection stones and had been inside my bedroom.

"Jesus," Kaderyn muttered, moving past the men to help me sit. "You projected, didn't you?" she questioned, not needing my reply to sense the truth.

"I'll get some tea," Noah offered.

"I'll grab bedding. You're not sleeping alone tonight in case the asshole tries to get to you again," Micah stated, making my stomach sink at the idea of him being close to me.

Within minutes, I had tea and a bed full of hunters that refused to hear reason and leave me in the bedroom alone. Noah curled against my back while Kaderyn laid on the other side, forcing Micah to take the floor alone. I rested my head on Noah's arm, and I felt safer than I had in weeks. Sleep came slowly, filled with nightmares of an invisible enemy that had marked me, and took great enjoyment from my pain.

Chapter Six

I awoke to the sound of voices in my kitchen. Stretching out on the bed, I tested my limbs before sitting up. Micah was still on the floor, staring at me as I peered down at him. His eyes were rimmed in red, and there was sadness in them. I opened my mouth to say how sorry I was for his loss, but the words didn't come out.

"Meredith was pregnant—seven months along. It was a boy," he stated, driving a knife into my heart. "We were married on the day you and I were supposed to have wed. Your father said she deserved to be married properly, and I needed to do right by her."

My stomach churned with the magnitude of the words he was tossing out. They'd planned our entire wedding together, after all. I hunted monsters, proving to the hunter guild that I belonged here while they fucked each other behind my back. My breathing grew labored as I stood, moving to the dresser to search through it for clothes.

"Tell me you hate me," he whispered, as if he didn't want the others to overhear him.

I didn't, because hate was a very strong word that I'd promised my father to only use when I truly felt it. Micah wanted me to scream and yell at him because I hadn't done it, not even when they'd been fucking in our home, on the island we would have used to prepare our meals.

Fishing out my clothing, I went to the bathroom, shutting him out. Tears fell from my eyes, and I wiped them away, chastising myself for allowing him to hurt me after all this time apart. I'd left Micah behind and hadn't planned on coming home anytime soon. I'd healed in my own way and had pasted myself back together with what little dignity I had left.

In the shower, I leaned my head against the tile, letting the coldness seep into my soul. I wasn't this weak creature that cried over everything. I barely cried at all, but I'd done enough in the last two days to make up for the months I'd spent angry, having meaningless sex with strangers to fill the void Micah had left within me.

I'd coped and ignored the failure of my past relationship. It had turned me into a better hunter, mindlessly operating on pure anger and rage. My father had demanded I return, but he hadn't removed Micah and Meredith from the guild, which caused a rift between us.

Had I wanted them reassigned? Yes. I didn't want a

reminder that my friend and my fiancée had fucked me over sideways and had been doing so for a long time. I'd been forced to examine every instance I'd found the two of them alone. Seven months pregnant, and I'd only been gone five fucking months!

I groaned before turning the water off, exiting the shower. Wiping the moisture from the mirror, I stared at my pale eyes and stringy hair. Exhaling slowly, I opened the makeup bag and started applying cosmetics to cover the bruises on my cheeks that hadn't healed. I'd need to check in with Bali and see what was up with that, since my body should have been healing already.

Once I had my face on, I peered down at the marking that started beneath one breast, slowly drifting down the side to my hip, where it moved toward my belly. Glaring at the thin black marks, I trailed my fingertips over them until a knock at the door caused a soft cry to escape my lips as I jumped.

"Everything okay in there? I got coffee on, and an omelet started," Noah called through the door. "It's filled with meat, just how you like it."

I rolled my eyes at my startled response. "I'll be out in a moment." I glanced at the tight tank top I wouldn't have typically chosen for myself. I preferred baggy clothes, but I hadn't bought any before leaving.

I hadn't purchased many clothes at all, but mostly because they ended up destroyed from hunting. I owned only a few pairs of jeans, camisole tops, and army fatigues. Grabbing the green army jacket, I slid it over my arms and gave my ragged appearance a once over before adjusting the jeans that hugged my hips.

Stepping from the bathroom, I smiled at Noah, who gazed at the outfit. "I'm guessing Kaderyn helped my dad shop for clothing?"

"Nope," she called from the other room. "Noah did that because he said you'd need something to wear when you came home. We all know you suck at buying things for yourself, even though there's such a thing as online shopping!"

"Yeah, I'm aware!" I shot back, grumbling as I exited the bedroom to find the den filled with people. Bali looked at my face, covered in makeup, and grimaced.

"Add more cover-up. You look like a battered woman, babe," he stated, standing from the small couch he dwarfed with his form. Kind blue eyes with thick black lashes batted innocently when I growled at his words. "Here," he said, handing me some pills. "These will help with the healing. I fear Ezekiel's formula doesn't go with your specific genetic make-up, but then nothing really does. Take two now and two in a couple of hours. It should remove the bruising on your face, but not the deep tissue wounds. Those look angry today, but angry means it's healing. I'm guessing the amount of damage you took has something to do with the slow healing process." He dropped four blue pills into my hand and smiled gently. "I saved five of the dying, but the rest..." his smile faded as he shook his head. "We have twenty-nine dead, Xariana. I wish I could have saved more, but the damage was substantial from the bombs that went off in the courtyard."

"It didn't look like a bomb in the videos. It looked like the cars exploded and then folded into themselves.

We'll have to wait for the forensic team to look closer at the scraps left from the detonations," I muttered, eyeing the omelet as my mouth salivated at the smell inside the room.

Accepting a glass of water from Noah, I downed the tablets and headed toward the table, only for Bali to stop me.

"You need to wait at least an hour before eating, I'm afraid," he informed, dashing my hopes of a home-cooked meal. Groaning, I turned, glaring at him. "I must insist unless you wish to vomit them and the meal up, Xariana. They're rather touchy with food in your stomach. You may have coffee, though."

Grumbling beneath my breath, I headed for the coffeepot, finding it empty. Sighing, I turned to see Noah holding out a cup with cream already in the mug. Smiling at him, he grinned back.

"I wasn't trying you without some caffeine in your blood," he stated, sipping from his mug.

"What would I do without you?" I muttered.

"What you've been doing without him for the last five months," Micah snorted, causing my stomach to twist into a knot. "Where have you been?" he continued, as if he had any right to ask me.

"Hunting," I snapped at him over the rim of the mug. "Not that it's any of your business, now is it? I'm sure my whereabouts were the last thing that worried you, what with the new baby and wife to keep you happy." I slipped out before noticing the uncomfortable silence that followed my statement.

"Okay," Noah slowly stated, and my attention moved back to him. "I have the funeral rites planned to be held at the mansion. I hope that is okay? I figured that you'd want it to be performed there, because it's where we usually hold them. I asked Kaderyn to find you something to wear since you don't own a dress and will need one for tonight."

"That's fine," I quipped, sipping the magical beans that turned me from a she-demon to human-ish. "It's where my father would have had the ceremony, so we will too. Plus, the cemetery is there. I'll grab the keys, and we can get some volunteers to move the caskets and things needed up to the mansion." It fucking hurt to say it out loud, knowing that we had lost a lot of good people last night.

My stomach growled, and with a longing look, I eyed the omelet before allowing Noah to drag me out of the apartment. Twenty minutes later, we were reviewing what little info we'd discovered during the night, which wasn't shit. If the Underworld was chattering, they were doing it silently.

Studying the images on the screen, I frowned. Doing a headcount, I deepened the crease in my forehead before standing up to walk closer. Turning, I moved back, grabbing the page of names I was about to call out over the air, ending the hunter's service to the guild.

"Son of a bitch," I snapped. "How the hell did we miss that?" I demanded crossly, kicking myself for not catching it sooner.

"What do you see?" Noah asked, coming up behind me to look at what I'd discovered.

"Twenty-nine people died, and five survived. There are seven women we have not found. Look at this," I stated, clicking the frame to the image right before the first explosion happened. "It was a distraction. They took those women when the cars detonated, but we missed it last night. Forty-two people were in the courtyard. They took them just before the first explosion, and then took my father before the last one occurred. It's a sleight of hand. First, draw the eye away from the purpose, and then remove them when the focus was elsewhere."

"Holy shit," he muttered beside me crossly. "No one even fucking guessed they were gone. How is that possible?"

"Easily," I mumbled, focusing on the scene in case we'd missed something else. "They're women that wouldn't have been missed until we did a headcount. None of the girls have family here. They're all orphans, varying in ages."

"Okay, so they took women. Why?" Micah asked, fixated on the crumpled form of his wife on the computer.

I switched the images, frowning as I studied a photo of Micah beside Meredith, lifting her into his arms. It shouldn't have hurt as much as it did, but learning the two had married and were expecting a child felt like I'd been socked in the gut. Through everything that had happened, I'd never seen that shit coming. It meant they had been fooling around for months while I'd been looking the other way. And the entire time, I'd been oblivious to the fact that they'd been together.

"Trafficking, maybe?" Kaderyn offered, pointing at another photo. "What the hell is that?"

I turned, focusing on the blurring image. Then, zooming in to enhance it, I peered at what looked like a streak of light on the monitor. The hint of amber made my heart race, causing a smile to play on my lips.

"Son of a bitch," I whispered. "Can we can clear that image up?"

"Let me try something, Xari," Forest offered, working his magic with the technology we had.

Luckily, our donors didn't blink at donating a ton of cash to keep theirs and our existence silent. It allowed us to buy the coolest toys and gear that made it a lot easier to catch creatures that were brilliant at hiding from the outside world. Unfortunately, they didn't like to remain hidden.

By the time Forest had finished, we had a partial image of the silver-haired male. Moving closer to the screen, I grinned.

"Gotcha ya, fucker," I grunted, turning to Forest. "Great job, kid." I smiled at him before placing my hands on his desk, and he flinched at my proximity. "I need you to go frame by frame and clean up each image. I don't care if it's a spec on the screen; we need to see it."

"I can do that, but I sort of want to be at the ceremony tonight. My aunt was one of the unlucky ones that didn't survive." He fidgeted while stating his case.

"Of course you can be there. Everyone will be there, minus those who offered to remain behind to guard the guild. Can you finish up after the ceremony or tomorrow morning?" I asked, hoping I didn't have to force him back into the seat when the funeral rites were complete.

"Right after the rites will be fine, ma'am," he whispered, swallowing audibly, and relief washed through him as I backed up. Slowly, I shifted closer again, leaning against his desk.

"What is scaring you, Forest?" I questioned.

"You're Xariana Anderson, and I am the one who has to count your kills every night. Most hunters bring in one or two kills a month, but you report several, if not double digits, ma'am. In all honesty, you freak me out a little."

I blanched at the laughter that sounded behind me. Frowning, I turned, glaring at my team. Shaking off the kid's terror of me, I snorted. "I earned my position here. Most people assume I gained my status from being the daughter of the creator of the guilds. I wanted to earn my rightful place based on my skills, not my name."

"You did, ma'am," he returned, nodding around the room. "No one here questions your skill or that you're one of us by right. It's just a lot of kills, and you're young. You're a year older than me, and you have more kills than anyone else, minus your father. It's an honor to even be in your presence, honestly."

I lifted a brow, then gave myself a mental shake. "That's enough honesty for today, Forest. You can go prepare for the funeral." Once he'd exited the room, I groaned as the others slow-clapped at me. "Stick it, assholes."

"I thought you were going to have the poor thing pissing his pants," Kaderyn snorted.

"He's a strange kid," I muttered absently, staring at the being in the image. "We need to find out why they took the women. Taking my father made sense if it was for ransom or a vendetta. This development creates an additional problem. I don't think whoever took them was planning to traffic them. Look at the outfit on this male. It screams money. He's wearing diamond cufflinks, dressed in an expensive suit, which doesn't fit an assault team or the type of slimy creeps that traffic women. They want them for something, and we have to figure it out. The clock's ticking."

Chapter Seven

We arrived at the mansion after dusk. Fires burned brightly against the setting sun, and a light breeze filled the area with the earthy scent of sage and lemongrass. Priests, Pastors, and other religious leaders joined us at the behest of families, given free spiritual reign over their parishioner's rites.

It was sobering to watch a mass funeral, knowing that so many folks I'd worked with over the years were gone. A sinking sensation filled my stomach, churning inside of me. Noah, Kaderyn, and a few others stood behind me during the ceremony, providing silent comfort to one another.

After the service, I'd remained at the ceremonial grounds until the bodies were salted and burned to nothing more than ash. This process prevented anyone from raising the dead from their afterlife, ensuring their eternal rest. It was the same procedure used while hunting, keeping the proof of the kill from human eyes or knowledge.

Music started, and Simple Man by Lynyrd Skynyrd echoed through the valley surrounding the mansion. My phone chirped, pulling my attention to the message, and my eyes narrowed on the name. It was from Axton, a local bar owner that served Otherworld creatures.

"I'll be back in a moment." I slowly made my way over the cobblestone walk and past the swimming pool that had sat empty for over twenty-plus years.

Stepping into the house, I smelled the musty scent of dust and time. My gaze slid over the covered furniture, and I swiped at the wall, turning the lights on. My attention moved around the den, slowly taking in the pictures that hung on the wall, topped by a thin layer of dusty film over the glass.

Lifting my head, I noted the elegant, high vaulted ceilings and crystal chandeliers reflecting prisms of rainbows onto the walls. Moving deeper into the room, I paused at the bar to examine a single glass with red lipstick on the rim. I looked around, studying the areas where the dust had been displaced.

I walked over to a console table near the couch and picked up a photo that had been cleared of dust, staring at the original hunters. My mother and father had started the hunter guild soon after attacks on humans had become rampant in these parts. Sandra, my father's sister, was one of the first to die. Hers was the largest memorial in the cemetery behind the mansion.

My gaze slipped over the faces as an eerily sensation of being watched crept up my spine, forcing me to glance behind me. Then, swallowing the unease, I turned back to look at the image of my mother. I was the perfect mixture of my parents, but where she was slender, I had curves, and her fair hair and skin contrasted with mine, which favored my father.

My phone rang, jolting me from my thoughts in the otherwise silent house. Sliding my finger over the screen, I held it up to my ear.

"Anderson," I muttered into the receiver.

"Hey," Axton's dark, silky tone wrapped around me, soothing me immediately. The man had a voice that could warm your ovaries and twist them into a frenzied need. "I heard about the attack, Xariana. I'm sorry that I didn't contact you sooner. Shit's been crazy over the past few hours."

"I imagine so," I snorted while moving back toward the bar, running my fingers over the surface beside the glass. I lifted it, scrunching my nose in distaste as I inhaled the lingering scent of gin. "You said you had information for me?"

"Yeah, but I also expected you to call me when I sent you the text. You enjoy making men wait for you, don't you?" he teased before pressing the receiver against his shoulder, causing static to fill the line. "Ana, no. Use the other one for tonight. He's coming, and I intend to impress, not offend."

"Who are you expecting this evening?" I inquired, intrigued to know who Axton wanted to impress.

More static sounded, and then Axton was back, ignoring my question. "You put on the bulletin that you wanted to know when anyone new was in town.

There are a few witches I haven't seen before, and I know they haven't registered with the immortal houses, either. There are also a few werewolves causing issues, and I recalled that you've had wayward packs thinking themselves above the rules."

"Conrad hasn't enforced them to register?" Conrad was the head of the House of Wolves and was responsible for all the packs in our area.

"He'd have to get his head out of Rhys Van Helsing's woman's ass," he snorted, sighing. "Look, I know the hunter guild is limping right now, but the moment you stop enforcing shit…" he let his meaning hang in the air.

"We're not faltering, Axton. I have two hundred hunters in residence and another five hundred a phone call and a flight away. I don't intend to shut down, nor do I plan to allow anyone to think otherwise. Send me the location of the witches and the wolves, and I will send teams to deal with them both."

"Doesn't work like that," he chuckled. "I don't give shit out for free, woman. I'll see you in an hour. Don't be late, Xari." Axton ended the call, and I groaned at the idea of going to his club tonight.

I had already borrowed a skater skirt with a thin, backless top from Kaderyn for the ceremony, so at least I was dressed for the occasion. The shirt was held up by a silver circle that adorned my throat, and it exposed the outline of the wings tattooed on my back. I'd thrown a suit jacket over the top and wore a pair of her stiletto heels that had my feet aching. I had taken extra time to cover my remaining bruises and fixed my hair in a twin braid that I'd learned from a YouTube tutorial on

Viking-style braids.

Sliding out of the jacket, I sat on the stool, peering back at the glass before typing off a group message. Within moments, Noah, Micah, Kaderyn, and Onyx were standing in front of me, waiting expectantly.

"Micah, go back to the funeral," I ordered, watching the stubborn jerk of his chin before exhaling in frustration. "Can you handle a mission?"

"I can keep my shit together, Xar. I need to be out there, not here, drinking my pain away."

I nodded slowly, turning to Noah. "Gather a small team of ten or so hunters," I smirked at the way his eyes narrowed. "Axton has information we want on the witches and a small pack of werewolves mucking around town. We can't afford to look weak right now. Have our team prepare for a strike, and we'll pray that we don't need them. Knowing Axton, his payment is going to be a pain in the ass to obtain his intel. I swear, he enjoys making my life hell."

"You should just handle the prick and show him who the fuck he's messing with," Micah snorted, staring me down with anger pulsing through the veins in his neck.

Micah would never have approved of the deal I'd made with Axton. But he had a pulse on everything happening in the Underworld chatter and a finger on the line of immortals that was priceless. Micah had demanded that someone else be assigned to the bar owner, but Axton and I both refused.

"I'll handle him accordingly, following the rules of the informant laws," I returned sharply, standing to fix my skirt before grabbing one of the whiskey bottles from the wall behind the counter. "Is everyone here fine with leaving early?" I asked, slowly rounding the bar to grab a few shot glasses. It was a tradition to toast to the fallen, and I needed a drink.

I watched Noah lifting the glass to his nose before lowering his eyes to my lips. "Gin? You hate gin," he muttered.

"And crimson lipstick, too," I offered, holding his gaze. "I'm guessing someone was here before the funeral." And that idea didn't sit well with me. Unless my father had a side piece, but that wasn't his style, and I hadn't ever known him to bring anyone here.

Once I'd topped off the shots, I held mine up in the air. "To the souls we lost and to the ones who remain on the hunt. We are the unwanted and unseen, yet the one thing that protects those from the monsters that live amongst them," I finished, clinking my glass against the others before downing it and enjoying the burn that slid down my throat. "Let's go hunting, ladies and gents."

Less than an hour later, we pulled up to Axton's club and exited the Land Rovers cautiously. Glancing down the long line that wrapped around the corner of the block where the club sat, I rolled my eyes. Axton had a flair for drawing a crowd to his club, and he was the main attraction. Music pumped from the ground floor, the only one that humans could access. Luckily, humans were only permitted on weekends due to the laws prohibiting their presence in clubs that accommodated the shady clientele of the Otherworld.

Axton catered to everyone, regardless of what chaos they brought with them. Of course, I'd protected him from being on our watch list by enforcing that he followed the rules. Unfortunately, it created more than one issue with his inability to stay out of trouble.

Bypassing those waiting to enter, I grinned at Carson, the bouncer, who narrowed his gaze on the group that moved past the never-ending line. He sneered, revealing fangs with a glimpse of crimson eyes as I stopped in front of him.

"We're expected," I announced, waiting for the vampire to remove the rope and allow us through.

"Your kind is an abomination that should have been dealt with at birth, hunter," he growled, condemnation filling each word.

"Maybe," I grunted, smiling impishly. "But your kind just keeps creating more of us. Perhaps if you and yours weren't so fucking sloppy, I'd be out of a job?" I returned icily, watching him for any movement.

Vampires, by nature, were shifty assholes that were cold and calculated. They also had super speed and the ability to lead by compulsion. Genetics usually protected hunters and half-breeds from being compelled to do anything by Otherworld creatures.

"One day, you're going to end up dead, and I will piss on your grave, Xariana," Carson sneered.

"Only if I don't take your head before that day comes. Now, open the fucking rope and let us in so we can figure out what your master wants from us." Carson was just a puppet to Axton, and I got off on reminding him of that fact often.

His eyes returned to crimson at the mention of his

boss, which caused Noah and Micah to step closer to me. The vampire removed the red rope and stepped back, allowing us to pass, while others waiting to enter bellowed their frustration. Tossing a withering glance over my shoulder at a female shifter that snarled, I wrinkled my nose before shrugging in response to the profanity that echoed down the line.

In the club, I peered through the people that turned, noticing our presence within their little gathering. Humans weren't allowed on this level, which meant everyone here was an immortal or half-breed. Sensing our arrival, creatures moved out of the path we were taking to reach the bar, where Axton was dancing.

I Wanna Be Your Salve by Måneskin was pounding loudly through the club. Axton was shirtless, with his sinewy, sleek muscles covered in a fine sheen of sweat. Jeans hung loosely on his hips, revealing the V-line of sin he promised those insane enough to crawl into his bed. He had tattoos on his sides that twisted in thin, black tendrils to his shoulder blades, drifting over them and back to where they'd started, just above the waist.

Women danced near the bar, each one reaching their hands up for his fingers to touch them. Snorting at his antics, I walked to where he had women swooning with the simple brush of his hand against theirs. The asshole knew how to create a frenzy of hormonal tension, which was impressive.

His ice-colored eyes met mine through the crowd that was parting, allowing us to pass. A sinful smile played on his full mouth as inky hair covered his forehead, brushing against his shoulders. Axton was a piece of masculine art, and the broody prick knew how to work it to his benefit. We'd never been anything more than business associates, and that's where our connection ended.

I wasn't into pretty boys or flirtatious ones that thought women belonged on their knees, awaiting their pleasure. I'd watched women crawl to appease this creature, and I'd also heard whispers of his sexually deviant ways. Neither of those things appealed to me.

Tension shot throughout the crowd as we cleared the pulsing dancefloor. My hackles rose, and I focused on a dark corner where a group of men sat bathed in the shadows. I could barely make out their forms, but sensed the immense power wafting from them into the room. No one approached their table, not even the servers.

A snarl sounded in front of me, yanking my attention toward the threatening sound. I slipped my hand to my back, flicking the safety off my weapon as a werewolf stood hovering above me. Startling blue eyes warned of his status as alpha, but that wasn't what made me reach for my gun. Instead, it was the rest of his pack slowly gathering around us.

"Well, shit, we going to play it like that then?" I snorted, knowing he'd hear me over the music still blaring through the room.

Chapter Eight

I didn't remove my hand from my gun, knowing that this asshole was salivating to end me. Bjorn, the alpha of this rogue pack, was known for causing problems, and the prick thought he was above the laws here. Everyone in the club held their breaths in anticipation of the impending conflict.

"You think you can come onto our turf and not get what's coming to you, whore?" Bjorn snarled, sending spittle flying as he fought his transformation. "I should bend you over and teach you where you belong, hunter. You're going down, and when I'm finished with you, I'll make sure to fuck your corpse, just for fun." He laughed coldly, closing the distance between us.

I squeezed the trigger, rapidly firing my gun with the barrel aimed at his dick. His agony-filled howl shot through the club, making my lips curl into a sadistic smile. He sliced his clawed hand through the air, but I captured it, his wide, blue gaze glowing as he struggled through the pain, trying to shift into his wolf form.

"I think you might need a new dick to get that job done, Bjorn," I hissed, holding the gun to his chin and pulling the trigger, watching the blood spray across the floor as he fell back. His beta shrieked at the loss of his alpha, and then all hell broke loose before Bjorn's corpse even touched the ground.

The air grew thick with power as his pack rushed toward us, promising violence for their alpha. Retrieving my second gun, I extended my arms, firing and downing two of the wolves easily. The bullets we used had silver casings. Though delicate, they efficiently ended their lives.

A female wolf collided with me, causing me to drop one of my guns to prevent her snapping fangs from reaching my face. I hissed, pushing her head back, and popped two bullets into her chest, spinning to kick another wolf, who had intended to take a cheap shot at me. Firing my gun in his direction, I groaned as it clicked with the sound of an empty chamber. Dropping it, I reached behind me, producing the small dual blades I'd been using since puberty.

He rushed toward me, forcing me to back up and slide to the side before twisting and cutting through his middle as if he were made of butter. Ducking to avoid a hand full of razor-sharp claws, I sliced up blindly, catching the arm with one blade before dancing away from the wolf howling in pain.

Noah and Micah closed in around him, both using their daggers to battle the fight. Knives were easier to control in confined spaces, and with the club packed with creatures attempting to take advantage of the chaos to remove more hunters, we shouldn't have cared who was caught in the crossfire. They moved swiftly, calculating the other's position before slicing through the advancing wolf, turning him into four pieces that splattered to the ground in a heap of blood and gore. Stepping back, I slammed into something solid. Turning, I sucked in a breath from the electrical shock that slithered along my flesh, making my teeth chatter from the contact. Dark, midnight eyes lowered to mine, holding them for a moment as we both peered at one another.

My body reacted in a visceral manner that left me internally fighting to take back control. My first thought was that this creature was a male incubus demon, which would account for the strange reaction to his touch. Only he didn't look like a demon. His eyes were a mixture of blues and purples that plunged into starry depths that gleamed like sparkling diamonds in the distance. He wore a fine suit, with a white shirt under his coat, unbuttoned to reveal the hint of a tattoo beneath it. His persona screamed mafia, but this area didn't have anyone like that of which I was aware.

Something moved behind me, but the male in front of me merely reached over my shoulder, never releasing my stare as I heard bone crunching. His body skimmed against mine, and I gasped at the raw current of power that his touch sent rushing through me. His lips brushed my ear, and then everything came back to life.

Spinning in place, I lifted my daggers as a wolf slammed into me, sending me backward against the male's solid form. Lifting my foot, I kicked the werewolf back, peeling myself off the man's expensive suit to swing the blades without a chance of causing him harm. I didn't know how I knew, but I realized that if he'd wanted me dead, I'd be so.

Noah, Micah, and Onyx fought off clubbers, while Kaderyn handled two werewolves fighting against the lone female. I whistled loudly, and she flattened her body against the floor to avoid my blades cutting the air from where she'd stood seconds before. Thrusting down and then up swiftly, I spun hard, slicing the wolves' throats, sending their heads rolling across the dancefloor.

Someone grabbed my skirt, tearing the material to reveal the tight shorts I'd worn underneath. I kicked my foot backward, pushing the sharp tips of my stilettos into flesh. Then, withdrawing them, I turned, holding my blade against the throat of the last wolf.

"Move, and I'll fucking end you," I hissed through clenched teeth.

"Fuck you, Anderson. You and your hunters are finished in this town. It is open season on you and yours," she snarled.

"Fucking try me," I chuckled, shoving the blade into her brain. Removing it, I crouched beside her lifeless form, wiping my knives on her jeans before standing and peering around the club.

Dead werewolves littered the ground, along with a few other creatures that had thought to intervene, trying their hand at a chance for fame by ending one of the hunters present. I gave a pointed look across the room, glaring murderously at the crowd that was slowly inching their way back toward the wall.

"Salt the bodies," I ordered, moving through the carnage to Axton, who watched me with a calculated expression burning in his stare.

Once I reached him, I smiled tightly as he waited for me to speak. Rolling my eyes to the bottles that lined his shelf, I tapped my fingers on the bar impatiently. Noah stepped closer, placing my sidearm on the marble top. I picked it up before aiming it at Axton, who narrowed his gaze on the weapon. Adjusting my aim, I shot the top row of bottles above his head, raining glass down onto him.

"Fucking hell, Xari! What the fuck?" he demanded, stepping away from the alcohol pouring from the shelves.

"I don't like being used, Axton." My voice was cold and laced with venom and resentment. "You set me up. You informed Bjorn and his pack that we'd be here tonight. His was the wayward pack you needed to eliminate, correct? I'm betting he's also the werewolf who opened a bar three buildings down from yours. You didn't want the competition, so you called me here to take care of your problem."

"And? It didn't break the laws you and your people placed, did it?" he demanded coldly.

Axton wasn't stupid by any means. He was a calculated asshole that would support whoever benefited him the most. If he had another benefactor to protect him from our wrath, he'd have taken it in a heartbeat. He hadn't made it to the top by being honest or caring about anyone except himself.

"I'm not your personal hunter, Axton. You don't get to call me, promise information, and then coerce me to do your dirty work. You pulled me away from the funeral rites of my brothers and sisters. And for what? So I could take out your fucking competition. You're a sadistic prick," I exhaled and peered over my shoulder as my team shifted nearer to me.

I could sense Axton's people closing in around us and knew they wouldn't be as easy to fight as the werewolves. I didn't wish for the situation to escalate, but I also couldn't allow him to think he could use me as his wild card when he needed one to play. Smoothing my hand out on the counter, I watched the hard lines of his face relaxing.

He knew I wouldn't fight him, but he also understood I wouldn't hesitate to bring down hell on his inky dark head. I was pissed, but he had the upper hand because we were low on ammo after dropping thirty or more werewolves inside the club.

"Your laws make it hard to deal with shit in the way I'm used to handling it. You didn't like Bjorn any more than I did, Xari." Axton braced his hands on the counter, staring at me through icy blue eyes surrounded by thick, lush lashes. "You think you're the only one who has offered me protection?"

"No, of course not, Axton," I snorted, not backing down or looking away from his gaze. "You're the manipulative prick who is always trying to get a leg up. You have no loyalties other than to the creatures you house inside this place. You'd probably sell out your mother if it brought you power, wouldn't you?"

"I already did that to that ice-hearted bitch," he

chuckled, walking to the only shelf that wasn't broken and carefully grabbing a bottle of scotch before turning back to face me. "You wanted information. I told you it wasn't free, hunter. Nothing is ever free, and we both know that is the cold, hard facts of this world."

"I don't need your fucking lecture." I stared him down unwaveringly. He was accustomed to women caving to his unworldly aura, but I wouldn't fall for that shit.

Axton leaned forward, pushing a drink toward me. My mouth watered, scenting the essence of the otherworldly drugs pulsing in the glass of scotch. I could smell the enticing amber liquid that urged me to take a sip, bringing my inhuman instincts to the forefront of my mind.

Half-breeds sold their soul to taste this shit, but I knew better. I understood the moment it touched my lips, my body would sing to release my inner creature. Smirking, I pushed the glass back, and his brow creased at my rejection.

"I don't drink that crap, Axton." I nodded to the alcohol oozing down the shelves behind him. "You may be able to persuade weak-minded creatures with the allure of that poison, but I'm not interested. You claimed to have information; let's have it."

Axton snorted, sliding his gaze to the right of us where the male I'd touched was sitting quietly, observing. My attention slid to his dark eyes that slowly scrutinized my face before lowering to my bare hips, then to my holsters that crisscrossed at my waist.

My stomach churned beneath his intense stare, as

if he was considering how easy it would be to end my life. Power continued to slither from his pores, alerting me he wasn't anything I'd ever come across before. Typically, I could pinpoint a breed within seconds of coming within miles of it, but this male was a mystery.

I took one quick sweep of his form and slid my gaze back to Axton, who silently studied me. Then he turned from me and walked around the bar, and the men and women behind me aimed their weapons at his unguarded back.

A quick shake of my head had them locking their safety, and the sound of salt shaken over the bodies of the dead seemed to diffuse the situation. I didn't need my team fighting this battle, not when I had Axton under control. He grabbed a glass and turned back to me, holding it up for me to see him pouring some clean, non-enchanted whisky.

Pushing the drink toward me, he glanced at the hunters cleaning up any signs that we'd ever been here. His eyes caught mine, studying my face, then shifted to the creature that had yet to move from the chair he'd retaken after the fight.

I'd never met or encountered anything like this male before, which bothered me. He wasn't just unnerving; he was exotic and oozed power that drew my attention. The hint of ink under his shirt made me want to know what lay beneath the scrap of fabric. I'd felt nothing like him, and touching him awakened something inside of me I thought had died from Micah's betrayal.

Lifting the glass to my nose, I inhaled the scotch while keeping my gaze on Axton. He gave me a crooked smile, slowly shaking his head.

"How come you don't respond to me like other females do, Xariana?"

"Because, Axton, I have self-esteem, and I refuse to be just another bitch you've bedded." I sipped the whiskey, enjoying the burn as it touched my tongue to slide down my throat. "You said you had info, and we're running low on midnight steam," I pointed out, setting the glass down and pushing it toward him. He started to lift the bottle, but I shook my head. "One drink is enough. I don't want you getting the wrong impression and assuming we're friends."

"You're such a bitch, and yet I've imagined fucking you on this very bar until you begged me to stop." Axton held my stare, challenging me to shy away from his crude mouth.

"You couldn't handle me," I returned icily. "You want easy prey that surrenders because you tell them to do so. I don't submit, ever."

His lips jerked up, and his eyes narrowed to slivers. "Ah, pretty girl. Every female submits when she meets the right man. You just haven't met him yet. We all know that asshole glaring murder at me wasn't the man for you. We just had to wait out that mistake. Didn't we, Noah?" Axton grinned at Noah, who was trying to ignore our conversation, and failing miserably. "You need someone who isn't afraid to play with the wickedness burning inside those pretty green eyes, Xari. You should have a man that will pin you down and fuck that fight out of you. One day, you will meet him, and you'll never need to wonder why women want a man to protect them." Scuffling sounded behind me as

Micah snarled a reply that I couldn't make out.

"Do I look like I need to be protected?" I sneered, turning my nose up at his words. I stood to my full height of five-foot-eight and tilted my head. "I do like the idea of a man fucking the fight out of me, though. It would intrigue me to discover if it could be done. However, I have no interest in an alpha male who wants to control his female. I want someone who isn't intimidated by the fact that my lady balls are as big as his. Now, give me the information and stop pretending to be worried about my sex life. We both know I'd come out on top if you took me to bed, and you're not interested in me anymore than I am you, Axton."

His blue gaze flashed with liquid fire before he ran his tongue over his teeth. "There's an entire coven of witches that slipped into town two days before the guild was attacked. They didn't register with Talia or any other coven. The House of Witches isn't aware of their presence here either. There are twelve of them altogether, which is a lot for one coven. The witch you need to worry about is Raven Thorne. She's powerful but young. She and the others are here because members of her coven came to our town a couple of weeks back, and never returned to Salem once their business here had concluded."

"You summoned me from our hunter's funeral service for wayward witches?" I snapped, glaring at him.

"And to murder my competition, which you did as payment," he snorted, smiling coldly before he crossed his arms over his naked chest, daring me to challenge him.

"Conrad will seek punishment for this slight. You can explain to him why you set me up to assassinate one of his packs. The House of Wolves don't take kindly to registered wolves being killed. Bjorn might have been a sleazy asshole, but he was here legally. Now he's dead, along with his pack, and your entire club witnessed their slaughter. When Conrad comes to me for answers, I will send him to you. You knew I was bringing a team, because you are fully aware that I am in charge of the hunter guild, and wouldn't be traveling anywhere alone. You didn't want to hurt me tonight; you just wanted Bjorn dead. He's been trying to gain access to your club for weeks, but your people haven't allowed him or his spies entrance. This evening, though, you permitted him in, knowing that he'd think he could kill my hunters and me to build his reputation. Expect a visit from Conrad. Have a pleasant night, Axton. Don't ever use me like that again," I growled, turning to leave the bar, but the sound that escaped his throat made me hesitate.

"You still think you're the one in charge, don't you?" he asked, causing my eyes to narrow in response. "Things are changing around here, Xari. Your father is gone, and everyone now knows it. How long before you lose what little hold you have in this city? Sure, you have the backing of the alpha houses, but not even they will challenge what is coming. Your glass castle is crumbling, princess. Your father's skeletons are being revealed, and with that said, you can get the fuck out of my club. You're not welcome or wanted here anymore. Our business arrangement has come to an end."

I smiled without allowing Axton to see how his words jolted me. Remaining in place, I tilted my head before scanning his expression. He wasn't backing down, and that told me he had found someone else more powerful than the guild to protect him. Licking my lips, I sucked my bottom one between my teeth, rocking on my heels.

"Careful not to cut your nose off to spite your face, Axton. There seems to be a lot of that happening lately," I muttered, stepping back while holding his icy glare. "We don't run or hide from our enemies. Our flag still waves, and it doesn't fade. You think we're weak, but isn't that what your kind said about the hunters initially? That we were just outcast bastards who wouldn't survive without your kind protecting us?" I smirked, and Axton's jaw pulsed as if fighting the urge to respond. "Who needed protection? You or me? Our deal protected you from me." He stepped forward, and the click of weapons being drawn and armed sounded all around us.

After a moment's hesitation, Axton grinned and pointed to the door. My team and I moved cautiously toward the exit, but the sensation of being watched niggled at my spine. Looking back, I glanced across the dancefloor and saw Axton with his back to us. The stranger's gaze was fully on me as he spoke in a hushed tone to Axton's treacherous ass, who turned at something that was said and smiled at me before I dismissed them both, leaving the club.

Chapter Nine

It took me less than an hour to discover the name of the male inside Axton's club. Kieran Knight. I'd made call after call to learn what people knew about the man and what he was, only to get shut down every time I brought up his name. It was frustrating and made him more intriguing than he should have been.

I fired up the laptop, settling down in the surprisingly comfortable chair of the small elegant desk my father had purchased for me. Xavier may have been rough around the edges with a tough exterior, but the man had lavish tastes.

He had furnished the apartment while I'd been gone, adding simple comforts that he knew I liked. The kitchen was filled with such things, including chamomile and Earl Grey tea. Everything was organic, which was my preference.

The tea kettle whistled, forcing my tired body to

the stove to move the pot off the burner, and I gasped as my fingers touched the metal. I quickly went to the sink and ran cold water on them before holding them against my lips. Grabbing two tea bags and a spoon, I headed to the little pink box of sugar and pulled out two cubes, adding them to the oversized mug.

At the desk, I placed my teacup on a coaster with a picture of Deadpool riding a unicorn. I stirred the tea before brushing my fingertips over the keyboard to type in Kieran's name to start a search. After a few moments, I frowned at finding nothing online about the mysterious male. Typing in my code, I entered a special area on the dark web reserved for the guild, the main source of information we relied on to catalog creatures. This was a resource shared by hunters across the globe, containing a database on how to hunt, kill, and control each breed.

Kieran's name brought up some pictures and the few details obtained on the guy. I skimmed through images, pausing as one came into view of him wearing only a pair of slacks. My gaze feasted on his sleek muscular frame, sliding over the tattoos that decorated his arms and sides in strange, ancient writing, following their beauty as they dipped below his belt.

Dark inky hair covered his head, but his was kept short where other creatures preferred their hair to be longer. I clicked on the next photo, which was a close-up of his face. His ears were pointed at the tips, giving away his fae heritage. But there was a lot of fae in Washington, with Hunter, the leader of the House of Fae, holding court in town. I studied Kieran's features, noting his full mouth and angular chin, then I focused on those eyes that I'd been unable to purge from my mind, staring up at the camera. They were a deep indigo, a mixture of dark blues that appeared almost amethyst in the light. My stomach tightened the longer I looked at them, twisting with pent-up desire. I needed to get laid if staring at Kieran's image was enough to make me respond in such a way that my clit pulsed.

Sipping my tea, I silently read through the information about him. There wasn't much, though. In fact, it was depressing how little was known about Kieran. He was a mercenary for hire, one that cost a fortune. He had unlimited resources and a reputation for never turning down a job. He also ran a shell company that hid his real identity from the human world, located here in Washington.

How had I never come across him? Adjusting in my seat, I typed in the address noted on his file into Google Maps, studying the three blocks identified as his location. Grabbing a pen and paper from the drawer, I wrote the information down and resumed my investigation of his photos.

Searching through them, I found one of him in a bed with a woman, noting that it was a still-shot of a video. Kieran was above the woman, and the look on her face was of absolute pleasure. Peering around, I pushed play on the image. Her screams ripped through my apartment, making me jump. I turned down the volume, blushing as he thrust against her.

My body heated, and like some creeper, I watched him fucking her until the video shut off. Then, swallowing down the urge to watch it again, I switched off the computer and shivered as I pulsed with need.

He'd been raw, brutally taking her, and shit if I hadn't responded like a bitch in heat.

Finishing my tea, I slipped into the shower, washing off the day's turmoil as I readied for bed. My body was strung tightly from stress, and I needed a release. Fighting typically eased the tension, but it hadn't. I'd yet to make any progress in finding out who had attacked us, and my father was still missing, adding to my anxiety.

Sure, it had only been one night, but what was happening to him? Was he in pain or being tortured? Was he already dead? What about the women that they'd taken with him? I'd followed his rules, burying the dead and worrying about what I could do in the moment. I couldn't find my father by myself, and tonight I'd probably fucked up my opportunity to find out any additional information from the Underworld.

Turning off the water, I slipped from the shower and wrapped a towel around myself. Inside the bedroom, I grabbed a fresh pair of panties and a soft cotton camisole with suns and moons on it. Searching the drawer for some matching bottoms, I frowned when I came up empty. I made a mental note to order some shorts to sleep in and snatched the brush from the vanity, starting in on my hair.

My phone chirped, and I reached for it, seeing Enzo's name on the screen. Answering, I paused as a feminine voice laughed.

"You doing okay? I didn't hear from you today. We were worried," Enzo began, not even bothering with hello.

"I'm fine. Thanks for checking in, though." I sat back on my bed, staring at the ceiling. "Axton turned on me."

"You want him handled? I can end him. Just say the magic words, and he's done here," he chuckled, knowing I wouldn't. The woman in the background squealed, which caused Enzo to hiss. "She's enjoying that shit, asshole. Try actually doing something that resembles torture," he ordered.

"You two need some serious ethics. You can't torment your staff," I snorted, hearing his deep, rumbling chuckle vibrating against my ear. I paused, feeling it pulsing through me. "Calm it down, Enzo," I whispered huskily, far from immune to their male incubus powers.

"That's it, spank that pretty ass until it's bright red," he purred.

I moaned loudly, holding the phone away from my ear. My thighs clenched, and everything inside me threatened to explode from the tone Enzo had used to seduce the female in their room. Regular incubus demons were unnervingly powerful with their pheromones and voice, but the twins took that shit to another level. My nipples hardened, and my eyes rolled back in my head.

"Shit, Xari? My bad. Don't tell your dad, or he'll have my balls in a sling," he groaned, adjusting the tone he used to continue speaking.

"You're talking to Xar?" Ezekiel asked, not bothering to adjust his voice. I dropped the phone, rolling over and grasping a pillow between my thighs, growling at them. Pressure built until I felt my body pulsing with the desire to release the orgasm they had accidentally forced to the surface.

"You dicks!" I snarled, pushing my face into the pillows.

"Voice, Ezekiel. She's edging. Xavier is gonna fuck us up," Enzo snapped, like it was his brother's fault I was in my current predicament. "Deep breathing helps stop the effects," he offered, exhaling slowly.

After a few awkward moments, I was able to stop biting the pillow. "You two shouldn't be calling me with a bitch between you! It's not healthy for me, or her, let alone safe!" I scolded, fighting my instincts to scream at them both. "Tell me what you assholes know about Kieran Knight."

"Where the fuck did you hear that name?" Ezekiel's tone went from playful to serious in an instant.

"Around," I lied, hearing them ushering their current plaything out of the room.

"Lie," Enzo snorted. "Where?"

"He was at Axton's club tonight, with a front-row seat to witness his betrayal. Axton assured me that our time controlling this city was at an end. I'm guessing he hired Kieran, and I like to know my enemies."

"You stay the fuck away from Kieran Knight," Enzo demanded, his tone etched with something I hadn't ever heard in it before.

"Who is he?"

"You don't need to learn anything about him.

You're not fucking with Kieran, little one. He isn't someone you want to mess with, understood? Agree, Xariana."

Sitting upright, I rolled my eyes and then screamed as the demon twins appeared in my room. Growling, I threw my pillow at Enzo, who stared down at me with a wide, owl-like expression.

"You're in your underwear," he pointed out.

"A warning would have been nice," I snapped, pulling the blankets over me.

"Your wards aren't working, and neither are the hex bags Talia made for your room," Ezekiel announced. "Did you disable them?"

"I have only spent one night inside this room. I should have realized that dad would have placed fucking hex bags everywhere," I snorted, staring at them before pausing. "You're fully dressed."

"You want us to undress?" Ezekiel smirked, grunting when Enzo elbowed him in the stomach.

"She's Xavier's only daughter, asshole. Xariana is so fucking off-limits. In fact, if you rated her availability from 1 to 20, she'd be a negative 30. So, stop flirting with his child. His only child," Enzo scolded.

Ezekiel snorted, and I echoed it, smirking at him when Enzo growled in response to our antics. Enzo moved to the closet, opening it to fish around on the top shelf for something. His hand came away with a sheer, empty bag, reeking of sage.

"You didn't remove the contents from these bags?"

he questioned, glaring at me.

"No," I answered, watching his eyes shift to black before turning to their usual soft blue.

"Truth," he announced, as if I'd even try to deceive him with his ability to distinguish the truth from a lie with his creepy demon mojo.

"Back to Kieran," I stupidly demanded, smiling as they both turned to glare at me. "He's been in town, and yet I have never encountered him. That in and of itself is strange, don't you think?" My tone was abrasive, but fuck it; they'd shown up in my bedroom after midnight. Neither one answered and avoided eye contact by seemingly finding the things inside my room interesting. "I found his address online."

"Dammit, woman," Ezekiel snapped, shaking his dark head. "We don't want you anywhere near that prick. Do you hear us? He's not the type of guy you should fuck with or piss off. Kieran is another level of fucked-up, all on his own. The leaders of the houses don't mess around with him. You get me? There are not many people we can't stop, and he's at the top of that short list."

I shivered at the warning and nodded slowly. I replayed how I'd reacted to Kieran and how the room had stopped moving the moment our eyes had locked after touching one another. I frowned. I'd never felt a sensation like it and had been shocked to experience that kind of power from a total stranger.

"You should visit Talia and have her make you some new hex bags. I will have the wards in here reestablished tomorrow morning. Be a good girl and get some rest, little hunter. I have girls working on the men inside the club, and we're doing everything we can to figure out who attacked the guild. It's only a matter of time before we have your father back, driving us all bug-fuck crazy with missions." Enzo leaned over to kiss my forehead. "You're exhausted and not healing because of it, brat."

"I know," I muttered, kissing Ezekiel on the cheek before he crouched in front of me. "No demon bullshit. I'm going to bed."

"Good girl," he purred, smiling as I felt myself falling backward. "Just a little help, though, to ensure you listen."

I sensed myself drifting to sleep, assisted by the powerful asshole that had knocked me out. I was so going to kick his ass in the morning when they returned to fix the wards. Rootless in a sea of blissful awareness, I smiled as I snuggled into the covers, being pulled up and over my slumbering form. Opening my eyes to tell the twins they could leave, I blinked, looking around.

"Shit," I muttered, sitting up to take in my surroundings. I wasn't in my room, or even on a bed. I was somewhere else entirely.

Chapter Ten

Pushing up from the wooden floor, I gazed around the large room with high ceilings. My brow creased at the lavish furniture and dangling chandeliers that sent prisms of rainbows dancing on the softly lit walls. Pictures sat on easels, mostly of women in different sensual poses.

Turning in a slow circle, I trembled at the power within the room. It was slithering over my exposed skin, reminding me I was clothed in skimpy panties and a spaghetti strap top. My stomach churned with unease, but I shoved it away while moving closer to one of the portraits.

A beautiful, full-figured woman with fiery red hair was reclining on an emerald French tufted chaise lounge chair. Her arm rested on her forehead, and piercing blue eyes held mine, momentarily trapped by their beauty. Lowering my gaze to her body, I smirked at the pose and the thin silver blanket covering her bottom half. Her smile was contagious, and much like looking at the Mona Lisa, you wanted to return the smile.

Sliding my attention to another painting, I moved over the wood floor on bare feet. Stopping at the next image, I frowned at the way the blonde female leaned forward, her heavy breasts pushing against the arm that covered them. Unlike the last portrait, she hadn't hidden her nakedness from the artist. Her smile looked as if she was keeping a secret behind her cherry-colored lips.

Scanning the area, I noticed someone had similarly painted several others. Creeping over the floor, I paused as one floorboard creaked loudly. Ignoring it, I continued deeper into the room, stopping in front of a portrait of a tawny-haired woman with tears running down her cheeks. Unlike the other paintings, the artist had captured her pain perfectly.

"You're either suicidal or incredibly brave," a deeply rich voice growled from behind me.

Spinning around, I gasped, discovering a shirtless Kieran with jeans slung low on his hips. His eyes lowered, slowly taking in my lack of clothing. My heart hammered against my ribcage, and I stepped back, bumping into the picture.

"It's only a dream," I whispered, shaking my head. I swallowed past the fear tightening my chest and throat. My arm caught on the edge of the frame, sending it clattering to the floor as I retreated from his imposing form. I kept him in front of me, continuing to backpedal away from him.

Kieran's mouth tightened while he watched me, inching further from him. I chanted the words out loud, knowing that he couldn't hurt me here. "This is just a dream," I repeated. One conjured from ogling him online, and the twins using their magical mojo on me. My back collided with something solid, and I cried out, watching as he crept forward, slamming his hand on the wall beside my head.

"Tell me, is this a fantasy or a nightmare?" Kieran asked in a haughty tone.

I shook my head slowly, taken aback by the question. Closing my eyes, I counted to ten and tried to redirect the dream to something less dangerous than being half-dressed and alone with Kieran. My stomach tightened, and my nipples hardened like they felt the heat of his gaze, and I opened my eyes, peering up at him.

His attention was on my mouth, causing me to clasp my bottom lip nervously with my teeth to stop the trembling. But then, those deep violet eyes lifted, and a wolfish smile spread over his full mouth. It wasn't friendly by any means, and it kicked my pulse into overdrive.

Kieran grabbed my arms and spun me around, pushing me against the wall. A cry of surprise escaped my lips before I could squash it down. One of his hands continued holding mine above my head, while the other slid down my spine, slowly maneuvering across my waist as if he thought he'd discover a weapon beneath my thin top.

His nose brushed along my throat, inhaling deeply before tracing over the pulse racing at the hollow column of my neck. Slowly, his fingers slipped under my shirt, running them over my stomach until they began moving upward. I moaned as they skimmed the globe of my breast, stopping at the barbell that adorned my nipple. Instead of continuing, he twisted the metal piercing, causing a gasp of pain to escape my lips.

"I'm only dreaming. He can't harm me here," I whispered huskily, wondering why it even mattered. He didn't seem inclined to hurt me as much as he was playing with me.

Deep masculine laughter rumbled against my shoulder, and a violent shudder of need slammed into my abdomen. Kieran's hand moved up and around my neck, and I blinked as my pussy fluttered, awakened by the simple action. He turned me again, and pressed me into the wall, placing his hand back on my throat. He didn't apply pressure, but continued to hold it, stroking my pulse with his thumb.

Kieran's dark gaze shifted to my lips, watching me as I studied him silently. This wasn't real. It couldn't be, right? If I was dreaming, what did it matter if I played along? The hand on my neck lowered and slipped under the thin strap that held my shirt up, breaking it easily. My breasts rose and fell, even as he moved the shirt lower, exposing one.

"Have you figured it out yet?" he asked, pulling his attention from my breast to my face.

"Figured out what?" I scanned his face in case I'd missed something.

"You're trembling," he growled huskily, leisurely exploring my breast. His thumb slid over it while he studied my response. He lowered his mouth, trailing heated breath over the thundering pulse in my throat as his nose skimmed my jaw.

The hand holding mine trapped above me, released and slid around my head and through my hair to yank it back. A sultry moan escaped me, pulled free by the feel of his warm lips against the sensitive skin on my neck. He wedged his foot between my thighs, parting my legs seconds before his head lifted and his eyes pierced mine.

"You're unexpected, woman," he whispered thickly, his tone filling with lust while he peered down the length of my body.

I ran my hands up his hard, perfectly etched chest, slowly roving over his heated flesh. If he cared that I was leisurely learning every line and curve of him, he didn't voice it out loud. Instead, he twisted my head to the side, hovering his mouth over mine, teasingly.

I waited for him to close the distance between our lips, needing to feel him touching mine. My body was on fire, achingly so. Kieran growled and moved closer. He didn't kiss gently; he devoured me. Our lips touched, and his hand cupped my jaw, demanding I open for him. He explored my mouth, his tongue tangling with mine until I moaned with the need for air. He released my hair and face and glided his hand behind my thighs, lifting me until my legs wrapped around his narrow waist.

Grinding against the growing erection pressed against my apex, he pulled his mouth away from my lips and studied me. My head fell to the wall, and an exhale of absolute desire and longing broke free from me. Kieran lowered his head, licking the piercing before pulling on it with his teeth, stealing a cry of pleasure from me.

He ground his cock on me, forcing it against my clit, threatening to send me careening over the edge. My stomach tightened as the storm built within me, moving down to my clit where he continued rubbing his hard cock. I slipped my hands through his hair, holding him against my breast as if I feared he'd break away from it.

He did, releasing it with a pop that echoed through the room. Then he dropped me, claiming my mouth hungrily while his hand roamed down my abdomen, and further down until he was cupping my sex in his palm. Kieran pulled back, staring down at me as we struggled to control our breathing.

"Do you taste sweet or as bitter as you pretend to be?" he asked, searching my face for the answer.

"Why don't you taste me and find out for yourself?" I taunted, emboldened by the fantasy version of this creature. His smile wasn't friendly, but his magical fingers slid beneath my panties, causing a moan to tear from my mouth as he flicked my clit.

"You want me to fuck you? Is that what you need?" He slowly moved his fingers through the arousal that drenched my core. "Bloody hell," he groaned, teasing my pussy that clenched with the desire to feel him within my walls.

"Yes," I purred silkily, leaning my head against the wall while holding onto his broad shoulders, knowing if he continued, my legs wouldn't support me.

"Tell me to fuck you," he urged, pushing his finger

into my pussy.

My entire body trembled, clamping down around the finger that entered my pulsing channel. He hissed, staring at me as he slowly withdrew it, sliding it against my sensitive flesh.

"Fucking wreck me," I whimpered, gasping as he pushed two fingers into my aching need. I was so close to coming that if he'd flicked my clit one more time, I'd be screaming my release for him already. "Fuck me, please," I begged, uncaring that my voice sounded like it belonged to someone else.

I abandoned his shoulders, sliding my hands down to his slacks to free his cock. He leaned his forehead against mine, watching my frenzied movements as I pushed my hand past his underwear, grabbing his silken cock while my other hand worked the button.

"I've missed you, Xari. Gods damn, I've missed you so much." The whispered confession caused me to lift my gaze to his in confusion.

"Don't you fucking leave me, woman," Kieran snapped.

I whimpered, holding onto him as he grabbed my throat, making me lean against the cool surface at my back as the sensation of falling encompassed me. His anger radiated through the room, and I shivered, riding the fingers that still stroked the fire inside of my womb.

"He's fucking dead," he sneered coldly, forcing my eyes to his.

I blinked slowly, searching the darkened room. I felt Kieran continuing to bring my body to orgasm, and I parted my legs and moaned, kissing his shoulder until I felt strands of hair touching my lips. I blinked again, listening as he murmured. A piercing pain began burning on my side, and I whimpered against the scorching agony. Sliding my hand toward it, I fought sleep to gain control of my mind as my mark began humming on my skin.

"I needed this tonight, too," the voice whispered, and then something pressed against my opening, just before I heard a masculine yelp of pain.

My eyes widened with horror at the familiar voice, and I screamed, fighting to push the intruder away from me. Anger sliced through me, and my body shook with rage.

"You motherfucker!" I shrieked, rolling off the bed as I trembled with murder rushing through my veins. "What the fuck are you doing?" I demanded as the bedroom door slammed open, and Noah shot inside with his gun aimed at the nude male beside my bed. "You asshole! What the hell, Micah?"

"You were moaning, and when I tried to wake you up, you were begging to be fucked, Xariana," Micah snarled back, uncaring that he was standing stark ass naked with his cock fully erect.

"I was dreaming! You have no right to be in my bedroom. How fucking dare you!" I screamed through clenched teeth. "How dare you!"

"You pleaded for me to fuck you. I believe the words you used were, wreck me," he sneered, glaring at me through the dimly lit room, fed only by the light coming from the hall.

"Get out of my apartment, Micah. Get out! Get out, now!"

"Go, Micah," Noah urged, reaching down to retrieve the discarded clothes on the floor to chuck them at him. "Go! What in hell were you thinking?"

"Fuck you, Noah. You're always the knight in shining armor that she'll never fucking notice. You will forever be in her blindside. Fucking prick."

"Go back to my room and sleep it off, Micah. You're drunk, and you've overstepped here. You should think about what you just fucking did and to whom you did it, asshole."

"Fuck you both," Micah sneered, forcing his legs through his sweatpants.

"I'll make you some tea," Noah offered, nodding at my shirt and lack of clothes. "You should dress in something else and shower if you need to. He's drunk and mourning."

"Which is exactly why he shouldn't be in my apartment, alone, much less my room," I snapped, peering at crumpled sheets before noticing my top had a broken strap. My attention moved to the shadows. The sense of being watched slithered down my back before I nodded, swallowing past the anger still threatening to choke me. "Micah buried his wife and child tonight, and then came to my bed? That's not okay."

"No, it's not. But at one time, you two were inseparable and depended on one another when shit got rough. I'm not saying what he did was okay, because it wasn't. There's no excuse for what just happened. I'm just reminding you that when you needed someone, he was your person, and you were his. Micah ruined that when he cheated on you, and he understands that, too. He drank a lot once you went to bed, and I should have stayed up long enough to ensure he'd gone to sleep."

Shaking my head, I didn't reply, because what Noah said was the truth. Micah had been an extension of me and my crutch. It was why it had hurt so badly to find him fucking Meredith on the counter in our apartment. He'd broken that trust and my heart in one single act of betrayal. That's the reason I'd left everything and everyone I knew to escape having to see them together.

"I'm going to shower, and then I'll meet you in the kitchen," I muttered, heading for the bathroom to remove Micah's touch from my flesh.

Chapter Eleven

Noah brewed some tea in my kitchen and had it ready for me when I exited the shower. He frowned at the oversized pajamas I wore. He'd been the one to order my clothes, according to Kaderyn. I scrunched up my nose, ignoring his creasing forehead.

"If I hadn't lost so much weight hunting, they'd have fit perfectly," I announced, causing his expression to soften.

"You want to talk about what happened?" he asked, pushing the steaming cup of tea in front of me as I plopped down beside him.

Shaking my head, I inhaled the soothing aroma of chamomile and frowned as a hint of bergamot and lemongrass filled the room. My inquiring stare slid to his, watching the smile that played on his lips.

"You love that scent," he explained. "I know it

calms you down when your anxiety is going full force." He shrugged like it was nothing.

"You didn't just purchase my clothes, did you?" I sighed, wondering how I'd missed it before. "You are the one who set up everything in this apartment, didn't you?" I asked, settling back as he squirmed uncomfortably.

"Your dad planned to move the stuff from your old apartment into this one. I thought you'd prefer new things, but you'd also need supplies that you normally had on hand. It's not a big deal, Xari."

I leaned closer to him, smiling. "You know what scents keep me calm, and remembered how I liked my sugar to be in cubes, not granules. You're one of the good ones, Noah Jameson." Sipping the tea, I moaned before placing it down and turning back to him. "It's perfect."

"Good. Now, who were you dreaming about?" he winked, and I wrinkled my nose at his teasing.

"You don't know him, but he was inside Axton's club tonight. His name is Kieran Knight, and he's a mercenary for hire, I guess."

"The prick that has a pulse on the shadows?" he asked, and I narrowed my eyes in confusion. "I forgot you weren't here when he and your father got into it several months back. But yeah, I thought they were going to kill each other a few times."

"And you didn't think that you should tell me about that?" I pointed out in irritation.

"No, Xar. A lot of shit happened while you were

gone, and we've barely scratched the surface on it." My shoulders drooped, and he frowned. "I don't mean that you've done anything wrong. You know I don't believe that," he demanded, sipping his tea, then grimacing as it burned his mouth.

I wasn't even sure why he was drinking it since he hated tea. Noah was part hellhound and part incubus demon. It left him with a hankering for meat and girls who enjoyed wall-banging. Herbal tea wasn't his thing, nor was anything that smelled overly obnoxious. It explained his attention to detail, though.

"You're doing what you're supposed to be doing. You know that. You tend to the living and handle what you can. You don't go ripping apart the entire town to find shit out. You do it within the order, and then you branch out. I just meant that we have a ton of crap that we need to sift through with a fine-toothed comb, but not tonight. Braelyn called, though, earlier. You had already gone to bed when she and Saint reached out. She said they'd get the Blackhawks ready to pick up the members of the fallen hunters families from the mouth of the valley in Montana. I called in a favor and have buses arriving first thing this morning. We will get them loaded and to the sanctuary when we wake up."

"It's three o'clock in the morning already," I groaned, rubbing my eyes. "Tomorrow is going to suck big time."

"I brought some of that chicory coffee you like back from New Orleans," he offered, giving me a crooked smile when I groaned in delight at the idea of drinking it. "Thought you'd like it since you skipped out on the trip due to your absence and avoidance of the base," he said, shrugging when I glared at his term for my break.

"I needed to leave here," I admitted, running my fingers over the rim of the mug while he nodded. "I'm sorry that this situation puts you between Micah and me. I know you're his best friend and mine. I couldn't be here, and see them every morning and night. I just had to go away for a while, and I hated that I didn't say goodbye to you or the girls."

"We didn't blame you for needing space, Xari. You did what you do best when you're hurt; you ran." Noah may not have wanted to admit it, but there was an edge of resentment in his tone. "Besides, shit happened pretty fast after you left. Your dad told Micah that he needed to do right by Meredith. She was already pregnant. A few months along when you took off," Noah adjusted in his seat, leaning forward. "I wanted to tell you, but Xavier was against it. He didn't want you running further than you already had."

"No, finding out in the middle of a shit-show is so much better," I muttered, fighting the emotion creeping up my throat.

"You should also know that they married on your original wedding date. It was convenient since you'd left, and they'd planned and arranged all the details for your nuptials." He lowered his head but chanced a glance in my direction. "Your father said it would just go to waste, and that since Micah had knocked Meredith up, he should man the fuck up and do what was right. I guess he'd already decided to come clean, but hadn't found the appropriate time to confess their relationship and tell you about the baby."

I shook my head, fighting the urge to run away before it broke me again. I stood abruptly, and he mirrored my movements, sliding his gaze from me to the door, judging the distance. I sniffed, taking a step forward to study the panic in his pretty gray eyes.

"I'm just heading to bed, Noah. Are you coming?" I asked, knowing he wouldn't take his sights off of me, worried I would run and leave him alone to handle the mess unfolding here.

"You can't blame me, Xar. You're a mother-fucking track star when shit goes sideways, and you think it might hurt you. You want me to stay?" he asked, scratching the back of his head.

"Did you plan on leaving my apartment tonight?"

"No, I was going to crash on the couch."

"The sofa isn't big enough to fit your ogre ass," I snorted. "Come on. You can pet my head and tell me I'm pretty until I fall asleep."

He chuckled. "I'm not petting you, asshole."

"Can't fault a girl for trying," I chirped, climbing on the bed to fluff the pillows. "If you snore, I'm smothering your ass. Fair warning."

"I'll return the favor if you do the same," he stated firmly, curling onto his side next to me. "I should have told you what happened when you left, but your calls were normally short, and only to check-in. We were all afraid of pushing you further away."

"I always come back," I admitted. "Even if I didn't want to, I would have. You're here, and this is my home. Our home," I murmured sleepily.

"I hear you, but not knowing where you were or if you were okay, wasn't easy on us, either. Now, go to sleep."

I smirked, curling up closer to the heat of his body. His arm slipped over me before his nose brushed against my ear. I missed being held, but with Noah, it wasn't sexual. It was just comfort, something we'd done on hunts when they'd gone sideways. We calmed one another and seemed to be pulled together through our shared pain. It was one of the things that Micah had resented about our relationship, but we'd never done anything wrong. Not like he and Meredith had, anyway.

Chapter Twelve

I woke to an arm crushing me and a tickle in my ear where Noah snored loudly in it. Groaning, I shoved him off of me and crawled out of bed, stretching before I tiptoed into the bathroom to relieve my body's morning needs. Staring into the mirror, I brushed my teeth, glaring at the bags beneath my eyes and the dark circles that accenting them.

After a quick shower, I changed into a soft pair of joggers and a loose tank top, then returned to find the room empty. Snorting and muttering under my breath, I went into the kitchen, grinning as the heavenly scent of coffee filled my nose, awakening my soul.

A knock sounded on my door, and before I could answer, Noah entered with clothes in his hands.

He shrugged and cleared his throat before speaking. "Micah is in my shower. Do you mind if I use yours?"

"Go for it, but the hot water takes a moment to catch up with the cold," I admitted, walking back to stalk the coffee pot. "Thanks for making the coffee." I sighed dreamily as it continued brewing. "I love that smell. I wish we had a place that made beignets like they do in New Orleans. My tits even miss the powdered sugar stuck in their cleavage."

Noah laughed while heading to the bathroom. When I heard the water running, I went to the sink, counting to twenty before turning on the hot water, listening for his violent cursing before switching it off. Smiling, I hummed beneath my breath, pouring two mugs full. I added creamer to mine and three sugar cubes to both before stirring them and setting them down to wait for him to finish showering.

I tapped my fingers on the table until I heard another knock at the door. Standing, I went to answer it as Noah called from the other room. Twisting the knob, I pulled it open to see Micah focusing on his feet until his sad eyes lifted.

"Look, Xari, about last night," he began, but paused, looking over my shoulder, hissing.

"Shit," Noah growled, grabbing his towel from where he'd dropped it on the floor.

"What the fuck?" Micah sneered, sliding his angry gaze to mine.

I opened my mouth to speak, but nothing came out as my eyes shifted back to Noah, with an owl-like expression. Damn, he wasn't playing around down there. I blinked, reminding myself how inappropriate that thought was.

"You're fucking him now? What's the plan, Xari? Fuck your way through the guild? Daddy isn't here to give you a gold star or stroke your fucking ego, so you're going to ride dick until you get that high he gave you with his praise?" he sneered, snapping my attention back to him.

"What did you fucking say to her?" Noah snarled, lunging.

"Fuck you, Noah! Always second best, asshole. You're nothing more than second-string, and you never will be! Do you like fucking my leftovers? She's just a whore now, anyway."

"I'll fucking end you, prick!" Noah growled, heading directly for Micah.

I jumped between them, shoving them both backward. "We're not fucking doing this!" I snarled. "You, cover your dick!" I shouted at Noah, swinging back to face Micah. "And you, you can fuck off. You have no right to come in here and judge me. You fucking cheated on me! I didn't choose her; you did. You got Meredith pregnant, asshole. You broke me, and how I fix myself after your betrayal is my choice and mine alone. You don't get to call me a whore. I was willing to give you every part and piece of me. You ruined us. You did this to me. If I want to fuck Noah, I will fucking do so without your input."

"Is that what you want? To fuck him now and be some bitch that gets passed around the base? You're better than that, Xariana."

"You know that's not who I am, but it's too fucking bad that's who you turned out to be. I was supposed to be your wife and have your children, remember? You chose Meredith, and now she's gone, and you are a widow. It's fucking tragic, but that doesn't change what happened. Deal with your shit somewhere else. It isn't my job to hold you or comfort you anymore. Stay the fuck out of my house and keep your criticisms to yourself. Your opinion of me and how I live my life no longer matters." I pushed him out and slammed the door, turning on Noah.

He started to say something, but I held my hand up while marching to the table to down the caffeine. When he tried to talk again, I flicked my finger at him, guzzling my drink.

"Did you even try to discourage him from thinking we had slept together?" I snapped, frustrated at both of them.

"We did share a bed," he snorted, reaching for the coffee I'd poured for him, uncaring that the towel hung low on his muscular hips.

"Not like that we didn't, jerk-face," I grumbled. "You know, Micah assumes we fucked."

"Do you care what he thinks happened? Because it didn't sound like you did a moment ago," he replied, taking a sip from the mug while holding my glare, a brow lifting in challenge.

Someone knocked on the front door, and I groaned, moving across the kitchen and throwing it open. "What now, Micah? You want to shove more insults down my throat for sleeping with Noah?" I demanded, pausing as Onyx and Kaderyn both glanced over my shoulder where Noah stood in his towel, gripping his mug with a smile that I wanted to slap off his face. "We didn't—"

"There's a body," Kaderyn stated, waving off my reply. "The sheriff is outside the gates, waiting for you. He said they found this a few feet from the corpse," she informed, holding up the wallet I'd given my father two years ago for Christmas.

My stomach shrank as my heart leaped into my throat. Tears burned behind my eyes, and my knees threatened to deposit my weight in a puddle on the floor. I grabbed for the door as she exhaled, sliding in to place an arm around me.

"Breathe, Xari. Just breathe. We don't know if it is Xavier or if the wallet was placed there to throw us off the trail. We won't know until we get there," Kaderyn said. "You need to get presentable, both of you," she grunted, peering into my kitchen.

"I'll get dressed, Xar." Noah walked down the hall and into the apartment's only bathroom.

Twenty minutes later, dressed in normal attire, with weapons decked beneath my leather jacket, I strode toward the front of our compound with everyone behind me, even Micah. It didn't matter how much we fought or what problems we had. When shit hit the fan, we had each other's backs and always would.

"Sheriff," I nodded, opening the gates to slip through them.

"Miss Anderson, wish I was visiting under better circumstances."

Jeffery Wheeler had been the sheriff of our town for as long as I could recall. He knew otherworldly events were happening, but he wasn't one to stick a foot into things on our end. Instead, he ran interference when needed and never asked too many questions because he didn't want the answers to keep him up at night.

"You and me both." I exhaled to stop the tremor of emotion in my voice. "You found this on a body?" I asked, needing to hear it from him.

"Yeah, we did. The remains were discovered early this morning, out by the canyon. We were training new cadaver dogs, and they got a hit. We didn't think it would be human, but it looks like it was."

"It looks like it was?" I echoed, swallowing to rid myself of the saliva building as bile pressed against the back of my throat.

"Yeah, the body was burned. I discovered the wallet tossed in the bushes. It's not uncommon for predators to take things from a corpse before disposing of it." He rubbed the back of his neck while explaining, eyeing the people around me. "You sure you don't want someone else to identify him, kid?"

"No, this is something I need to do."

Sheriff Wheeler nodded in understanding, pushing his fingers through his salt and pepper hair. Wide hazel eyes flecked with gold slid to mine, and he frowned.

"You guys can follow us up the trail, and we'll walk you to the body. I can buy you a few moments alone with it, but the feds have called in a special team from Seattle to handle the case. We had a ride-along with us, and your dad would always make sure nothing was left behind as evidence. I didn't think twice about agreeing to this fed coming here."

"It isn't your fault, sheriff. If it's my father, I will take care of the body once it's returned for burial," I whispered thickly, unable to hide my emotion.

"Damn, Xariana. Your dad was one of the good ones, and this world needs more men like him. Not less." He wiped at his eyes, sighing and hiking his thumb over his shoulder toward a younger police officer standing beside a man in a fancy overcoat. "That's my rookie, Tanner, and the other one is agent Abraham Lincoln with the feds. I'm guessing his parents thought it would be cute, but he's pretty much a fucking prick that thinks we're nothing other than a few patrol officers."

I grunted before smiling at him. "Maybe we should give him a tour of our city at night," I offered, watching the sheriff's lips jerk up in the corners.

"No one should be out at night in this city, kid. Not you, not us, and not him." He cleared his throat as he headed toward his blazer. "I'll lead you up the mountain since we're not supposed to advertise where we're training, according to Lincoln. Like the people here don't already know how to avoid crossing our paths?"

"Obviously, someone didn't," I informed, nodding to my guys to get the Land Rovers as my gaze clashed with agent Lincoln. He slid his cool amber stare over my face, pausing before turning and saying something to the rookie. "This is becoming a shit-show."

"More than you having sex with Noah?" Kaderyn asked, barely controlling the disappointment in her tone.

"I didn't fuck Noah, Kaderyn. He showered in my apartment because he spent the night after Micah tried to fuck me. Is this going to be a problem?"

"No, but what happened before, with you and Micah—it ripped our team apart, Xari. We lost you, and that fractured the group. We've all been together since we were in diapers, so losing you caused a rift in the team. So next time something happens, send the other asshole away. You're our glue. Understand? Without you, no one checks us or puts us in our place. No one tells us when we're being fucking petty or stupid, or that it will be okay when the sky is falling—and girl, it's fucking falling on us all."

"You will be fine."

"Asshole," she muttered.

"Bitch," I returned.

"You're both being childish," Onyx injected, pushing us as we started toward the vehicles coming our way. "Kaderyn's right, though, Xar. You're our fucking duct tape, and without you, we were falling apart. It's good to have you home again."

Chapter Thirteen

The drive up the long, winding road to the canyon was filled with silent tension. A team of hunters were a mile behind us, and would scout the area once we entered the site where the body was found. If it was my father, someone was more than likely waiting for us to come upon the remains. I wouldn't chance walking into a trap, not when lives depended on the fact that I wouldn't make rash decisions.

"What if it is your father?" It was the question everyone was thinking but was too afraid of voicing out loud. I slowly slid my attention to Micah, frowning at the question.

"Then we bury him, find out who did it, and make them pay," I informed softly, fighting the pain that flashed through me at the thought.

It could potentially be my dad in this canyon, lifeless and discarded like trash. The thing bothering me was, where were the women? The sheriff hadn't mentioned finding more corpses. Our attackers didn't take any other males, but they'd stolen several females from the compound. So if the remains are of my father, that would mean the kidnappers decided to keep the women, or they were somewhere out there, undiscovered.

"I want teams scouring these woods either way. Even if this isn't Xavier, someone is dead in this valley, and we need to gather all intelligence and information to figure out who they are and why they died. Their family deserves closure. No one should be left wondering what happened." I stated firmly, shoving away all emotion as the sheriff pulled off the highway and onto a back road.

"Maybe we should go in first?" Onyx offered, her wide, midnight-blue eyes narrowing, creasing her forehead. She pushed the dark blue hair from her face, turning to look at me as we hit a bump. "You shouldn't see him like this."

"I disagree," I said with more bravado than I felt. "If it is my old man, I need the closure this will give me. I also want to find out what they did to him so that I know exactly how to repay the ones that harmed him when we hunt them down and end them."

Our vehicles pulled off the road onto a shoulder, which was already crawling with police. Slowly forcing my heart to stop beating painfully against my ribcage, I slid from the car and waited for the others to do the same.

"I want eyes on everything; branches, broken twigs, and debris," I ordered softly, keeping my voice down so the officers near us wouldn't overhear. "Something or someone came through here to discard the remains. Look for the path they took. I doubt they entered from the road."

Walking toward the sheriff, I waited for him to make quick introductions of the other officers. Lincoln smiled, nodding at me as I offered my hand to shake. The hair on my neck rose, and I peeked a glance at his coat, noting every weapon he had stored beneath it. For a federal agent, the guy had an alarming amount of firepower under his jacket.

"This is Xariana Anderson, our victim's daughter," Jeffery stated.

"Alleged victim," Lincoln corrected, sliding silver eyes over me.

"Either way, it's not pretty up there. It's about a mile's trek to the body. My officers have been watching the scene and the area around it since we were notified. I hope you don't mind hiking up? I'll be taking the four-wheeler, but Tanner here will guide you and the others up the trail behind me." Jeffery nodding at Lincoln. "He enjoys walking, so he'll be joining you with his sunny disposition."

"Understood," I grunted, sliding my attention back to the agent who had yet to take his eyes off of me. He wasn't human; that much was obvious. I smiled tightly, slowly turning to Tanner. "We will follow you."

Tanner was young, barely out of the academy from the looks of it. He was gangly, with shaven hair similar to a soldier's cut, indicating he had some military background. His uniform was pressed, and there wasn't a speck of dirt on it. The young officer took pride in his position, and it made me want to smile, but the thought of what we were about to see prevented that.

"I've got to warn you guys. It isn't pretty. I've been on a few calls like this, but I lost my lunch when Wheeler forced me to look at this one," Tanner admitted, rubbing the back of his head before grabbing a pack and hefting it over his shoulder.

He stumbled from the weight, and I watched in silence as he righted himself. He walked to a police cruiser, opening the door to release a K-9 officer. A quick pat on the shepherd's head, and we started down a narrow trail, forcing two people to walk shoulder to shoulder.

I'd chosen to walk beside Lincoln, who I was willing to guess wasn't an agent of anything. He didn't carry himself like one, and his freshly polished shoes with dirt crusted to the soles told me he hadn't been prepared to observe the dogs at their secret training facility, as indicated earlier. His shoulder brushed against mine, and I turned to study the way he tensed at the slight touch.

I felt an electric current that only came from being near one of my kind. Lincoln's gaze hadn't wandered to me, but his posture had gone stiff as he walked surefooted through the overgrown path. If he'd felt it, he played stupid rather well.

We rounded a corner, and my foot slid through some mud, sending me precariously close to the edge. Lincoln grabbed me, pulling me against him to keep me from toppling over. My breath caught in my throat, and my heart pounded from our proximity. His hands slowly released my waist, fully aware of the guns on my hips.

Silver eyes flashed with intrigue, but he simply fixed his coat and tie before starting forward again. He didn't seem fazed by being surrounded by hunters, which was worrisome. Only someone suicidal or one who knew they'd survive the encounter wouldn't show some flicker of worry. I wasn't sure which would be worse. Suicidal people were unpredictable. Knowing Lincoln could escape meant he was powerful, and I had no idea what the hell he was. I also didn't think he was out here alone. I'd sensed someone watching our movements the entire time we'd been on the trail. It had little to do with my team flanking us, or the scouts hidden in the thickly treed forest.

A babbling brook and water falling against rocks could be heard through the trees ahead of us. Insects chirped, uncaring of the hunters in the woods. The sounds of the dog's feet clumsily crunching brush alerted me that other creatures were also within the area. The K-9 officer leading us wasn't padding through the thicker terrain, indicating coyotes or wolves were being drawn in by the scent of the corpse. Predators wouldn't care what their meal was made of, as long as they got to eat.

An eagle sounded above, and I glanced at the sky, seeing the hawk of our hunter, Clara, flying beside it. It squawked twice before diving lower to avoid conflict with the eagle. I turned to find Lincoln observing me closely, and I released a sigh of relief, knowing that other teams were out looking for the trail our killer had taken.

"You don't seem all that upset about identifying

your father's remains," he uttered in a thickly accented voice, which he hadn't used until now.

"Allegedly," I informed coolly, smirking at the disgruntled sound he made in his throat. "For all we know, it could be a hiker that wandered off the trail."

"And yet you identified your dad's wallet, which was found yards away from the deceased," he pointed out crassly, scrutinizing my reaction.

Lincoln wasn't hard on the eyes, and his height gave him an advantage over most men. His hair was light-colored, and the sharp angular lines of his features spoke of Norwegian descent. He didn't have the woodsy scent that werewolves carried or the rich, exotic smell of a vampire, I noted, still trying to identify his species. He lifted his hand, checking his watch, exposing tattoos that covered his forearm from the wrist up.

"My dad loved hiking this canyon. He could have dropped it here during one of his treks," I offered after a moment. "We don't have the most honest citizens in the world, but they're not the worst, either. I prefer to hope and believe he's out there alive somewhere, and not a burned and bloodied corpse."

"Hope is nothing more than a false narrative derived by dreamers to strengthen their resolve against the brutal truth, Miss Anderson." Lincoln didn't bother to hide the heavy accent that reminded me of Leif Knight, which meant he was probably Norwegian by birth, just as I had suspected.

"Is that Norwegian or Danish origin I detect?" I asked, unwilling to discuss hope with a total stranger.

"You have blue eyes. Should I assume you're Norwegian?" He was blatantly ignoring Tanner, who was still rattling on about the woods. "No, because they're cosmetic, and you wear the contacts to hide the fact that your green eyes are not human." He smirked, fluidly changing his accent to Middle Eastern, shifting my attention to his full mouth. "The simplicity of your face and form give you away, hunter. You move gracefully and are defensive. Your senses are greatly heightened, which is why you have yet to stop tracking others through the forest by sound alone."

I peered around the trail, realizing we'd been left behind while I'd been distracted by the puzzle Lincoln presented. I pulled my handgun on him, but he'd done the same. My chest rose and fell as I cleared everything else from my mind, focusing on him and the situation.

A gun barrel pressed against the back of my head, and his lips twisting into a smile until a pistol was pressing against his as well. I grinned, holding my gun ready as no one made a sound or moved a muscle. The noise of feet crunching beneath brush had sweat trickling against my temples.

"Who the fuck are you?" I demanded coldly.

He snorted, never looking away from me. "I could ask the same of you." Lincoln, or whatever his name really was, wasn't afraid to be shot, appearing to believe he could survive it. That was never a good sign.

The sheriff broke through the trail, swearing as the scene came into view. One of Lincoln's people aimed his weapon at him, forcing me to point my other handgun at his man. It was a stalemate, and we knew it, but Jeffery didn't.

"Which agency are you with?" Lincoln changed tactics.

"Who says I am with any agency?" I fought the strain it took to hold two guns pointed in opposite directions. Sweat trickled down my neck, and the tension between us was thickening, which meant sooner or later, someone was getting shot.

"Let's all calm down," Jeffery demanded, holding his hands in the air.

My gaze slid to the tattoo on Lincoln's wrist, and a smile twisted my lips. "E.V.I.E. huh?" I asked, watching his stare zeroing in on my bare arms. My tattoos weren't visible unless I wore a backless shirt.

"You?" he asked, glaring at me with the look of a killer. "Hunters guild?" he questioned, tilting his head.

"Indeed," I replied carefully.

"Same team then, little girl."

"Not entirely," I stated, as we lowered our weapons. "I should call Rhys Van Helsing and have you sent packing for being in our territory."

"Rhys doesn't lead E.V.I.E. anymore, Miss Anderson," he growled, nodding at his people to lower their guns.

A quick jut of my chin had my hunters following suit. One of Lincoln's men still pointed his weapon at Jeffery, causing my hackles to rise.

"The sheriff is one of ours. Lower your fucking weapon, now," I hissed, watching a pair of crimson eyes slide toward me. "I will not ask you again."

"Do as she said," Lincoln ordered. "I take it you're in charge? You're a little young for the role, aren't you?"

"Younger than you, Abraham Lincoln, but then you did die in 1865, so—." I smirked, rocking on my heels. Scrunching my nose, I paused, allowing him time to give me his real name, but he merely smiled. "So, who is in command of the offices in Seattle?"

"If he wanted you to know, you'd know," he stated offhandedly. "You think something inhuman killed the poor sod up the hill, and that's why you're really here?" Lincoln's demeanor eased to a causal conversation while dodging the question.

Swallowing down the urge to laugh at the absurdity of it all, I shook my head. "No, and yes," I elaborated while keeping certain aspects to myself. "My father, Xavier Anderson, went missing a few days ago. It could be him, but the chances of his kidnappers murdering him and leaving the body to be found are slim. The attack felt personal, and that normally comes with a message sent back with the dead. Since they abandoned the remains in the woods with predators circling, I'm guessing this is just a supe's killing ground."

Lincoln's expression softened, but only a tad. Jeffery swallowed hard before clearing his throat. He nodded toward the trailhead, and everyone holstered their weapons as Tanner's clumsy feet smashed through the underbrush.

"As I was saying, Xariana," the sheriff started softly. "It's a rather grisly scene, so you need to prepare for what lies ahead."

Tanner paused at the sight of the newcomers, slowly sliding his gaze through them before speaking. "I thought I was moving too fast, but you guys never seemed to complain about the speed. I was an Eagle Scout, so I'm fluid motion on the trail. They used to call me Eagle Lightening." I blinked as Lincoln's mouth jerked up in the corners.

"Follow me," Jeffery stated, sidling closer to me while we moved into the clearing where the deceased was located. "We didn't touch anything or move it. Your father always asked me to leave the weird shit alone, so I did. I put tape up, protecting the scene, and told our guys to stay off and away from the ground surrounding it."

I paused at the edge of a large hexagram that circled the remains. In the middle was the charred body, its hands staked into the dirt. I didn't even need to pass the barrier to know this wasn't my father. Instead, this was someone who had pissed off the witches, and they'd left him out here as a sacrifice for the creatures in the forest and the carrion birds, as a warning.

Looking at the others, they cautiously moved into the circle, unable to see it beyond the spirit realm. They couldn't tell where the candles had been, burning on each point of the hexagram. Sage still hung thickly in the air, which told me the body hadn't been here very long. His death looked recent.

"What can you see that we don't?" Lincoln asked, drawing my attention to where he stood, studying me closely.

"Everything," I grunted, slowly shifting my focus to the treeline, noting the wolves waiting for their meal.

They weren't werewolves or shapeshifters, though, just a pack of hungry wolves driven here by the scent of a kill.

"Not your father, I take it?" Lincoln asked. "And my name is Lynx, or at least it's what my friends call me."

"Not my father, and not your name," I returned, backing up to get a better look at the display the witches had left behind. "We're done here, Sheriff."

"You don't need me to clear the area so you can figure out what did this?" he asked.

"No. I know what did this and exactly who did it." I nodded at the wolves. "You're finished here, too. They won't let you take the kill out of here. He's an offering to nature, a meal promised to them for staying away during the sacrifice. If you try to take his corpse, you have to kill the wolves. There are also birds of prey surrounding us right now, waiting for the pieces they'll leave behind. Insects are swarming, knowing even after the birds fly off; they'll eat. His legs were severed and placed against the knees. If you got closer, you could see his sexual organs were harvested. He trespassed against a witchling, and her sisters came for vengeance. Do not touch him, sheriff. Clear your people out, and make it look like a staff error, so those waiting on their food can eat. Whoever touches the remains not only has to deal with nature, but the witches that left him here will seek them out, too. That is precisely why one doesn't fuck with witches. Witches don't leave anything to chance, and nature gets what it was gifted in the end. Be it your men or this one, the forest will feed tonight. Don't let it be your people, please," I stated softly in warning, holding his hazel stare.

"Jesus Christ, kid," he muttered, covering his mouth with his hand. "It doesn't explain your father's wallet being here."

"It does," I returned. "The witches knew I'd come, and they ensured it to be so. I'm here to protect you from touching that corpse. If I hadn't shown up, you'd take it with you back to the morgue. One of your men would have died here, and I'd be at their door to enforce our laws protecting humans. It was also a message, indicating they wish to talk to me."

"They couldn't leave a fucking note?" he asked in frustration.

I cleared my throat and turned to the wolves, who let loose warning howls into the air. Shrugging, I took a step back from the circle, scrunching my nose.

"I speak asshole, and I'm fluent in what the fuck. Now, do as I said so that I know you are safe from harm. We're on our way to visit some witches. I'd prefer to be reassured that you understand the gravity of what I am saying."

"I get it, but I don't like it, Xariana. I appear to be the biggest idiot when shit like this happens."

"Better to look bad than be dead, wouldn't you agree? There are lots of times that you're the hero, too. Take the bad with the good, because life doesn't give a shit about any of us in the end. You'll be a hero again, and this will be forgotten. Besides, no one else wants to be sheriff of this city. You have job security."

I turned toward Lincoln, or I guess I should call

him Lynx, and nodded. "Mystery man, I'd say it was a pleasure to meet you, but it honestly wasn't. I have a feeling I'll be seeing you around. Let's hope it's on good terms, and that eventually, I'll have your actual name." I lifted my hand and rotated my finger to show my team that we were moving out. Talia needed a better way of communicating that didn't have me hiking into the canyon to receive her message.

Chapter Fourteen

Standing outside the House of Witches, I tapped my boot over the cobblestone driveway, where I'd stood for over an hour. Talia appeared sometime later, and I lifted my head, zeroing in on the witches walking with her toward the gates.

The house they'd claimed, appeared small and had dark aesthetics to keep humans from getting too close. Gothic wrought-iron gates with massive gargoyles enclosed the exterior courtyard. Beyond that, a small Victorian cottage sat behind the giant weeping willow trees that stood guard. Delicate arches rested between rounded columns on each side that tapered into points high above, with the witch's mark etched in the glass above the door at the entrance.

Once I stepped into the courtyard, I would cross a barrier that would reveal the house's secret, revealing that the structure seen on the outside was a magical illusion. The inside was huge, flowing into large elegant rooms with wings that stretched out in all directions for miles and miles.

The witches had their own rules and decrees unto their own but agreed, albeit loosely, to follow the laws set by the hunters. I'd once walked through a forest with Morgana. Talia's carefree, wildly spirited daughter. Women had danced naked beneath the moon, singing while indulging in sin and drink.

The gentle scent of sage and chamomile tickled my senses as Talia, the oldest witch here, smiled softly in greeting. My attention slowly roved over the firetruck red hair and emerald green eyes she conjured to mask her aging. If she had any weaknesses, I'd yet to discover them. Morgana squealed from within the house, and I couldn't help but smile at her excitement.

"You got my message!" She clapped her hands as Talia frowned, narrowing her darkening gaze on her daughter. "I knew you would come, Xari. I told you, mother. I merely needed to leave it where that old stuffy human would see it, and he'd call in the real hunters." Morgana's singsong voice echoed through the yard, causing the homes across from them to tremble as if in an earthquake.

"Morgana has missed your visits, Xariana. We all have," Talia admitted softly, her smile forming a firm, thin line of her lips. She nodded at the gargoyles, who jumped off the gate, shifting into men as they opened it for me to enter.

"Thank you, gentlemen," I murmured absently, ignoring the fact they were naked in their human form. Talia had collected them as a debt owed to her family, and while it appeared the gargoyles weren't valued, they were.

Morgana slammed into me, forcing the air from my lungs as she wrapped her arms around me, hugging me tightly. "You just vanished, bitch!" she snapped, yanking back to stare at me. "I almost burned the guild down to find you, but your dad was all, 'She needs space, and give her some time to come to terms with what happened.' Absolute horse shite, if you ask me. You should have let us handle Micah and Meredith and made them vanish."

"I missed you, too," I chuckled, hugging her back. "You were right. The other witches on this continent are whiney bitches that wouldn't know real witchcraft if you shoved it up their vagina and pulled it out of their ears."

Talia snorted, nodding her head in agreement. "Bunch of lazy hussies, the lot of them," she muttered beneath her breath as we started toward the entrance. "Your father said you'd need some things when you returned. I had them prepared in advance when the winds shifted, and your scent was upon it, girl."

"He told you I was coming back?" I asked, turning to wave at the hunters that stood across the road, banned from entering the House of Witches by Talia herself. Not that it was an actual home, but since everyone else had one for their breed, including Rhys's woman, they'd taken the name and hung a plaque on the gate.

"No, you daft child. I told you, I smelled you on the wind," Talia snorted before shaking her head. "You're going deaf because you never set those blasted phones of yours down long enough to hear."

"I left mine in the car," I stated plainly. "A certain witch loathes those damned contraptions," I smirked, and her shoulders shook as she chuckled at me, spouting back her own words.

"Goes to your vagina," she chirped before cackling. "You'll never have babes if you stay on those retched things. How are you to meet a man? How are you to experience the world the mother created for us if you never set it down?"

"Men suck, children are a pain in the ass, but this world is beautiful," I replied, watching her turning to look at me, narrowing her calculating gaze.

"You've met him, then?"

"Who?" I asked, feeling as if she could see my fantasy unfolding on my face.

"The man who teaches you that not all of them will suck," Talia replied. "No, you haven't met yet. One day you will meet a man who you will want to throttle. Pummel him, and if he gives you that fire back, come to me, and we'll make a spell to have the sodden prick fall in love with you forever," she promised, studying me. "Oh, you thought I would give you advice on romance? Men are jerks, darling. If you don't know that yet, well, you're a lost cause."

"Mother, she's young. Xariana isn't even twenty-five yet. She's a child," Morgana chuckled, patting my shoulder. "So, what the hell is all over you?" she surprised me by asking.

"What?" I wiped my face off before looking down

at my hand.

"You're marked," Talia snorted, pointing at my stomach. "You didn't realize you were marked?"

Frowning, I narrowed my eyes before lifting my shirt. "This shit? You know what it is? If so, get it off of me, please."

"It cannot be removed." Talia moved closer to the scrawling black vines that pulsed as she neared. She reached out and was about to touch it, and I yelped as pain ripped through my stomach. "They're inside of you, Xariana. You've been marked by darkness, and it intends to claim you for now. It hasn't spread to your legs, correct?"

"No, but it's below my breast, on my ribcage, and covering my abdomen," I admitted, watching the inky substance pulse as if poised to attack Talia if she touched me. "Why doesn't it seem to like you?"

"Because it knows I would try to remove it, and in doing so, you'd die. It's warning me by harming you. It wants you alive. That's a good sign, but it doesn't explain why or to whom it belongs. You haven't come across a dark practitioner lately, have you? Or a male witch that you shared amorous actions?"

"No, and hell no," I snorted, as Talia and Morgana's eyes snapped up to meet mine with venom. "It's not personal. As you've said, if they wanted me to love them, they'd merely need a spell to enforce those feelings. I'm a hopeless romantic at heart," I elaborated, aware of how touchy witches could be about their own.

Dropping my shirt, I scrunched my mouth up, twisting it sideways. "You had my father's wallet?"

I pried, knowing they didn't take him. But they were much like Axton, with a pulse on the underworld chatter. But, of course, theirs came in the form of favors that generally ended up with me naked in the woods, luring something that could kill me out of the dark, creepy forest.

"Yeah, Xavier was here a few days ago," Talia admitted, nodding to where the orphaned child, Mindy, was standing, her eyes following me like prey.

"Soothsayer, succubus, and gypsy aren't a good combination to breed. Add in witch genes and an enhancement spell that no one can break, and you have that little asshole. She swiped it from his pocket when he was here," Morgana scolded, and I fought a smile as the small child stuck her tongue out at her. "Keep it up, and I'll find a way to remove that enchantment and turn you into a snail, feeding you to the wolves for dinner."

"You're cursed," Mindy stated, stepping away from the southern-style wrap-around porch that appeared the moment she moved. "Day wants your womb, but night would like your life. One wishes to breed you like a dog, and the other prefers to hurt you. Which one will you choose? Both have sinister desires for the daughter who was hidden, kept from her kind. They're here, tick-tock; they've already started your clock. Games are afoot, and pieces are in play. Which king shall you slay, and which will you lay?" she whispered in a multilayered voice that sent the creeps rushing down my spine.

"Be gone, brat," Talia snapped, shooing the child away. "You never know if she's reciting a warning or if the little monster wants you looking over your shoulder for the rest of your life. She takes great joy in scaring the shit out of people."

I shook off the kid's words and sat in the chair in which they beckoned me. Once I was settled, tea started hissing in the kettle beside me. I peered down, watching it lift by magic and pour into a floating cup before three sugar cubes were dropped in and a spoon began stirring.

"Something else is on your mind. Best be out with it," Talia stated, her sharp gaze studying me.

"Do you recall when I was little, and my father first brought me here?" At her nod, I frowned, peering around the yard.

"The night terrors, or the time you projected for days, and Xavier couldn't get you to return to your thin, frail body, Xariana? I remember both times, and how panicked he was at the thought that he would lose you forever. There is nothing your father wouldn't do to keep you from harm, even when it was from yourself, which he worried most about."

"That's just it, Talia. He can't protect me from what I am. Nobody can, and while he tried, it hurt to be cut off from that part of myself. My guild still doesn't know the extent of what I am, nor does anyone else. Do you? He killed everyone that knew my secret to keep me safe from them. What if I was what our attackers came to retrieve, but they took him because I was hidden? I think your magic worked, and those that attacked didn't know who I was. My guess is this; I am marked because I am Xavier's daughter. I'm the only thing that could be used to get to him. I was mixed in with the guild, concealed, along with several other children. It's known that I am his daughter, but I believe they think I was switched with another, and that his actual child is hidden within the hunter guild."

Talia nodded, pushing her firetruck-red hair off of her shoulders. "It is possible, but why not take you when they abducted him? From what I understand, they only kidnapped your dad."

"It isn't known, and I would appreciate it if you didn't tell anyone else—" I paused as she pushed her fingers against her lips for silence. Her hands touched, and she created a circle around us, ensuring my words wouldn't leave the barrier. "Good?" I asked, watching her nod softly before she flicked her finger, and the teacup floated to me. "When the guild was attacked, I thought he was the only one taken. Upon reviewing the video footage, we noticed that several girls my age, and one mouthy little asshole hunter, had also gone missing. The first explosion was used as a distraction to take the girls. The second blast went off, and my father vanished with a male with silver hair and amber eyes. The women they took had similar coloring to what they assumed I would have had from birth if it were not for the subtle changes I inherited from my grandmother regarding my hair color. My eyes are an anomaly."

"Yeah, and you cover them up with cosmetics, forcing people to wonder what is real and what is fake," Morgana teased, smiling tightly at me. "I know they're green, and that when you're mad, they turn a startling lime color. Remember, inside the Forest of Truth, nothing is hidden. Your truth was revealed, and it was terrifying and exhilarating simultaneously." She looked over her shoulder and sighed. "Your hunters are growing weary of the time, and yet you've just arrived."

"There's a lot happening," I admitted. "What can you tell me about Kieran Knight?"

"The Keeper of the Shadows? That you should stay far away from him," Talia hissed, like his name was a curse.

"I think I may have projected into his house." I sheepishly sipped the tea as she spat hers out at my admission. "It was totally a sex dream, and the hex bags weren't working. They were punctured and emptied inside my room before my arrival. Anyway," I waved her horrified expression away with a hand. "So, the dream felt real, and I was into it, big time—. Don't look at me all judgy, Morgana. I was here when you took on three imps and both gargoyles, and I even held your beer while you banged the pricks." I muttered, looking pointedly at her. "Back to the story. I woke up to Micah on top of me." Both women peered toward the hunters, glaring at the male in question. "I'm not sure what's real and what isn't. I don't know if I was with Kieran or if I had conjured him into my thoughts as Micah tried to do things to me. Apparently, I begged Kieran to have sex with me, and Micah thought I was begging him to fuck me."

"That's quite the predicament. Did you weaken after you woke?" Talia inquired, noticing the way I frowned. "You were under a compulsion to sleep. Weren't you? Those fucking demon twins and their powers muck everything up."

"Yeah, so, I'm not certain," I admitted, shrugging.

"You could confront Kieran and see how he

responds to you being in his face," Morgana offered. "Finding out the woman of your dreams is real is never an easy thing to ignore."

I nodded, but Talia sputtered. "Absolutely not! Kieran is a monster. In fact, he is the boogeyman of our circle. He lives in the shadows, and you never even see him coming until he pulls you into them. By then, you're dead, and it's too late to save yourself. So you stay far away from that creature, Xariana Sunny Anderson. You hear me? Heed my warning because no one here can prevent him from getting to you if you step into his world. Take your pills and replace the hex bags." A bag dropped into my lap, and then my chair lifted and tilted, and I slid off. "You are a smart girl. Listen to the ones telling you to avoid him. I know I'm not the first, and I won't be the last. If you're curious about him, it ends here. Only death comes to those who cross that man."

"Do you have a girl here named Raven?" I asked, changing the subject. Both witches closed off their expressions, causing me to groan. "Look, I don't care if she is here or if she's hunting. My only issue is that she needs to register. It's only a name on a slip of paper that makes her legally allowed to be here. That's it," I fumed, pissed that they'd shut me down like everyone else. Who the hell was this prick?

"Raven is a good girl," Talia snorted. "Raven is like you. That one is my blood, and the blood of my blood is immune to your laws."

"No, they're not," I stated firmly, knowing I was flirting with certain pain. "Your sister tied men up with their entrails because they asked her to dance. She cursed half of the town, forcing them to masturbate because she couldn't find a shlong large enough to scratch her itch. Your mother blew the forest up, and it took a lot of magic to get that crap fixed before the humans woke up in the morning to find it missing. Your family, and I say this with the utmost respect, is fucking insane, and when they show it, the entire town becomes a shit show that is one clown away from becoming a circus. Tell Raven to register, because you realize I will catch her outside these gates. I always do, Talia."

"I'll suggest it," she sniffed indignantly, which meant she wasn't getting involved.

"You know I hate chasing, right?" Her chin jutted up into the air, indicating this visit had reached its limits of hospitality. "I love you both, even if you are assholes that make me hunt." I frowned, turning on my heel as they chuckled behind me.

Reaching the gates, I turned around in time to notice Mindy watching me. Her head tilted, and a wicked grin played on her lips as she glanced at a witch I'd never seen before with raven-black hair with fluorescent-blue strands woven through it. The girl lifted her hand and waved at me with a saucy smile spread over her cherry lips.

"Catch me if you can, bitch," she cooed, allowing the wind to carry the words toward me.

"Oh, sugar tits, I don't need to capture you." I drew my gun and shot through her palm before she realized my intent. "I just have to see you to make my point. Register. It protects you from other beings and them from you. It's the law. Have a good day, though, Raven. Oh, and I'd bandage that. It looks painful." I shoved my pistol back into the holster while Talia cackled at Raven's horrified expression.

"That bitch shot me! She could have killed me," she snapped.

Talia patted her back, snorting. "If Xariana wanted you dead, Raven, you'd be dead. She shot your hand as a courtesy to me and my home. That wasn't a miss. She was aiming at what she hit." I shook my head, listening until the sound of them talking dimmed to murmured bickering.

"I'm leaving." I turned to nod at Talia, who observed me from the shadows, a worried crease on her forehead.

"Blessed be, child. May the earth watch over you and keep you safe and protected," she whispered, allowing the prayer to carry to me. "Next time, shoot them in the knee. I love watching them drop when you do that to them."

Chapter Fifteen

My team and I returned to the compound long enough for us to change and gather more hunters. I'd chosen a pair of jeans that weren't tight but made my rounded ass look damn good. My leather boots complimented them, stopping just below the knee, and were loose enough to hide blades in their interior. The leather jacket I wore covered a plain, white t-shirt and concealed the twin 9mm Ruggers with custom grips, perfect for my small hands. Finally, I pulled my hair back in twin braids that started in the front of my head and wrapped around the back. It was the ideal attire for a hunt.

The call about demons openly feeding had come in less than thirty minutes ago. Apparently, Axton had decided to revise the rules of his club, allowing human patrons inside every day of the week. Disturbance calls began lighting up the police switchboards within hours of the rule change. We were notified immediately and were heading into town.

Standing on the Main Street strip that moved through downtown, I watched a lone female coming out of the club. A few moments later, a group of men trailed behind her. Her body language suggested she'd over drank and was having a hard time staying upright. One man slipped in beside her, moving his arm around her back to steady her on her feet.

I signaled my team to move ahead of me, not waiting for the woman to be drained of life before reaching the next block. Then, stepping from the sidewalk, I started down the road slowly, watching the arm at her waist, noting the pulsing tattoos. That alone gave away this predator's breed and that he was preparing to feed on her.

Sadly, until he made his move, we couldn't intervene on her behalf. Passing another club, I gagged at the stench of stale alcohol and sweat. Music played from several clubs, each one fighting to draw patrons into their interior.

Passing a lavish restaurant, I turned, peering inside. Midnight eyes locked with mine, but if Kieran recognized me, he hid it well as he helped a beautiful brunette into a long, white jacket. Focusing on the road, I paused, noticing the woman was gone from sight. Unfortunately, so were Onyx and Noah.

My hackles rose, and I stepped back, scanning the shadows when the doors of the restaurant opened, and Kieran and his date walked out into the evening air. I strode past them, hearing his date hiss at me.

"Half-breeds are so disrespectful these days,

darling," she whined, causing me to look in their direction as my brow rose in agitation.

Dismissing them, I searched the darkened street with the sensation of eyes burning into my spine. A whistle sounded, and I stopped cold, turning to see Axton standing in a dimly lit corner. He smiled, but there was something wicked dancing in his gaze. Looking back at where Onyx and Noah should have been, I swallowed down a growl as a demon slinked from the shadows, waving at me before pointing up to the top of the old brick buildings.

"You can save one, maybe. If you're fast enough, half-breed," he sneered, laughing menacingly. "You cannot save them both. Your choice, but I'd make it quickly; they're about to swing. Who do you choose?"

I peered up, staring at Noah, before shifting my gaze to Onyx. Both were held teetering over the edge of two separate buildings. I could see the thick rope wrapped around their throats and knew what the demons intended to do.

"Decide," he snarled, and Noah and Onyx screamed as I pulled my guns, never taking my eyes from them as I shot the ropes holding them suspended over the side of the buildings. Dropping my weapons, I made the split decision to use one of my suppressed abilities. I would do anything to save my friends—even going against my father's wishes, teaching me long ago that many of my natural traits should be kept hidden for my safety. I ignited my power and threw my hands in the air, calling water from the ground. When they splashed safely into the levitating pools, I grabbed my dagger, thrusting my arm out and cutting through the throat of the demon that had ordered their death.

"Both, bitch," I snorted, snapping my finger to release the water that had saved my teammates from dying.

The air beside me shifted, and I dropped, grabbing my gun to aim at a demon trying to stab me with a wicked-looking blade. Then, continuing to roll until I got my legs beneath me, I pushed off the ground with both guns fixed toward the darkness. I narrowed my gaze on Axton, who watched with a dispassionate expression.

Noah and Onyx rushed toward me, both reaching into my boots to retrieve blades as they took up positions around me. "That was a neat trick. Are we going to talk about that?" Noah asked.

"Not today." My heart pounded, and blood echoed in my brain at the thought of exposing some of my power to the growing crowd. It would be handy if the toys they had in Men in Black existed in real life. Instead, I would need to relay to the press what to release in the morning news to cover this shit up. Typically, we played the whole film crew shooting a movie scene downtown card, donating a crap ton of money to the city to create a trail.

The shadows started to pulse, and I groaned. Werewolves and lone creatures slithered out, murder burning in their eyes. This hadn't been a tip or an honest citizen calling it in. It was a fucking hit someone had paid to put into play.

"This is going to suck," Noah muttered.

"If we go down, we do it together," Onyx yelled,

her tone holding hope that we weren't about to be mauled to death.

"Fuck that," I said. "The teams are in place already. We will all survive this. Ain't no one got time to deal with that bullshit this week." Growling, I fired the first shot at a wolf that walked off the sidewalk and onto the street. "If any of you assholes have a brain, you'll run. Step one foot off that curb, and you get what you got coming to you. Understood?" I called over the music, still pumping from the bars.

When our pursuers advanced as one, I rolled my eyes. Idiots. My gun exploded, sending bullet after bullet at each creature without prejudice. A wolf barreled through the others, his body contorting with the change, marking him as an alpha. I popped off a round, breaking formation to take a head shot. Noah saddled closer to my exposed back, shooting in the opposite direction.

Onyx screamed, and I spun, firing one last time before my guns were empty. Removing the daggers connected to my wristbands inside the sleeves of my jacket, I sliced through the attacker's torso, repeatedly stabbing him. Jumping, I landed on his shoulders, hooking my feet through his arms, sending my body over the front of him, causing him to sail through the air. Landing upright, I kicked high, slamming my heel into one wolf's head while twisting mid-jump and thrusting my knives into another.

The sounds of tires squealing over asphalt should have pulled my focus from the fight. It only took a second to end up dead, and I wasn't dying in the street like a dog. Round-kicking a new assailant, I used my weight to force him to bend. Rising, I balled up my fist and hit him in the face, smirking when he smashed against the concrete with a sickening crunch.

The scent of copper filled the air, and the smell of death clung to my skin. I spun toward the cars that had sped to the scene, smiling as Rhys, Cole, Eryx, and the twins exited the vehicles, joining the fight. Exhaling, I whirled around as something whizzed toward me, striking my body. Another object hit me, and pain sliced through me. I felt Noah grab me, yanking me back and swearing beneath his breath.

Staring at my stomach, I swallowed the pain while studying the arrows protruding from my abdomen. Noah leaned me against a car and peered between us. I groaned, fighting the discomfort and nausea that fought to be free. Then, snatching Noah's blade from his waist, I pushed him away and stabbed the demon coming up behind him.

The pain made my head swim, but I refused to go out like this. Swinging my gaze over the bustling crowd, I saw Axton watching, but all of his excitement had vanished. Instead, his eyes bore regret, sliding over my features. Blood dripped from my nose and mouth as I coughed violently, and he closed his eyes briefly before shaking his head at someone behind me.

Turning, I found Kieran facing his date, who held a bow in her hand. The smile on her face was victorious, and she laughed before meeting my stare. She vanished before I could give the order to attack. Kieran didn't laugh. His intense gaze slid back to me, finding me standing and glaring at him.

Reaching down, I snapped off the fletching end of

the arrow and gripped the iron tip protruding from my back, pulling it out of my flesh. I didn't make a sound, and never broke eye contact with Kieran as I removed the arrow. Then, turning, I tossed it on the car beside me, looking back at him and seeing his eyes narrowed on the second arrow, dangerously embedded near my lungs. Repeating the steps, I pulled it free and heard Noah cursing as he cupped my cheeks, forcing me to look at him.

"Rhys and the others are here to help us. They found out about the hit on you," he glanced down while speaking and gasped. "Xariana, what the fuck?"

I laughed, watching the horror spread across his face. He pushed me back against the vehicle, grabbing the broken arrows slathered in my blood. I heard shouting, and I looked over at the crew that had shown up to assist us.

"She's a fucking child," Rhys snapped, his tone echoing against the buildings for everyone to hear. My heart leaped to my throat at his words.

"Xariana needs to be guarded. She's too fucking young and weak to be out here alone. You should have had her beneath your protection the moment her father went missing. She isn't strong enough or mentally prepared to lead the guild!" Eryx snarled back, shoving Rhys.

"Fuck you both," Cole interjected, crossing his heavily tattooed arms over his chest. "Xariana is easy prey out here. You both fucked up. Xavier is going to have all our asses when he returns, and you damn well know it. She's too young and shouldn't be out here fighting at all!"

It fucking hurt that they were saying all these things, let alone where everyone could hear them. My eyes burned with tears, threatening to fall and give away the pain caused by their words. I wasn't weak or a child, and none of them had ever expressed these concerns before now.

They continued arguing amongst themselves, belittling my standing and skill level, and I felt each blow like a punch to the gut. But I ignored them as more cars pulled up, and people poured out to listen to the immortals that I'd fought and bled beside, quarreling over how weak, immature, and young they thought I was.

My body hummed with disappointment, but more than that, betrayal. Someone touched my shoulder, and I turned, staring up at Conrad and Ian, both peering past me to where the men argued. They moved toward their comrades, but when they got close, they joined in the dispute unfolding, agreeing with them.

"What the fuck is happening?" A red-haired female whispered, causing me to focus on her. She rubbed her hand over her round belly and then glared at Rhys. She rolled her bright blue eyes and then met mine, a soft smile tugging at her lips.

"They're arguing over who fucked up by allowing someone as young as me to hunt," I answered with thick emotion.

My gaze slid to the shadows, and I saw glowing green eyes staring at my extended team. Producing my gun, I aimed and waited for his attention to turn toward me before pulling the trigger. The men immediately stopped arguing, turning to stare at me before moving their gazes to the dead demon on the pavement. Fucking demons and their meddling.

I slid my weapon into its holster and crossed my arms to prevent anyone from seeing how badly my hands were trembling. It may have been a demon that spread discord, but it wouldn't make them say things they didn't believe.

The people I'd fought beside for years believed I was unfit for my role. They thought I shouldn't be leading during my father's absence. Rhys said he'd started a hunt on his own because he didn't think I couldn't handle the more challenging parts of what needed to be done.

Eryx planned to force me to the mountain with Braelyn and Saint to hide like some weak female needing to be sheltered. I'd saved his ass more times than I could count, and I wasn't half bad at math. Ian had a castle, one he wanted to push me into visiting until things blew over. Conrad intended for his omegas to caudle and pamper me so that I wouldn't grieve alone.

Ezekiel and Enzo thought I was doing a shitty job of enforcing the laws. That I was failing, but not one of them had the balls to say that to my face. They worried that my mental stability wasn't enough to deal with the loss of my father and the others. They felt I should be put in time out and taught how to handle the business aspects, as my dad had done.

I turned toward the Land Rovers parked at the end of the block, pausing as Rhys grabbed my shoulder.

"Xari," he started, but I yanked my arm away from

him.

"Save it, Van Helsing. I have bled with each of you and walked into battle, not knowing if it would be my last, and I never cowered. We have hunted down monsters that made the ones here tonight look fluffy in comparison. I have saved several of you from sure death and never bragged or asked you to repay that debt. A demon might have caused you all to argue, but he didn't make you say the things that you said. He only caused you to reveal your true feelings." I began walking again, aware the other hunters were following me.

I didn't wince or shy away as I passed through the crowded street. People didn't move out of our path, or give us the wide birth they normally did, either. Of course, I'd just had some of the biggest named immortals in the area calling me a silly kid, playing an adult game that would get me killed one day. The sad reality was, they were right about that last part. I lived by the blade, and I would die by it, but it would be my choice.

No one said anything as I walked beside Onyx, making our way past all the onlookers. I sensed eyes on me, but I didn't care to look or see who was staring. Disappointment rocketed through me, my gut twisting as I replayed all their shouted words. This was the lowest point I'd ever felt, even worse than discovering Micah fucking Meredith on my counter.

At the Land Rover, Noah opened the passenger door for me to slide inside. Resting my head against the seat, I gazed out the window, finding Kieran watching me from the shadows. His intense gaze narrowed while he stared, slowly searching my face, before he smiled coldly. My heart fluttered as we drove away, speeding through the city streets and back to the compound in dead silence.

Chapter Sixteen

The next morning, I woke before the sun rose. In the silence of my bedroom, I dressed in black, loose-fitting joggers, a tight top, and running shoes. I didn't fuss with makeup or do anything fancy with my hair, leaving it to hang down my back in soft ringlets. Then, carefully, I wrapped my holsters over my shoulders and slid my guns into them. Once done, I gently reached down, gathering the iron-laced explosion packs into the pockets of a waist trainer. Exhaling, once they were all in place, I attached the pulse monitor to them and connected the device, grabbing my jacket to conceal the bomb around my waist.

Slipping out of my apartment, I quietly closed the door before starting down the hallway, using the master combination to bypass the command center as I exited the building. Inside the parking garage, I sighed in relief at not having to explain why I was awake at this ungodly hour or to admit where I was going.

Pausing at the main entrance, I reached up to grab the keys for my father's Ferrari 812 GTS. It was his favorite car, matte black, with red interior, and the only one he owned that wasn't an SUV of some sort. He'd never let me drive it, and had hardly driven it himself since he'd purchased it.

Often, when we would infiltrate a trafficking ring, you'd had to play a rich aristocrat, needing fancy things as part of the rouse. The Ferrari had been one of those necessary purchases. It was perfect for my plans for today, requiring the speed it offered for what I was about to do.

Using the keyless entry, I closed my eyes, sliding my hands over the smooth exterior. "Okay, daddy," I whispered. "If you're dead, and you're here, I'm going to need you with me on this one. You know, so I don't join you in the afterlife and all that jazz. Also, I want you to forgive me if I wreck your baby," I muttered, frowning at the fact that I was talking to air.

The idea that he could be dead made my stomach churn, but knowing that I was about to do something incredibly stupid but brave wasn't helping that either. I'd been raised to never allow someone to threaten a member of the guild. If they did or slighted us in the eyes of others, it had to be addressed. Axton had to know his bullshit stunt wasn't okay, and I couldn't take a chance on anyone getting hurt because of it.

Sliding into the soft leather seats, I grimaced at the pain of the wound from the iron arrow tip that hadn't fully healed. I'd taken the pills that Talia made for me, doubling the dose after using my powers last night. It was becoming harder to hide what I was, and I wasn't so certain I should be doing it anymore with everything happening.

Pushing the ignition button, I savored the sound of the engine, allowing the vibration to ease my fears. Then, pulling out of the parking spot, I drove through the underground garage, waving at the hunter who'd started to protest until he saw who was behind the wheel. He stepped closer, but I didn't stop to talk, choosing to rev the engine while exiting to the ground level.

Engaging the remote that opened the outside gate, I moved past and closed it before hitting the empty side streets. It was early enough that traffic wasn't an issue, and wouldn't be for the next hour. Heading toward Axton's club, I silently prayed that whatever god catered to half-breeds would listen.

I arrived a short time later, staring at the front door and the vampire guarding it this early in the morning. Axton had some serious trust issues he needed to work through, but maybe they were warranted after his stunt. I parked in a spot reserved for his distinguished clientele, frowning when I saw the Bugatti La Voiture Noire beside me. My jaw dropped, and a low whistle escaped my lips.

Who the hell did Axton know that could afford to buy this eighteen million dollar, one-of-a-kind masterpiece, once owned by Bugatti himself? It looked like the freaking Batmobile or something out of a James Bond movie. What it didn't look like was an automobile you'd find in our city.

I slid from the seat, closing the door, and pocketing the keys. Stealing my spine and asking the gods for strength to pull this off without dying, I started toward the entrance. The vampire guarding the door turned, giving me a sinister smile that fluttered over his lips. Using my speed, I plowed into him, knocking his head against the wall. Then, moving back, I allowed him to slide in front of me before I kicked him, sending him sailing through the heavy wooden door.

I walked through the hole I'd made with the vampire's body, stepping over him to enter the club. A blur of light rushed me, and I thrust my hand up, sending a creature hurtling backward through the bar. Then, with another burst of speed, I slammed into Axton, withdrawing both of my guns and pointing one at him and the other at whoever was at my back.

"Fuck around and see what happens, Axton," I sneered, staring at him coldly. "You want to find out what I'm wearing, asshole?" I hissed, sensing another presence behind me without needing to look. "On my waist is an iron bomb, one that detonates if my pulse slows or stops. I'm willing to bet most everyone in here is fae, and if this thing goes off, you're all dead."

"What the fuck are you doing, Xari?" Axton asked, his eyes wide with panic, understanding that I was serious.

"Did you think you could call in a hit on me and that I wouldn't retaliate? Only, unlike you, I don't send anyone else to deal with my issues."

"Walk away, hunter," Kieran hissed behind me.

"We can all go our separate ways once I have delivered my warning," I bit out through clenched teeth.

"I got the message, Xari," Axton growled, sliding

his icy-blue gaze to my waist, flinching when he realized I hadn't been bluffing. "Don't do anything stupid or something you'll regret. We will all die if that thing goes off. All half-breeds are created from some sort of fae, woman. You're not immune."

"Nor am I scared to die—not at all, asshole." I chuckled, allowing him to see the craziness I was feeling in my soul. "You want to take a chance and gamble if I'm playing? Go for it, Axton. Let's see who is willing to die for their cause. You're a greedy, self-serving prick that takes whatever deal is best for him, not worrying about who it hurts. So tell me, does it look like I'm afraid of death or that I'm fucking around right now? Dying is easy. It's a simple matter of it all ending and everything just being finished."

"You're fucking insane," he hissed.

I laughed, sucking my lip between my teeth as a gun pressed against my temple. I could see Kieran in my peripheral vision, indicating I'd been wrong to assume it was one of Axton's lackeys coming up from behind. He released the safety, and I smiled while holding both guns tightly. I tilted my head to stare at him, finding angry black eyes on me.

"You're not getting out of here alive, little girl," he whispered coldly.

"And neither will you, Master of Shadows. Do you want that pristine record to remain so? You'll lower your gun, allow me to deliver my message, and we'll all walk out of here in one piece. If my heart slows or stops, you're all coming with me to the afterlife, Knight."

The tic in his jaw only made the prick hotter. His darkly intense eyes slowly lowered to my mouth before lifting to hold my stare. The sound of boots moving over the floor echoed through the now empty bar, and my pulse rocketed as I felt a ripple of power slithering through it.

"Kieran, I'm calling in my debt. Do not kill her," Enzo's voice was death incarnate. Kieran's lips tipped into a wicked smile. But there wasn't anything pleasant about it.

That intensely visceral stare slipped from me to where the footsteps had paused, seeing the situation unfolding. Slowly and methodically, Kieran lowered his gun, still looking at Enzo, before glancing back at me. The bastard looked pleased about something, and that sent warning bells ringing in my mind.

Turning my attention to Axton, I grinned smugly. "If you ever order a hit on my people or me again, I will fucking end you. I don't care if I go out five seconds after you. Do you understand me? You'll finally get that date you keep asking for, but we'll be having it in the afterlife. Look me in the eye and tell me you comprehend what I am saying. I won't give you another warning. The next time you do something like this, you won't see me coming. It won't matter who the fuck is guarding your back, either. No one, and I mean fucking no one, threatens my team or me," I snarled, pushing the gun against his chin.

"I get it, Xari," he whispered, anger pulsing through him.

"Good." I stepped back, lowering my guns and placing them in their holsters.

I braced for impact, but it never came. Instead, I turned on my heel to discover Rhys, Cole, and the twins, Ezekiel and Enzo, standing behind me, loaded to the teeth with weapons. I didn't stop for conversation because I sensed Kieran's need to murder me. It pulsed through the room, slithering around me as I walked toward the gaping hole in the door.

A flash of light flew at me, and I smirked, using my abilities to stop it cold. It slammed into the decorative wall of water, slowly sliding through it, bursting into flames, and turning to ashes before it touched the floor. I rippled with raw, unfiltered power that begged to be released. The problem was, if I played with it too much, it would call to others like me, and then we'd all be damned.

Ducking through the rubble to exit the club, I ran at full speed to reach the Ferrari, getting in quickly and backing out of the parking lot. Hitting the side street, I heard Kieran's car before I saw it in my rearview mirror. It figures that he would own the freaking Bugatti. I removed the bomb from my waist, placing it on the seat beside me as I entered the highway, pushing my foot on the gas pedal, and gunning it. I couldn't outrun him; that much was a given. But I needed to get him on the interstate, further from civilization.

A mile out of town, another sleek sports car pulled out ahead of me, but it didn't stop me or block the road. He must have had the same idea of getting far away from the city. Suddenly, the vehicle slowed, forcing me to do the same. The Bugatti didn't let up, making my stomach roll and churn with unease.

The car in front sped up, and I followed suit. They

were fucking playing with me. I glanced out the side window, slowly trying to gauge the distance to where I needed to be. Swerving into the other lane, I barely escaped a head-on collision by jerking the wheel, moving back into my lane.

I did the maneuver several more times, fighting the urge to vomit as I looked for a way out of being entombed in the sports car. The sound of horns blaring distracted me for a moment, pulling my focus from the mile markers. The driver ahead of me began decelerating, and I slammed the brakes when I noticed the marker number I'd been trying to reach. I jerked the wheel, turning off the highway, looking over my shoulder to see them pass by me.

Smiling, I peered in the rearview mirror as Kieran reversed his sports car to follow me. I grabbed the remote and began entering the gate code as I flew down the street. I'd never driven over ninety, but the engine opened up, and the countryside went by in a blur as I raced blindly down the winding road.

My father's mansion came into view, and the sleek sports car following me sped up the moment Kieran saw it, too. I pushed the Ferrari to its limit, knowing that if he caught up, he would do whatever it took to keep me from entering the gates.

My blood thumped loudly in my ears, and everything around me seemed to stop as I reached for the one button that would ensure I made it to safety. The nitrous hit the engine, and I shot forward at a dangerous speed. Closing my eyes, I prayed hard that I wouldn't get onto the property, only to end up exploding or something insane.

Kieran's car came up beside me when I got close to the gate, forcing my attention on the driver as fear ripped through my mind. His glare promised pain, but the Ferrari jerked forward and entered the last leg of the nitrous before it began easing up.

"No. No. No, come on," I pleaded, holding the shaking steering wheel as the Bugatti slowed, sensing that I was losing control.

I saw a police cruiser at the mansion, and it made my gut twist into knots. I could make out Jeffery's form leaning against it as he witnessed the race to the estate. My body was trembling, and fear consumed my mind as I glanced in the rearview mirror. Kieran bumped the back of the Ferrari, causing it to swerve, threatening to send me rolling into the field in front of the property.

He backed off, allowing me to correct my vehicle as it crossed the threshold of the gates. Once I was inside, I pushed the control, engaging the tire spikes that would prevent Kieran's car from entering. Then I exhaled in relief, slamming on the brakes and sliding sideways as I squealed to a stop.

I opened the door and rushed to close the fence, reaching it at the same time as Kieran, who stopped short, sensing the spell protecting the boundary of the land. He paused at the barrier, glaring at me through narrowed slits. I grabbed the gate, walking toward him with my body quaking from the power I felt rolling off him in angry waves.

"You think you can hide from me? I am everywhere, hunter. I am in the shadows and the one thing that will get to you. The spell protecting you has a time limit, doesn't it? And the witch that placed it here, she isn't inside. I can only hear two hearts beating right now. That means eventually you will be unprotected. No one fucks with me and walks away unscathed."

I swallowed past the threat and gripped the iron bars of the fence, staring him down, un-phased that he could tell that I was terrified. Fear made creatures unpredictable. Add to it that I was a woman, and you had a bad combination.

"I don't doubt that you will do as you say," I admitted, shivering when he clasped my hands, holding them to the iron. It told me he wasn't willing to touch it, and that my imagination hadn't played tricks on me. A shiver ran up my spine as his hand caused electricity to rush through me. "But I just walked into a club you were protecting. I did it with you standing by and unable to stop me. Adding to the insult, I'm not even at my best, having been weakened by your girlfriend's cheap shot with the arrow last night. You're not as terrifying as I thought you'd be. In fact, I'm not afraid of you at all." I was, of course, lying through my teeth, but I had his attention. "I did what I set out to do, and you looked the fool while I did it. Kill me if you want, but heed this, asshole. The moment you end me, you inherit my curse. You would never be able to hide your secrets or suppress your true nature from anyone or anything ever again."

"Who said I wanted to murder you, Xariana?" he smiled, testing my name out on his tongue.

My nipples hardened, hearing it uttered huskily from his lips, and my thighs clenched as I struggled to push away my body's response to the sadistic prick. Kieran's dark gaze lowered to my mouth, sliding absently up to meet my eyes.

"It would be a waste to kill something like you. There are many other satisfying things to do to you, other than to end your pathetic life, hunter. I can get to you anywhere, at any time I want. Enzo took away my choice to kill you, but it won't protect you from me— no one can save you, Xariana Anderson. I own this town now, not you. You just fucked up, little girl. Your friends can no longer help you; I won't allow it. There isn't a single creature inside this state that hasn't hired me at one time or another and owes me their loyalty."

"So what? You're cutting me off?" I snorted, whimpering as his grip on mine tightened until my fingers ached from the pressure.

"Something like that," he smiled, but it was calculated and had the hair on my nape rising. Glancing over at the other driver that had just exited his car, Kieran shouted, "Call everyone indebted to me, Ender. Declare Xariana Anderson on the do not help list. I want her exiled from everyone she's counted on in the past. Not one person is to assist her, or I will call in the life debts owed to me."

I didn't look away from the haughty expression burning in his stare. I knew what a life debt was. He'd just cut me off from the otherworld altogether. If he called in that debt, he could order that person to murder their family, and they'd be spellbound to do so.

I swallowed the fear creeping up my throat, briefly closing my eyes before opening them to glare at him. I'd responded to Axton's betrayal the way my father had taught me, but it had cost me any and all help to find my dad. Kieran's grip eased, but he didn't release me. Instead, he trailed his thumb over the pulse on my wrist and smiled roguishly when he found it racing.

"There's a reason people don't fuck with me, little one. I have collected debts since the moment I took control of the shadows, never chancing to lose a fight. You're cute to think you're on my level, but you're not. Ask for my help, and I'll find your father, Xariana."

"Never," I whispered in reply, hating that he was threatening me as my body heated from the simple touch of his fingers.

"Why not? The shadows see everything. I know who attacked your guild. Do you?"

"No," I admitted, shaking my head slowly. "But I won't ever ask a monster like you for a favor."

His touch wasn't innocent. I could feel him learning me, seeing if he made my pulse race. He was allowing his shadows to slither over every inch of me. It was erotic, yet terrifying at the same time. His heady scent was fucking me harder than I'd ever been fucked. A tremor rushed through me, and I licked my lips to speak, but his eyes dropped to my mouth, and a wicked spark lit his expression.

"We could make a deal, you and me, Xariana," he encouraged, searching my face while I shivered at the sensation of his shadows.

"Never," I whispered huskily, not immune to his power. How had I missed it? He had touched me, and that had allowed him to bypass the magic, working his shadows against me. "You don't need money. And if that's what you demanded, I couldn't afford to pay you. You don't require power, and I wouldn't give you any even if I could."

"There are other ways to pay for my services," he offered, slowly tugging me closer. He pulled me against the bars, brushing his nose along my cheek. "I have identified your attacker and who is responsible for your father's disappearance. You need me, and I want something from you, Xariana."

"Let me guess. It will only cost my soul to get that information?" I gasped as he captured my bottom lip, nipping it painfully, forcing a moan to escape me. One of his hands slipped through the fence to slide around my neck, holding me in place.

"Your soul is worthless to me," he murmured, releasing my lip to peer down at where he'd drawn blood. "Souls are messy and aren't worth the trouble of dealing with or collecting."

Lifting my gaze to his, I licked the wound he'd inflicted and stared at him. Kieran may not want my soul, but I had a feeling it would be shattered either way once he'd finished with me. His fingers slowly roved over my neck, sending pressure pulsing between my thighs. He knew how to fucking work someone over. I'd give him that.

"Then what would you want from me?" I asked, holding his midnight stare that sparkled with amusement.

"Come to me, willingly," he urged, shifting his attention to something behind me. He lifted his hand, cradling my face while his thumb traced over my jaw. Every part of me was responding to him, and I prayed he couldn't scent the arousal his touch conjured. "You know where I live, Xariana. Meet me at my home, and I will tell you my price. If you refuse me, I will let you walk away without hurting you, although you will still pay for what you did today. Like you, I have to respond to the slight against my investment. I can either be your darkest desire or your fucking nightmare. Which one I become depends on you and your response to my offer," he murmured, pulling me closer. "Don't make me into your enemy."

He released me, stepping back and spinning on his heel without a backward glance. My attention shifted to Ender, and a cold, calculated smile stretched across his mouth before he turned, following his master to their vehicles.

Kieran paused at the lifted door of his outrageously expensive sports car, smiling. "Don't make me wait too long for your decision. You won't like your punishment if you keep me waiting. Goodnight, hunter. I look forward to sitting down with you to discuss our future."

Chapter Seventeen

Kieran had gone, but he'd left a small force of men behind to guard me for the evening. Sitting at the bar with the sheriff, I peered down at the pictures he'd brought out for me to examine. He didn't mention the incident at the gate, or that I had been street racing down the road. Jeffery hadn't batted an eye at any of it, in fact.

"These were taken out by the old mill." He pointed at a blurry image.

Looking at the photo, I squinted, then lifted it to the portrait on the wall. "When was this taken?"

My entire body still buzzed with the adrenaline coursing through it from my encounter with Kieran, who had left me whirling, and on uneven ground. He'd said he knew who had attacked us, which meant I'd be going to him one way or another. I intended to make him wait, though. I wasn't jumping simply because he'd demanded I do so.

"Last night," he snorted, sitting back to light a cigarette.

"Don't light that in here," I complained, watching him tap it on the counter. "We can sit outside. Pick your poison."

He held up the cigarette, smiling sadly. "This is my poison. But I don't suppose you'd have any scotch or bourbon on hand?"

"Both," I grinned, pulling out a cigar from my pack, filled with Braelyn's herbal remedy. He lifted a brow, and I shrugged. "It's Washington and legal. It's also not weed, old man. It's a simple herbal concoction that soothes the monster within, taming it, per se. A friend grows the herbs, and we supply them to the werewolf population to ease their itches when the moon rises."

"You're a wolf?" He scrunched his forehead in thought.

Laughing, I shook my head. "Much worse, I'm afraid."

"Insanely enough, I asked your father what he was, and he replied with the same answer," Jeffery chuckled, collecting the file he'd brought for me to inspect. "Lincoln didn't leave town, by the way. He was asking a lot of questions about you directly. Either he wants to date you, or he's suspicious of you, kid."

I swallowed at his use of the word kid, which was something my old man said all the time when talking to me. My gaze flicked to the wall, staring at a photo of the first crew of hunters before going to the bar and grabbing two bottles to hold up for him to choose.

"I'll take the scotch, but you do realize that bottle is two hundred and fifty years old, right?"

Snorting, I rolled my eyes. "Did you know we have some hunters that are older than this alcohol? Some worked in the distilleries even when they were made." He whistled, following me outside where I uncovered the chairs, folding the covers that protected them from the elements.

"Your father brought me up here once," he admitted. "Told me how you were born in this house, right upstairs. He wanted to torch this place to the ground because he said it was filled with ghosts."

"He couldn't burn it down." I turned to look at the elegant house he'd purchased for our family, only to abandon it soon after. "My mother helped design it. She insisted on the large windows to allow natural light into every room. Plus, the basement is a vault containing artifacts and weapons that would blow the minds of both scholars and the ATF."

Pouring two glasses to the rim, I chewed on the end of the cigar, not bothering to light it. Instead, I picked up the pictures, staring at the familiar feminine form and image I'd seen a million times before, bodies lying lifelessly at her feet. Exhaling, I thumbed through the photos, hearing vehicles coming up the road, turning to see a line of Land Rovers passing Kieran's men, staked out on the opposite side of the fence.

"You said this was up by the old mill? It's been closed down for a few years, right?" I questioned, as the gate creaked open.

"Three years now, or thereabout," he nodded, pulling out another picture before placing his cigarette into the ashtray, stretching to hand me the photo. "There's been a ton of asshole kids up there over the years. They were mostly partying and causing trouble. These images, though, they're recent. The symbols made me think it was some kind of ritual."

"It would be if they were drawn correctly." I tapped the top of the star on the spray-painted symbol. "This tip being outside the circle would make the entire thing invalid. How many bodies did you say you recovered?"

"Nine. Seven females and two males," he stated, exhaustion clearly in his voice. "Each one had their eyes and tongues removed. Again, it hinted at a ritual. Your father taught me how to spot it to avoid bringing in the feds. Guess I missed it this time. That isn't even the weirdest thing we found." He sat back, staring up at the sky. "There were babies left behind."

My blood turned to ice, and I leaned forward as Micah, Noah, Onyx, and Kaderyn strode over, sitting down with irritated expressions. Smirking, I returned my attention to the sheriff.

"So, how many dead infants were there?" I wrinkled my brow when he exhaled and sat up, staring directly at me. My team exchanged glances and settled into the other chairs on the patio.

"None were deceased," he admitted, grabbing his glass to take a long swig from it before continuing. "They were all alive and just laying beside the female's bodies. I had Brodie do the autopsies. He's the guy your father planted in the morgue. He said the women hadn't given birth and that he didn't find any markings." At my confused look, he elaborated. "When a woman gives birth, it leaves a shotgun pellet-sized mark on the pelvic bone that won't fade. It's a sign of the trauma she experiences in childbirth when the ligaments tear. It wasn't present in any of the women. The men and women were young and riddled with iron bullets, which is officially their cause of death. Someone shot each one and then removed body parts from them. Including their wombs." He downed the rest of his drink before lighting up another smoke. "This fucking job is going to put me in the nuthouse sooner or later."

"Where are the babies?" I asked, and his eyes snapped to mine.

"They vanished, and I get to explain that one, too. We sent them to the hospital to be examined, but they never arrived. The officer I assigned has no memory of ever signing for the infants or riding with them in the ambulance."

"So," I frowned, peering down at the woman once more. "You have nine corpses, seven missing babies, and a huge fucking mess of paperwork you don't know how to explain?" I clarified, tossing the cigar of herbs to Noah, who caught it without looking away from me. My team was angry that I'd snuck out, and I was willing to bet they were itching to tell me all about it once Jeffery left.

"Yup," he laughed, but he sounded tired, and I didn't blame him.

Leaning forward, I tapped the photo of the woman. "Do you know who she is?"

He shrugged, closing his eyes before rubbing them. "I was hoping we could find her in your database. Your dad allowed me to use it when shit like this happened. That woman, she knows something. She's my only lead."

"You don't need the database to identify her," I admitted. "Her name is Sandra Anderson, and she's been dead for twenty-five years. Her grave is sitting in that yard. It's the tallest tombstone, to be exact," I snorted, pointing over his shoulder at the cemetery. "She's my aunt, and one of the reasons my father formed the guild to hunt down creatures that preyed on our race. Sandra is his reason for hunting, or so I was told. The original hunters were a small organization. They alone hunted inside this town, knowing what else was out there preying on humans. Eventually, they started picking up more members. But not without tragedy happening along the way." I accepted the cigar from Noah, puffing on it as I closed my eyes.

"Sandra was on a hunt one night, and a lot like me, according to my dad. She was wild and preferred the thrill of hunting alone. She reported a strange occurrence that she couldn't explain." I shivered as my dad's words echoed through me. "Hunter became the prey, and the thing stalking her was incredibly fast. It moved through the woods unseen, tracking her. It played with her, leaving wounds on her flesh with each renewed attack. They tried to locate her, to figure out where she was in the forest, and when they finally found her, she was in the same spot she is buried now. They couldn't move her, as if the earth had claimed her. My father dedicated the grounds as a hunter's cemetery in her honor. It can't be Sandra in that photo because she was salted and given final rites."

"And you're certain she wasn't able to return from the grave?" Jeffery asked, shaking his head at his own question. "Jesus Christ. This is one of those times I wish I didn't know shit like that was possible."

"I understand it is hard, but the work you do helps us, too. You being aware of our existence makes it easier for us to do our job. Plus, you'd really hate us if you didn't know, and we met at crime scenes too often," I chuckled, and his eyes sparkled at the irony of it all.

"You sound like your old man, Xariana." The sheriff finished his drink and stood. "I'm going to head out. Keep the pictures. I made you a file so that you could help me with this one."

"Tell your staff and the media that the children were taken into protective custody. Have Brodie send me a full autopsy report from all the victims. We will be back at the compound tomorrow." I stood to walk him to the gate, and the others rose with us, following me to the edge of the property line. "If anything else turns up, don't hesitate to call."

"Will do, but you sure you want me to leave you with these guys? They look upset about something," he asked seriously, glancing at my team and then at the men standing guard outside the fence.

"I can handle them," I said, waving at Kieran's men as they stared me down. They weren't leaving, and I had a sinking suspicion that the moment I left the property, they fully intended to take me to their leader. "As for my team? They probably just heard about me threatening to blow up a club." I shrugged when his brows shot up in surprise. "It's okay. It wouldn't have made a ruckus, or much of one, anyway."

"Alrighty, then." Jeffery waved and was no sooner in his car when Noah rounded on me.

"You want to explain what the fuck you were thinking this morning?" He demanded, forcing me to dismiss the intense stares of the others to answer him.

"Axton put a hit out on us, so I took a play from my father's handbook. He needed to feel the fear of the gods, even if for only a moment. I was not about to allow that one to slide, and I didn't. I walked in with an iron bomb strapped to my chest and told him exactly how it would go down if he ever did something like that again."

"Well, then, that's perfectly fine," Onyx groaned sarcastically.

"See, handled," I snorted, starting back toward the estate. "We have bigger issues to worry about right now, other than to focus on what could have occurred. I wasn't hurt, and while I have a feeling that's still up in the air until Kieran decides how best to punish me, we have to figure out if ghosts are resurfacing. I am beginning to doubt past events that my father said happened, and we have a house to search through for clues. If Sandra didn't really die, and my dad hid secrets, we need to know."

"Back the fuck up," Noah hissed. "He intends to punish you?"

"I kicked a vampire through the door at the club, used my power to reach Axton, and held a gun to his and one of Kieran's men's heads. He apparently cannot kill me because Enzo called in a debt, and that, too, is an issue. I'm starting to wonder if that wasn't the plan to begin with. I think Kieran let me reach Axton, because he's very powerful and could have stopped me. I believe he knew I was coming, adding another piece to the puzzle."

"It would really be nice to get answers instead of more fucking questions for once," Micah snapped, sliding his gaze toward the men outside the gates. "That explains those assholes."

"Yeah, that's also a problem. We have limited amount of time before the hex bags I placed around the property expire, and no one can be here when they do. No one," I whispered, stepping into the house I'd been born in, yet never been beyond my bedroom or the main rooms.

Chapter Eighteen

Inside the house, I was forced to explain my actions of that morning. I'd given my team the play-by-play and endured their disapproval of going to the club alone. I didn't blame them for being upset, but it needed to be done. Noah was the most vocal about it, and we'd agreed to disagree on the subject.

An hour had passed since the sheriff left the property, and in that time, we'd barely scratched the surface, searching the house, when I discovered a huge office that I'd never known existed. My father came up here a lot, but I'd always assumed it was to get away from the pressure the hunter guild placed on him.

Walking to the desk, I opened a drawer, withdrawing several photos of him and my mother together, yellowed with age. In one, he was holding her on his lap with his hands around her pregnant belly. Behind them sat my aunt, looking at them with a sadness that tugged at my heartstrings. I frowned, seeing dark circles beneath her puffy eyes.

She must have been crying before the picture was taken. Her green eyes were red-rimmed and swollen, and her hair was a mess of braids, some tied together to prevent them from falling into her face. Baggy clothing hung on her slender frame, and her expression was unguarded.

Sandra had wanted what my parents had; that much was obvious. It wasn't uncommon for hunters to push their needs away to do what we did. It was part of the reason why I'd agreed to marry Micah. I craved the family we could have created, but I had also been terrified of it as well. I'd even doubled up on my birth control agent to prevent myself from becoming pregnant. Had Sandra been like me? Was she driven by her desire to prove she belonged here, forcing the things she might have wanted in life to the background and second to the cause?

Flipping through the pictures, I found another of her with my father. He was laughing at something, causing her face to light up in response. I wish they were here to ask what had been said, to know what had brought her so much joy. In a different photo, all three of them were seated in front of the house, and my mother was staring at my aunt with an expression that made ice slither through my spine.

My father seemed uncomfortable, not looking at either of the women in his life, but then I'd known him to close down when there was discord. I'd been on the end of that look a lot growing up. I often asked him about my mother, only for him to shake my questions off and change the subject. I had pegged it as grief and a difficult topic for him to discuss with me.

Putting the photographs back, I ran my hand through the drawer, pausing as my fingertips touched something metal. Pulling it out, I stared at a skeleton key that looked as if it had been plucked from another era. My gaze slid around the room, but there was nothing that the key would fit.

Closing the drawer, I opened the next one below it, withdrawing an old ammo box. Undoing the clasp, I peered inside, glowering at more keys. The man had probably kept every key he'd ever discovered in his lifetime. Placing it back in the drawer, I heard it hit against metal. Slowly, I pulled the tin case out and stared down at the remaining contents.

Getting up from my chair, I crouched, running my hands along the inside. The drawer was a lot deeper than it appeared to be. Pulling out the few scraps of paper, I gazed at the locking mechanism I found, and chuckled. I grabbed the skeleton key off the top of the desk and pushed it into the lock, watching as it sprang open.

Humming started within the office, causing the hair on my neck to rise as the light went out. The room shifted to reveal a hidden wall of books. One of the larger volumes on the shelves moved, exposing a door. Looking around, I stood and walked over to it with the key still in my hand.

A tremor of apprehension slithered into the pit of my stomach. I pushed the skeleton key into the lock, hearing it click as it opened, sending a thick layer of dust into the air. Fanning the particles from my face, I peered into a dark room, brushing my hand along the wall in search of a light switch, finding none.

I went back to my father's desk and retrieved a flashlight, and entered the room. Shining the light inside, I paused, seeing two cribs. One was covered in plastic, while the other had pink blankets coated in a fine layer of dust. Glancing at the wall, I swallowed down the urge to sneeze, taking in the images of children that covered it.

Moving closer, I scanned the faces and frowned when I saw myself with several other familiar people. My aunt was holding me in one, her lips touching my forehead with a radiant smile lighting her eyes.

"That's impossible," I said out loud. Sandra died before I was born, and my mother had followed her during my birth. "What the hell, Dad?" I muttered absently, searching the other images.

There were more photographs of my aunt and me and ones that also included my father. My heart thundered in my chest, and my mind raced with the implications brought to light. Had he faked Sandra's death to hide something? Or had my dad hidden her from the world as he had done with me?

Why would he grieve her loss if she wasn't dead? Every year on the day of her death, he disappeared for twenty-four hours to mourn the sister he'd lost. I had been invited once when I was little, and his grief seemed genuine. He'd taken me to places they'd gone as children, showing me their world, even though we'd kept to the shadows to see it.

I slid my hand over the other crib and sighed,

noticing the bookshelves that lined the wall. Reaching up, I grabbed a familiar tonic bottle that still smelled like the pills I took to this day. Had he hidden me in here? Or was this for another child like me? If there was a second child, was it altered to remain hidden from the monsters, too? Frowning, I set the thin brown bottle back onto the shelf and looked around with the eyes of a hunter and not those of a daughter.

The bassinets contained silver chains meant to hold the babies safely within, a common feature when having fae children, as many could teleport. Without them, the infants could vanish, frequently harming themselves in the process. The coverlets were worn, and someone had hand-stitched them with love. Reaching into the first crib, I removed the soft green blanket, noting the colors in each bed did nothing to help identify their sex. Holding up the fabric to smell, I sneezed, rubbing my nose with the back of my hand before returning it to the crib. What had I expected? If it was from my infancy, there was twenty-two years of dust on the material.

My father had once told me about a time when I'd vanished on him. I'd been two, and he'd put me down for the night, but I hadn't wanted to sleep yet. I'd teleported, leaving him terrified and unable to locate me for hours. When he finally found me, I was outside beneath the full moon, watching the stars in the guild's courtyard.

After that, he chained me to my bed to prevent me from teleporting anywhere else at bedtime. This is also near the same time he met up with Talia and concocted the pills to hide what and who I was from everyone.

I lifted my hand to my ear, skimming over the piercings that ran up my lobe. They were the same as my mother's in every image of her inside this realm. I inspected the room one last time, then stepped out and back into the office, pulling the door closed behind me.

Most people would freak out about finding something like this in their father's things. I wasn't one of them, since I knew he liked to keep secrets, and I was one of those. Leaving the office, I snorted at the images that hung on the walls.

The man had taken random photographs and tried to turn them into art. Studying one, I narrowed my gaze on a building in the background. Knightly Industries was painted on the windows, and the symbol of the moon and stars, with an enormous wolf between them, held my attention. The same logo sat on the industrial park sign in another photo he'd captured and framed.

"Finding anything?" Noah asked, easing up beside me. "Other than dust, that is?" he grunted, leaning against the doorframe.

"No." I churned the question over inside my head, wondering if I should tell him about the baby room, deciding it could wait. "I'm focused on upstairs because we can't access the basement since it takes a combination of his and my blood to open the lock." I squinted as the largest picture came into view. A sign stating, The Anderson Day and K. Knight Foundation, sat on what looked to be an orphanage's gate.

I pulled out my phone and typed the name into the search engine, and sighed when it came back with nothing. Noah studied me and then lifted his gaze to the image, noticing what had gotten my attention. He stepped forward and took the photograph down, and frowned.

"That's not a coincidence, is it?" he asked, holding the picture up, pointing at the sign. "Tell me that isn't your grandfather's name, and K. Knight isn't Kieran Knight?"

"Wish I could, but I honestly have no idea what the hell it means," I mumbled, peering at the other photographs. "I thought they were just random photos my dad took, but look at the names on them. You and I both know better than to assume this is a coincidence."

"Do you think your grandfather knew Kieran Knight or someone related to him?"

"I don't know anything anymore, Noah. I believed my aunt was dead, and yet she's popping up everywhere now. First, in the photos the sheriff had of the old mill, and then today, I found one of her holding me as an infant. Of course, that's impossible because I was told she passed away before I was born."

"You think she was turned?" he asked, placing the picture back on the wall.

"No idea." I yawned while stretching. "You guys should head out, though. I don't think it's wise to remain here much longer. I used the hex bags Talia made, but the potency is unpredictable. They were initially crafted to protect my bed, but I placed them here instead, to safeguard the estate. I don't know how long we have on the bags, or if they'll last until morning."

"We've all talked and decided we're not leaving you here alone," he snorted, nodding to the stairs.

"There are enough beds for us all to stay here, so pick one. I'd remove the top blanket, though, before lying on any of them."

"You guys need to be at the guild, not here," I complained to his retreating form. "You're being obtuse."

"Night, Xari. I'll see you in the morning." He jogged up the stairs, meeting the others, who smiled down, daring me to argue.

"Stubborn assholes," I groaned, glancing at the bar that had a nightcap on it. "Thanks for the drink."

"Figured you would need one," he called back, heading down the west wing of the large upper level.

Chapter Nineteen

I peered at the rising sun from the bed on which I'd slept. I'd tossed and turned most of the night, haunted by nightmares of Kieran doing lavishly sinful things to me. It eviscerated the myth that you couldn't die in your dreams, because I had. Once on his dick from coming so hard, I expired, dying on the spot, and the second time he'd used me for target practice, then played with my corpse.

Prying myself from the hard mattress, I sat up, staring at a shadow that slipped through the balcony doors. Clearing the sleep from my eyes, I blinked, trying to focus on the form exiting the bedroom. Standing, I grabbed one of my guns from the holster and chased after it.

"Stop!" I screamed in warning as it leaped onto the railing and then to the ground. "Son of a bitch!"

Rushing toward the glass door, I slid through it

and jumped over the balcony, slamming against the hard dirt. Groaning, getting to my feet, I followed the pathway into the heavily overgrown garden.

I hated running, especially without my magical caffeinated beans flowing through my system. My body ached, screaming in pain as I ran barefooted over the bushes covering the earth. I wasn't stealthy or even anywhere close to being silent.

Branches smashed beneath my steps, and I entered the yard looking in each direction before running to the open gate, growling at the knowledge that whoever was here had slipped into the woods. I crept forward, forcing the pain from the fall to take a backseat as I tracked down the person who had been inside the house.

A branch broke to my left, and I shifted towards the sound. I released my safety, readying the weapon to fire at whoever had been stupid enough to be spying on me. Rounding a large boulder, I paused as my heart hammered in my ears, coursing blood through my veins.

Scanning the area, I started forward again, checking each crevice of the rocky terrain as I trailed through the forest. I could hear feet crunching through the path at my back, alerting me that my team was coming in hard and heavy on my heels. Birds chirped, and ravens squawked deeper in the forest, stirred up by the movement of my team.

Fighting to regain control of my breathing, I slowly slipped behind one of the large rocks, easing around it to ensure I wasn't heading into a trap. I slid through the mud and barely contained the urge to groan as the slimy earth stuck to the bottom of my feet and between my toes.

Coming out on the other side of the rocky gorge, I glanced down at a boot print left behind. Smiling at the irony of it irking me and leaving a trail to follow, I started down a narrow pathway. Creeping around a corner, I felt the barrel of a gun pressing against my forehead as I stared into moss green eyes, trembling while also holding my pistol aimed at her head. I didn't buy into the fact that this woman was blood, because my father wouldn't have deceived me. He wouldn't be that guy, since it would sever our trust if he had lied to me about something this important.

"Who the fuck are you?" I demanded through clenched teeth, glaring at her.

"We need to talk, Xariana. Your life is in danger," the woman whispered, removing the gun barrel from my head, even though I didn't return the favor. "You don't trust me because you don't know me. I understand that more than you think. If they took your father, then they're here looking for what he has concealed from them. They will come for you. You need to stay hidden, do you hear me? Remain in the light, Xariana, and away from the shadows, for he hides within them. God, you're so beautiful. You look like my mother. Did he tell you about me? Did he tell you who I am?"

"He told me the woman you're pretending to be died many years ago, and I believe him. So, I will ask you this one more time before I pull the trigger. Who the fuck are you?" I carefully noted each detail of her face was a dead ringer for my Aunt Sandra.

Branches crunched from multiple directions, taking

my focus away from her for a second. I turned back, staring at the air that was vacant of anything or anyone. Noah burst into the clearing beside me, his footsteps barely making a sound over the dried-up vegetation. He paused, aiming his weapon in the same direction as mine, turning to look at me.

I blinked slowly, searching the area until Micah approached from the path where we had our guns aimed. Silently, I lowered mine and exhaled the air I'd been holding in my lungs. Either I was going insane, or I'd just come face-to-face with a ghost.

"We need to get more salt," I stated, turning to Noah, who frowned before sliding his attention through the empty forest around us.

"Who the hell are we chasing?" he asked, putting the safety on his weapon before shoving it into his jeans.

I did the same, pushing it into the waistband of the yoga pants I'd found in my mother's dressers. My body ached and would be bruised from jumping from the balcony. It hadn't seemed that far down, but I could feel the bruises already spreading.

"How the hell did you get past the door? Kaderyn was at the back, and I was at the front," Onyx grumbled, scratching her dark head.

"I jumped out the window," I admitted.

"You jumped from the second-floor window?" Micah asked, creasing his brow as he pushed his gun into the holster.

"Balcony, but yeah," I grunted. "I didn't land

gracefully either." I limped back to the path, grimacing when I stepped into the mud again, but I stopped, staring down at the boot print. Kneeling in front of it, the others paused to inspect it.

"I'd say size thirteen, easily," Noah said, while holding his foot against the imprint. It was larger than his, and the shoe didn't look to be name brand. He peered around us, slowly scratching his head before he spoke. "Was the person you were chasing inside the room you slept in, Xari?"

"Yeah, I woke up and saw a shadow in the curtains. They jumped, and I followed them out here," I confirmed, keeping the fact that it was my dead aunt to myself.

"You didn't see them?" Kaderyn asked, moving behind Micah to look around for more prints.

"No, just the shadow. Then it leaped over the edge, and I gave chase. I haven't even had coffee yet. You think I'd be out here if it wasn't something I thought should be hunted down?" I muttered, slowly starting up the hill to the house.

"You haven't been sleeping well, Xari," Noah snorted, shaking his head when I opened my mouth to argue. "We understand. Trust us, we know. There's a lot of shit happening, and everything is crashing down around us. Your dad's missing, and that should take priority, but we don't have a clue as to where to start looking. We have every motherfucker we know out helping to look for him. You ran a grid search for clues, and it came back with nothing. We have bodies piling up and people shutting us out because they think they have a new savior in town. Right now, you're under a lot of stress, and we get it. Let us help you. You should be delegating jobs, and you keep forcing everyone to remain in teams. That isn't helping."

"Noah is right, Xari. You need your team, and we're here to help, so let us. You can't do this one alone," Kaderyn stated, enforcing Noah's words. I looked at the others, watching them nod in agreement.

"He's my dad." I swallowed past the tears in my throat. "I am doing what he would do."

"You're not Xavier, though. Are you? You're his daughter. You can delegate tasks and send out teams. But you have to stay healthy, and you're hardly sleeping. You are barely eating, living off caffeine and protein bars. Hell, you walked into a fucking club of assassins wearing a bomb!" Micah exploded. "You're not immune to iron, Xar. You're not, and you can't tell us you are. We are your fucking people. Don't shut us out. That's all we're trying to say. Let us in so we can help."

"I just saw my dead aunt," I blurted, watching their jaws drop at the words I'd been holding back. "Yeah, so what can you do about that? I'll wait while you formulate a fucking plan to get an exorcist up in this bitch."

"You're certain it was her?" Noah pushed his fingers through his dark hair, staring at me like I'd grown a second head.

"I had my gun on her forehead while she held hers to mine. It felt real to me. She told me I was in danger if my father had been taken. Then she vanished, disappearing into thin air. It sounds insane, and even more so when said out loud."

"It's not impossible, though," Micah stated, coming to my defense.

"It doesn't make sense. My father mourned Sandra and started building up the hunter guild to protect us from the kind of creatures that killed her. We say our purpose is to guard the humans, but organizing the guild was the only way to stop us from being hunted down and exterminated. We are a smear on the faces of the full-breed races, and they loathe us. So we gathered and got stronger. We learned how to band together and become a force they couldn't murder outright. Yes, we stop our own from killing humans so that they don't join the others who want us dead, but it didn't start like that. The first hunters killed some pretty bad things, and those beings threatened to make us pay. I think they're carrying through on that threat now."

"It's been twenty-five years, though," Kaderyn argued, her eyes narrowing when I merely shook my head.

"To them, time is nothing. It moves differently there. I don't know how different because my father never told me about it. I read it in his books and from the archives in the hunter guild. I think we're about to be in the middle of a war that we're ill-prepared to wage against beings that want us all dead."

"Then we need someone strong enough to help us against them," Onyx muttered, starting toward the house.

"Yeah, we do," I admitted, frowning as Kieran's words echoed inside my head. At least Kieran's men had left, and I hadn't had to deal with his men on top of my dead aunt. A ghost was bad enough, but a bunch of alpha assholes weren't something I wanted to deal with before coffee.

Chapter Twenty

I'd been busy the past three days delegating hunts and scheduling people to patrol areas of the city and forests. I hadn't gone back to the estate to see if my aunt reappeared. My focus was on doing what we could to protect the community. I'd spent nine hours on calls with dignitaries at the other hunter guilds. It was an endless task that was exhausting and frustrating. I wasn't sure how my father handled it without losing his shit.

I'd fallen into bed each night, depleted to the point that if I dreamed I couldn't remember them. Talia sent me a care package, and in it was a letter stating that martyrs never went down well in history. Some asshole always made fun of them and smeared their names.

I'd snorted, calling her the moment I'd finished reading her message. Only she didn't answer. The next day I decided to stop by, but when I reached her house, it was eerily silent, and the gate would not open for me or allow me to pass. There was no sign of anyone outside, and the gargoyles hadn't moved or transformed to acknowledge my presence.

Changing courses, I'd gone to Enzo's club where the bouncers blocked my entrance. They told me the twins were indisposed and then sent me away. It wasn't until I'd pulled up to the Van Helsing estate that I figured out why I wasn't able to access any of my allies.

Kieran had cut me off from any and all help. Cole had chuckled, leaning his heavily tattooed body against the gate, and promised me that if a blood debt didn't bind them, they'd be helping me. He had at least informed me they were still on the hunt to find my dad, but that all communication with me had to end.

By the time I returned to the compound, I was livid. Kieran, the sadistic prick, was making sure I had nowhere to turn except for him. I exited the Land Rover, pausing as Axton's lengthy frame came into view. I glared at him, crossing the parking lot to where he waited on the other side of the fence for me.

"What the hell do you want?" I snapped, already exhausted from the day I was having.

"I need you to know that it wasn't me, Xari. I didn't put a hit out on you. I was told to be in that alley, and that I wasn't to warn you, aid you or look away from you." Leaning closer, Axton laced his fingers through the chain links of the fence. "I've known you a very long time, little one. When have I ever cut you off? I am merely moving with the flow and trying to survive here. I wasn't the one that set you up. I would never do that to you. If I planned to murder you, I would do it with the respect you deserve. Kieran isn't fucking around, though. He's here for something, and he won't leave until he has it. Are you hearing me? He showed up and confronted Xavier, who wouldn't back down, and now your dad is missing. That's what happens when you fuck with him. If the Underworld had a mafia, he'd be the leader."

"Do you believe Kieran took my father?" I asked carefully.

"I think this wasn't the first time they have crossed paths. Kieran comes when it is time to collect his payment for a debt. He hits hard and fast. I think your father owed him, and when you refuse to pay Kieran, you vanish, and he sees it through to the end. One way or another, he always gets paid. The other option is that your father made a deal with him, and he will be held in the ether until it is settled. Once the terms have been agreed upon, he'll come home. And one day, sometime in the future, Kieran will collect."

"My dad wouldn't form a deal with Kieran. Not when the cost could be blood. I am the only relative he has, Axton," I pointed out, watching the weariness burning in his gaze. "You think he is here for me? That my dad refused to kill me, and so they took him, intending to murder me?"

"Until Enzo called in his debt, yes," he stated, pushing his hands into his pockets. "Now that Kieran can't order your death or kill you himself without breaking an agreement, he's stuck. All he can do is wait for it to happen without interfering. So if Xavier has struck a deal, and you were part of the terms to be paid, then he will remain in limbo until it has been completed."

"Awesome," I groaned, pinching the bridge of my nose. "I can't believe my father would do that. What could he possibly gain from it?"

"Your father was an average half-breed who built an empire. Look around you, Xariana. He's a fucking legend in his own right. How? Because he's invincible?" he snorted. "I asked him one time how he'd gotten to where he is. He told me that deals with the devil have advantages."

I turned his words over inside my head, knowing that it was possible, but not plausible. My dad taught those classes, never to bargain with creatures. There was always a cost to be paid, and they struck where it hurt the most. He'd enforced that thought into our young minds.

"Look, I get it, murderous beauty. You don't want to think Xavier would do that because he's your father. Ask yourself this, though. Why is Kieran here now? Your father is missing, and Kieran is benefitting from it most. He's slowly undoing everything Xavier has worked his entire life to achieve. Kieran doesn't need power or this city. Yet, he's taking it from you. He's put out a citywide ban on anyone attempting to help you or the guild. The only person that refused his order was the fucking sheriff. Kieran runs E.V.I.E. now, too. He infiltrated the organization, discovered it was catering to half-breeds, and then turned it into a full-breed hunting unit. He's leveling the playing field, and you're not ready to take someone like him on, Xari."

"Rhys stepped down as the leader of E.V.I.E. because the vampire population shaped up the moment

Ian returned to be the face of the House of Vampires. He moved his castle here, stone by stone, no less. The twins called in their debt, making them vulnerable now, right?" I asked.

"I don't know," he admitted, slowly shaking his head. "It depends on if they had an arrangement with Kieran and what they owed to him. You'd have to ask them about the specifics. If they did reach a bargain, then they're on the list of assets that could be wielded like a weapon against you. If they refuse, Kieran could force them to kill their blood relations."

"And there's only the two of them left alive," I muttered, hating myself for being in the scenario where Enzo and Ezekiel had either called in or made that deal because of me.

"Yeah, and while Rhys wouldn't mind offering up some of his siblings, Kieran can dictate who he wants dead. Talia and her brood, they'd go to war to protect each other. So you know who he'd demand she kill. The one she loves the most—Morgana, and I realize you're attached to that saucy bitch, just as I am."

"And you?" I asked, watching the way Axton smiled.

"I have no family. I settled my debt, and I paid it in blood. I didn't hire him to guard me or protect me from anything, Xariana. I was given a choice to watch you die or send you away. I chose the latter and played the part expected of me. Kieran wasn't pulling those strings, though. It was another person that wanted you out of the picture in a bad way. I can't say who because that ends with me dead. Just know that I didn't want to be involved. You're in way over your pretty head." He smiled sadly, then took two steps back before turning to make eye contact. "I'll see you around, hopefully."

"Hey," I said, stopping him. "Thank you, Axton."

"If I were you, I wouldn't keep Kieran waiting much longer. He isn't a patient man." He walked down the road and across the street toward his dark SUV. The interior light turned on as the door opened, and I grimaced at the sight of his pasty driver. He flipped me off, and I returned the one-finger salute, then blew a kiss at the car.

I began walking to the guild's entrance, sensing a disturbance and pulling my guns from their holsters, aiming at the spot where I'd felt the air change. I didn't wait for anything to materialize or appear. Instead, I opened fire hearing the howls of pain as bullets rained from my pistols. Hunters piled out of the building, staring at where I shot, hitting something.

"Shoot!" I snapped, as brass casings pinged on the concrete.

"What are we shooting at?" Noah asked, marching up beside me as he fired his pistol in the same direction.

"Look," I whispered, not knowing if he'd hear me over the firing squad's response to my orders. Blood was dripping from the empty space, which meant whatever was there was feeling it. "They can bleed. We can kill them!" I yelled, reloading my gun while the others continued their assault.

I slid my gaze down the line, watching as some of the hunters broke formation. My hackles rose, and my stomach sank as one of the women vanished.

"Pull back and stay together!" I shouted, praying they heard me. "Fuck," I snapped as more women disappeared. I turned my attention to where the invisible assailant walked, visible only by his blood trail, and I continued to shoot as the air pulsed, causing my vision to blur until I stopped firing.

Blinking, I saw my father materialize beside a bleeding, tall, ethereal-looking creature. He glared at me with a murderous, calculated expression. I lifted my weapon, aiming it at him, and his eyes began to glow fluorescent blue. Strange lines slithered on his arms, and I swallowed down the fear at seeing those markings. Pointed ears peeked from beneath his hair, and I noticed he had elongated canines as he spoke to the male next to him in a foreign tongue I couldn't translate. I tightened my finger on the trigger, following his movements.

The being beside him turned, staring at me. He started walking in my direction, but a blur of smoke ripped through the courtyard and rammed into the creature. Someone was pulling me backward as I fought to keep my eyes on my dad.

I opened my mouth to shout his name, but Noah pulled me inside the building and slammed the door closed. People were screaming all around me, and blood was pounding in my head. My heart shattered at the implications. What the fuck just happened? How had he appeared as a full-blooded fae? My mother was full-blooded, not my father. I was only two-thirds fae, according to my bloodwork.

"Xari!" Noah screamed, slapping my cheek.

I swatted his hand away, staring around the room

at the people crying. "We need to gather all the iron we can find," I whispered. "You will take control of the guild, Noah. I can't lead us anymore. My father betrayed us all—as his daughter, I can no longer lead the guild. Sound the alarm to let everyone know we're fighting the fae. They'll be back. This won't end until they get what they came for."

"And what the hell is that?" Micah asked, his gaze sliding over my face.

"I don't know," I admitted. "I have no fucking clue."

My father created the hunters guild to protect the humans and us from the fae. So what was he thinking? He was a half-breed that had once lived within the fae realm and had left it behind when he'd met my mother, and they'd fallen in love. I knew he had stolen something from the fae that they desperately wanted back. So how could he be aligned with them now— attacking us? He started this war when he'd taken their princess as his bride, stealing some of their artifacts and the one thing that ensured they wouldn't have the numbers to attack the guild. Yet here they were, with my dad driving the attack. Nothing about this situation made sense to me.

Chapter Twenty-One

After handing the keys to the kingdom over to Noah, I decided I needed to see Kieran. His doorman escorted me into a lavish office where I had been waiting for over an hour, pacing the floor and fighting the ball of nerves growing in my belly. I looked at the clock on the wall for the hundredth time, bristling at being forced to wait inside a locked room for the pompous prick.

My heels were killing my feet, but they were a perfect match for my black dress with ruffles. Noah ordered me to take a day off, and I'd quickly been talked into a mundane shopping trip with the girls that had been a huge waste of my time. I'm not used to dressing up. The garter was cutting into my waist, and the nylons itched along my thighs. But I'd been told they were an essential part of the outfit, as was my hair, which I'd wrapped into a bun to conceal my weapons.

I'd expected a full body search, but Kieran's guards merely ushered me through a surprisingly beautiful courtyard, and locked me here. The bastard had exquisite taste, and I wouldn't mind getting the name of his designer.

The office was painted in a shade of midnight blue, making the white furniture pop in contrast. There was artwork covering an entire wall, with paintings that looked almost lifelike. My attention moved from one to another, slowly scanning a portrait containing a deep valley filled with intricate flowers and glowing lights.

Frustration at being made to wait was running through me, and I had a feeling he was doing it on purpose. The door opened, and I turned, intending to unleash my anger on him, but he stood in the doorway, shirtless, covered in beads of sweat that rolled down his well-defined chest. The words caught in my throat, and I closed my mouth to prevent the moan that threatened to escape instead.

Kieran Knight was fucking gorgeously built. His body was a work of art, with sinewy muscles that curved perfectly together, dipping into his sweatpants. The intensely dark stare that clashed with mine left my heartbeat thundering, and all coherent thought escaped my brain, sliding right into my vagina.

"You made me wait." His icy demeanor made me nervous as he stalked closer to me.

His scent was enticing, carrying none of the stink that should have clung to him from the sweat. I'd been around enough men training to know that they fucking stunk after working out. However, Kieran only smelled of dark masculinity with a woodsy undertone and something else that caused a pulse between my thighs.

"I'm a busy woman." He walked toward me with a predatory glint in his stare as men entered behind him. I paused as they drew their weapons and aimed at me. "You said I wouldn't be harmed," I reminded carefully, fighting the urge to run.

"Go to the desk and place your hands on it, slowly," he demanded in a no-nonsense tone. "If I were you, I would refrain from making any sudden moves until they have disarmed you, Xariana."

Holding my palms up, I did as he asked, trembling at the reminder that I was here alone, with my enemy, and I was only now rethinking my decision to come here.

I placed my hands flat on the wooden surface, spreading my legs apart slightly. Kieran shifted to stand behind me, gradually reaching across my waist to search it. When he touched me, I felt his raw power and trembled as it ran through me.

He slipped his hands over my abdomen and around my back, unzipping my dress, causing me to shiver as the cool air caressed my spine. I considered arguing against its removal, but I didn't think he'd care if I kicked and screamed over him taking it off at this point.

"Raise your arms, slowly," he commanded while reaching for the hem of the skirt, lifting it over my head. I obeyed, holding my breath while doing what I was told. A guard stepped up next to us, placing a metal box beside me with my purse already inside. "Now put your hands where you had them, and don't fucking move."

"Is this really necessary? I didn't come armed," I muttered, irritated. Wickedly dark laughter was the only answer I received as it slithered over my exposed spine.

His fingers slipped into my hair, removing the needle daggers that Onyx had worked into my bun, making them seem more ornamental than deadly. Both were tossed into the steel box. His hands slid over and down my arm before lifting it to divest me of my charm bracelet filled with nasty hexes. Carefully, he placed it into the box before doing the same to the other wrist.

Kieran ran his fingers over my shoulders, creating a storm of flurries inside my stomach, tracing them up to my neck. He unclasped the necklace containing a small vial of iron dust, putting it, too, into the metal container. Gathering my hair, he laid it over my shoulder before sliding his magical fingertips down my back, stopping at the garter belt with bells attached to the lace, ripping them free, and adding them to the growing pile of weapons. My heart raced, violently pounding against my chest as my breathing grew ragged.

Heated breath drifted down my spine as he lowered, grabbing my ankle and lifting my foot to withdraw the hidden daggers from the heel of my shoe. He did the same with my other foot, pausing to fan his breath between my legs. Clenching them against the sensation it was creating, I closed my eyes, willing my labored breathing to calm.

Rising from where he'd removed the weapons, he spun me around to face him, grabbing my hands and placing them on the desktop. He studied me for a moment, as if he could see my mind churning with fear. I didn't look away from the challenge burning in his hauntingly beautiful gaze.

He gradually lowered his eyes to my bra, smiling when he found it straining from my erratic breathing, running his fingers over the piercings beneath the cups. Turning his head, Kieran spoke in a foreign language, and the man beside us removed the box filled with my items and left with the other guards.

Once they'd closed the door, Kieran pulled down the cups of my bra while holding my stare prisoner, tracing his thumbs over the decorative jewels that pierced my nipples. The air in my lungs stopped as a violent tremor passed through me. Lowering that hypnotic gaze to my bared breasts, he gently replaced the lace and stepped back, sliding his eyes over my body.

"Sure you don't want to do a cavity check, too?" I asked, blanching as the words escaped me.

"If you want me to play with your pussy, just ask." He turned on his heel and moved to a cupboard, opening it to retrieve a bottle of water.

I examined the muscles of his back, feasting on them while I remained stationary. I didn't dare move because I wasn't certain my legs would support me. I had never been strip-searched, and he'd known where I'd hidden every weapon. Swallowing past the thickness of my throat, I watched him remove the cap before downing the contents all at once.

"I don't like to be kept waiting, Xariana. I'm also not fond of being lied to," he stated, turning to look at me. "Get dressed," he commanded, gliding his intense stare over me one last time.

"I don't appreciate being given demands or ordered about." I turned, grabbing for my clothes only to be spun as he stepped up behind me, gripping my arms to force me around. He released me, grasping the back of my thighs and slamming my ass onto his desk, hard.

"Yes, you do," he whispered huskily, taking a step closer until he was pressed against me. He placed his hands behind me, sliding his nose against my neck. "You're turned on by it, hunter. You smell like a woman that enjoyed being thoroughly searched. Not knowing whether I'd hurt you or let you live sent adrenaline rushing through your veins. As I said, I don't care for liars. You can lie to yourself if you wish, but your body tells me another story. Now fucking get dressed. I'll return shortly."

I blinked as he pulled away, searching my expression, and then laughed coldly. He turned, walking to the opposite side of the office before opening a door and vanishing behind it. Grabbing my dress, I slipped it over my head, reaching back to zip it up.

I heard the sound of running water, and I sat fixated on the open doorway, watching steam billow out. Was he showering right now? My curiosity was up, but I wasn't stupid enough to move closer, no matter how inviting it might have been.

Crossing my arms over my chest, I rested on the desk, staring at the open door to the clock and back. I didn't have time for this bullshit. I had places to be and shit to get done today. Turning around, I perused the files on his desk, glancing every so often at the steam still flowing out of the bathroom.

Leaning closer to the files, I shifted one for a better

view before a hand slammed down against mine. I gasped, shaking as I realized Kieran had fully intended to catch me snooping.

"I've killed people for less, hunter," he whispered in my ear.

"I'm sure you have," I uttered through quivering lips.

The smell of soap and freshly sprayed cologne surrounded me, and the heat of his body pressing against mine was doing things to my mind. His hot breath fanned my shoulder as he brushed his lips along the delicate skin on my neck.

"You're trembling, little girl. Are you afraid or excited? I can't tell past the scent of your body calling to mine," Kieran laughed wickedly, and released my hand, slowly tracing his fingers along my spine to slide through my hair. He grabbed a fistful, using it to turn me around to face him. His other hand gripped my jaw painfully, tilting my head so his mouth was against my ear. "I want to hurt you."

I shuddered, unable to ignore my response to his words. But instead of fear etching through me, desire rushed to the surface. My stomach fluttered, filling with butterflies, and my thighs clenched together, warring with need and fighting for control. My nipples hardened into pebbles, and my breath hitched at the pressure of his fingers on my jaw.

He examined me, dropping his hungry gaze to my mouth, trailing his thumb over my lips, and spreading the lip gloss that coated them. My spine arched, and I sighed against the need to taste him. My teeth chattered, and the shudder turned into a violent quake that rushed through me.

"Do behave long enough for me to get dressed so that we can discuss our coming arrangements, unless you don't mind having this conversation while riding my dick?" His words came out like gravel that scraped over every nerve ending in my body.

"Clothes are good," I whispered, opening my eyes to peek down at his massive frame. "Holy shit."

"Be a good girl for me, Xariana. Don't move a fucking muscle." He put my hands on the desktop again, brushing his heated lips against my cheek as he spoke, "Or I'll show you how I treat bad girls that can't fucking behave. Tell me you understand."

"I understand."

He was naked. Completely and utterly naked.

There wasn't a lick of clothing on him, and he didn't seem to be embarrassed about that fact in the slightest. Not that he needed to be. The man was made for sin, and my eyes couldn't help but slide down his sleekly built chest, pausing at the V-line that ended in a bed of dark curls. Nestled beneath them was a thick cock that hung between his thighs, larger than life, even though it wasn't hard. Licking my dry lips, I ripped my focus from his penis, finding him smiling cruelly while I ogled him. My mouth trembled as I tried to produce some kind of insult, but couldn't come up with one that wouldn't sound fabricated.

He dismissed me, walked back toward the cloud of steam still escaping the opened door of his bathroom. My greedy eyes feasted on the curve of his ass, and a groan of regret slipped from me. I quickly glanced at the artwork, forcing me to look anywhere other than where he'd vanished.

The man had ink everywhere, and it was perfectly placed to lure the eye to each tattoo. The ones on his hips curled up his sides, flowing onto his chest beneath his pectoral muscles. His shoulder blades were also covered in markings that I wanted to taste with my tongue.

Kieran reappeared, pulling on a crisp white shirt over the wealth of bronze flesh. My stomach tightened, and I blinked slowly to dispel the heat rushing to my face. I'd stared at the man's cock like some hussy that hadn't been raised well, and now I was molesting the rest of him with my eyes.

"Take a seat," he ordered in a firm tone, nodding at the two chairs inside the office.

Pushing away from the desk, I started forward, and he watched every move I made, no matter how minuscule. Sitting in the high, wing-backed chair, I crossed my legs, fighting the pulse he'd caused between them.

"You and I know that the only reason I'm here is because you have taken away all my other resources in the search for my father. You said you know who took him and where I could find him. Just give me that information, and I'll be on my way."

"I don't think I'll be telling you what I know just yet. Consider it part of your punishment for making me wait after I graciously invited you to my home. How the remainder of your reprimand unfolds depends on you, hunter. You fucked with me, and I fully intend to fuck you in return."

My lady bits jolted at the statement, thoroughly agreeable to volunteer for that to happen. Swallowing audibly, I nervously played with my fingers, biting my lip while staring at the pictures on his wall to avoid peering at him. I wasn't admitting that I might like being beneath his massive body, but it had merit as a punishment.

I needed to find someone, and end the ache he'd created between my thighs on them. My entire body was taut with the need to feel him against me, punishing me in a dirty, wicked way that would leave a painful ache between my thighs.

"How would you suggest we handle your disobedience?" he asked in a raspy tone. I narrowed my gaze on him while his back was to me as ice clinking against glass met my ears.

"You could spank me," I offered breathlessly, watching his head shake.

"Like a disobedient child?" he queried, turning to stare at me with one dark brow raised in his question.

I shrugged, not bothering to elaborate. But then I did, even as I attempted to swallow the words that blurted out. "Some people are into that type of thing. I don't kink shame. Everyone has needs, and what they do is their business."

"I asked you how you'd prefer to be disciplined. Not how you think others want to be tortured before they're fucked, Xariana."

"And I asked you where I could find my father. I guess neither one of us is getting a direct answer today. But if I had to choose right this minute, I'd take a time out. I don't mind that option, and I could really use a break. In fact, I read three books when I was last there."

Kieran made a strangled noise deep in his chest before walking over with a drink in his hand. Offering it to me, I silently accepted the glass, bringing it up to my nose. I took a sip, and the taste of cedar and oak danced enticingly inside my mouth with a trace of something else. I took another sip, swirling it around my tongue to get the full flavor of the drink. My father had taught me how to appreciate things that most people didn't. Whisky had been our thing, something he'd enjoyed sampling with me once I'd been old enough to drink.

"What is this?" I questioned, shifting my attention to find him fixated on my mouth.

"Scotch whisky," he grunted, joining me in the chairs.

"I knew that, but it doesn't taste like Macallan," I pointed out, fully aware I sounded like a whisky critic.

His eyebrows pushed together, and a smile played on his lips. "Glenfiddich Vintage Reserve. It's also made and distilled in Scotland. The bitterness you taste is a hint of dark chocolate. It sells for roughly one hundred thousand dollars, because only sixty-seven bottles were ever filled."

"My father would love this shit," I blurted, hating the pang of regret that swelled in my chest, recalling that he may have betrayed us.

Kieran didn't respond, choosing to ignore me. "I

was thinking I would kill your people."

The blood left my face as I turned to stare at him. "Kill me. I did it. They're innocent."

His expression danced with amusement, like a predator knowing he'd drawn blood. "Too easy. You'd feel it briefly, and then the pain I want you to feel would end. There would be no enjoyment at watching you suffer."

"What do you want from me?" I asked, narrowing my eyes on him as the whisky turned sour in my mouth.

"I want a lot of things from you," he admitted, letting his gaze roam down my body before returning to my face. "I wish to own you."

I exhaled, setting the glass down before standing to let him have it. "You are insane. I am not something you can own, asshole. I am a person. You cannot own another being."

"Everyone has a price, Xariana. There is always that one thing they would sacrifice their life to protect. You just offered me yours in exchange for your hunters. I intend to have you one way or another. I'm offering you an easier option than I would anyone else."

"Screw you!" I gasped as something grabbed and jerked me back down into my chair. My eyes rounded, and he smiled at the fear escaping me as dark, wispy tendrils of what looked like smoke wrapped around my legs, arms, and waist, forcing me to sit. My chair slid over the floor until I was directly in front of him.

Panic shot through me, and my heart hammered against my ribcage, threatening to leave bruises from the intensity in which it thundered. Kieran didn't hide in the shadows, gathering intel. Nor did he have people passing information to him, through the shadows, as I'd assumed everyone meant.

No, this asshole controlled the shadows!

Chapter Twenty-Two

"We're having a conversation, and we don't need to label our relationship at this time," Kieran stated, sipping his drink while holding my stare. He enjoyed the fear escaping my pores, thickly filling the air between us. "I will own you. The only question is, how hard do you intend to fight me before it happens?"

"You're insane, Kieran. I am not yours."

"Not yet, but you will be. You trespassed on me twice, and there will not be a third time. Much like you, when someone fucks around with me, I strike back. You, though, have interrupted my business. Most people wouldn't dare do something so suicidal, and yet you didn't hesitate. In fact, you threw it in my face that you'd done it. So, choose which of your friends will die, and don't lie to me about who means the most to you. I already know the answer."

"Nope," I snorted, glaring at him as the shadows

released me. Their touch was like his, seductive and enticingly erotic. "I bet those are handy during sex," I offered, turning to watch them slink back into the corners of the room.

"Would you like to find out?" he asked softly, narrowing his eyes to slits. He clucked his tongue, and they raced toward me all at once.

"No!" I squealed, watching as they paused inches away from my skin.

One tendril crawled up my arm, sending a shiver of desire rushing through me. I gasped, closing my eyes as another moved along my thigh, caressing me like a feather on the delicate flesh. Opening my eyes once more, I found Kieran focused on the wisps of dark matter that slipped beneath my dress, stroking me there.

"You need me more than you think you do, hunter."

"The only thing I need from you is the location of where I can find my father." I grabbed the armrests and squeezed as the inky wisps continued sliding along my inner thighs. His dark violet depths burned with lust, and he swallowed audibly, dispersing the shadows instantly.

"Do you know what attacked you last night?"

"It was the fae," I snapped, fighting the need to rip him bare and take what he offered.

I needed to find a stranger, ride him until I got off, and leave him. Meaningless sex was simple, and it wasn't messy. There were no emotions involved, and I preferred that to any meaningful relationship that could end badly.

"You didn't think I knew what was attacking us? I am not stupid. I understand they believe we have something that belongs to them. But they're also taking women."

"Indeed, they are," he confirmed, lifting his glass before that dark, sinful stare lowered to where my thighs clenched tightly together in response to his shadow's touch. "But have you guessed why?"

"My father left me with a fae woman once. She told me a story about her homeland. It was a fable, or what she called a sad tale, of what had spread through their land. She had abandoned her home because the fae men craved to procreate, but couldn't. Their world had lost something it needed very badly. They would brutally rut on their women so violently, in fact, that they wound up murdering their mates. They discovered that half-breed bastards, like me, who they didn't care to claim, could bear their children. So, I imagine they're here to take women like me to breed. What they don't know is that we were warned, and most females in the guild choose to be sterilized to prevent that from happening. Many didn't want to have families since we are considered filth by your race's standards."

"Are you sterile, Xariana?" he asked, and my cheeks flushed. "I didn't think so. How long before you are among the women they take, tied to a bed and fucked until you conceive a child for one of the fae? You can't stop them, and you know it. I had to step in last night because I don't like anyone fucking with those I intend to punish."

I blinked, recalling the shadows that had sent the fae running. Kieran had been there, but not to save me, just to prevent me from being taken, so it didn't ruin his plans for me. Chewing my lip, I narrowed my gaze at his calculated stare.

"You desire what they are after, don't you?" I questioned, turning the information over in my head. "Your coming to town wasn't by chance. It was a choice. You're here to find what they want, aren't you?"

He nodded his head, finishing his drink before his shadows lifted me in the air without warning, depositing me onto his lap. Kieran's fingers slipped over the outside of my thighs, and I wrapped my arms around his neck. It was that, or I would have fallen in a tangle of ungraceful limbs on the floor at his feet. My stomach coiled, and my nipples pressed against the constraints of my dress, wanting to be sucked and tasted by this sadistic prick.

"Nothing is ever by chance, little huntress. Your father knew what I was, but he refused to listen to me. Now he's in the hands of his enemies. I thought they were here for you, his only child, but they're not even a tiny bit interested in you, but I am," he purred, gently rubbing circles on my thighs. "You will be mine."

"No, I won't." I watched the seductive smile that played on his lips. "You may try, but you'll lose this fight, Kieran."

"We shall see, won't we? If you get desperate enough to find Xavier, you will agree to my terms." He sat back to look up at me. It forced me to adjust in his lap, regretting it when I felt his cock lengthening against my heated junction. "I don't like the idea of breaking you, but I will. I need you to understand this. I will do whatever it takes to get you."

"If you want to fuck, just ask," I snapped, feeding him his own words.

"It isn't about sex," he whispered, moving his hands until he gripped my hips. "Sex is meaningless, and I can get it from anyone, and at any time I wish. I want you on my team to hunt for me."

"You have trained killers on hand, asshole. You are the head of E.V.I.E.! You don't need me. Snap your fingers and your hunters jump to do as you tell them. I am not the sort of creature who jumps because some pompous prick demands I do so. Also, I don't need your dick."

"My sources tell me otherwise, Xariana," he rebutted, using my full name like he couldn't taste it enough on his tongue. I started to argue, but he placed his hand on my lips, picking me up and carrying me to his desk, and sitting me on top of it as he stared down at me. "I have it on good authority that you ran away from here because you caught the man you planned to marry, fucking your friend beside the wedding cake you were there to try." Kieran chuckled.

"Dodged that one, huh? I didn't run," I lied, biting my lip nervously, feeling him growing erect against my pussy.

"You did, and I'm not saying I blamed you. I'd have ended them both, but that's me. You are not as old or calculated to have considered that recourse as punishment. Tell me, did he satisfy your needs? Was he enough of a man for a creature like you that holds such rage and uses it against whatever crosses you?" When I just stared at him, he smiled. "How well did he fuck you, little girl?"

"What kind of question is that?" I blurted, appalled he would ask something so personal. "That's none of your business."

"I am making it my business by asking you, right here. I think a woman like you would need someone who isn't afraid to pin you to the floor and fuck you like the dirty little bitch you really are. A man who isn't worried about going to war against your tight little body," he growled raspily, lowering his lips to press them against my ear. His hands tightened on my legs, forcing them to lift onto the desk. "You are violence that detonates without warning, yet you're also very delicate when you're not covered in bulletproof vests. There's a softer side of you that craves to be manhandled while treated with respect. You don't require some asshole to dominate you or prove you're the weaker one in bed. You just need that control taken away long enough that your mind quiets and your body can feel what is happening to it." His lips slid over my throat, causing my breathing to become erratic and sharp. Kieran's hands left my legs, sliding around my back to unzip my dress.

I shuddered, frowning at his assessment of me. "I don't think we should be discussing my love life, or lack thereof, Kieran." I closed my eyes at the feel of him against me, moaning softly when his fingers danced over my spine. "I also don't want to discuss what I need or don't need in bed. This isn't a sex education class, and I sure as shit didn't sign up for one today. You're not offering to be my sugar daddy or fuck me." His hand twisted through my hair, forcing my head to the side as he dragged his heated breath over my skin. "Let me rephrase that. I'm not fucking you."

"Not yet, you're not," he hissed, licking over the pulse thundering at the base of my neck. "Decide, woman. Will you willingly be mine, or will I be forced to make you do what I require of you?"

"You won't change my mind," I murmured, unable to stop the moan from escaping my lips. He chuckled darkly, slowly pressing one hand against my throat, while the other tangled in my hair, tilting my head until I was staring up at him.

Shadows slipped around me, pushing my legs apart, allowing him to press against the wetness he'd created. My arms were forced above me, and his mouth slammed against mine. Pressure started at my pussy, causing it to ache with the need to be filled with what he offered.

Kieran Knight didn't fucking kiss. He devoured. He ravished. He obliterated. His shadows held my jaw as his tongue captured mine, dancing with it until I moaned hungrily against his heated kiss. His fingers pressed against my core, sliding beneath my panties to find the proof of my need. I gasped into his lips, slowly rocking on the finger that teased my sex.

When his lips left mine, and the shadows pushed the bodice of my dress down for him to drag his heated mouth over my breasts, I blinked, watching the image of us in the mirror's reflection. The shadows were coming from him, gradually sliding from his spine to slither over my body. A shudder rushed through me as I saw them forming wings before closing around me, bathing me in their illuminating wickedness.

"What the fuck?" I snapped, pushing away from him. He didn't release me, holding me against the hardness in his pants. His eyes burned into mine, and I fought to regain thought and my breathing, neither of which I could control right now. "No."

"You want me," he reminded, sliding his finger over my clit that pulsed to reach the final goal. "I want you. It's not fucking complicated, Xari."

"No," I reiterated, shaking my head as I pushed him. I needed space to reclaim my composure. He was pissed. "I'm sorry, but I said no."

"We'll play it your way, then. Ender," he called, and I saw a male move through the wall to enter the room. He smiled coldly, raking his gaze down my body like I was beneath him. "See Xariana home. Make sure nothing happens to her on the way there."

"I don't need an escort." I slid down from the desk as Kieran backed away from me. "I can get there myself."

"I protect what belongs to me." He smiled with an expression that sent ice shooting down my spine.

"I am not yours. I don't work for you. I said no."

"We'll see. You'll change your mind when you're ready to find your dad." He searched my face briefly before turning to Ender, then glancing back at me, he licked his finger. I opened my mouth to protest, but he moaned, and my pussy fluttered with disappointment that I hadn't waited until I'd at least come before rejecting him. "You're not bitter at all. Strangely enough, you taste fucking delicious."

I shook my head, remembering his question in one of my dreams. My heartbeat pounded in my ears, drowning out the sounds as my vision swam. Startled, I turned, grabbing a glass of whisky to down it before heading for the door.

"I'll see you soon, Xari. When you decide the better alternative is to work for me, you will get on your knees and beg. Remember, I tried to do this the easy way, to make this gentle on you, but unfortunately, you've left me no choice."

Chapter Twenty-Three

I decided I wasn't ready to go home. Instead, I fully intended to scratch the itch that Kieran had started. So, I asked Ender to take me to one of the lesser-known clubs in town. I peered around while a silent, broody bouncer waited by the door. Ender objected to me coming here, but I'd shot him down, telling him my intentions for the evening.

A man I knew liked to rough girls up for fun caught my eye, and I smiled. He was a wolf that I'd had on my list for months. He hadn't crossed the line into murdering anyone, but he left them pretty abused after he'd finished using them. Unfortunately, the guild only got involved when rape or murder was committed.

Strolling toward the male, I grinned when he turned, slowly dragging his lecherous gaze down my body. Frowning, I reconsidered taking him into the storage room, but I needed to get my cravings under control. I shuddered, then snorted when he opened his mouth, releasing the scent of stale beer.

"Let's fuck, asshole," I growled, snatching his hand to tug him into the abandoned room that held the kegs. This place didn't sell enough beer to go through many, which left that area unoccupied.

"Damn, baby," he hissed, grabbing me and pushing me against the wall.

My head hit the wall, and I turned narrowed eyes on him as he reached into his pants, freeing his flaccid cock. Groaning at my misfortune, I slipped my panties off over the garters and held them. He lifted his hand, cupping my neck, and shoved it down, forcing me to watch him stroke and tease his cock into a solid state.

I grimaced at the tiny little fella trying to make an appearance. It looked like he hadn't graduated from tortoise school, too shy to leave his shell.

"You want a piece of that, you fucking bitch?" he snarled, yanking me up by the hair.

"Today, asshole. I don't have an endless amount of time to waste on you," I snorted, watching the anger sizzling over his features.

He turned me, painfully slamming my face into the bricks before lifting my dress. I stared up at the ceiling, slowly counting down while he continued to work his shaft, failing to get it up. It was probably because he indulged in too much alcohol and not enough vegetables. His fingers slid against my pussy, and I grit my teeth, closing my eyes. A pain in my side started, and I held in a hiss until he screeched, releasing a blood-curdling scream, and I spun, my stare growing wide in horror.

I saw him fall to his knees, his body contorting and jerking at an odd angle before it exploded. Shocked, I blinked, staring at the mess at my feet. Then, reaching up, I wiped a trace of blood from my face and scratched my head as I narrowed my gaze on his remains, frowning as goop bubbled up from the floor.

I lowered my hand to my side, and a sinking feeling entered the pit of my gut. My mark had once reacted to Micah touching me, too. Only it hadn't murdered him. It didn't respond to Kieran at all; in fact, it had buzzed in approval. This poor asshole, though, he'd gotten an explosive reaction.

Struggling to calm my horror to a minimum, I slipped from the room into the bar. Shielding my face from the cameras, I found Ender standing at a table, his fingers flying over the keyboard of this phone.

"Finished already?" he asked lifting his stare with an amused smile.

"Mistakes were made," I admitted, exiting the club.

"Did you get what you came for?" He chuckled, shoving his phone into his jacket, observing me with laughter in his eyes.

"I don't want to discuss it," I groaned, slowly moving towards the parking lot. Leaning against the car was the jerk that had put me in the situation. A smug look covered his face. "You fucking marked me, asshole. It was you in the woods! Wasn't it? You fucking touched me with your shadows, and now I am cursed!"

"Mmm," he said, sliding his stare gradually down to my hand, still holding my panties. His lips curled into a knowing smile, and he inhaled deeply, nodding his head. Ender grunted, leaving us while I glared at him. "You won't be fucking anyone else while we work together."

I opened my mouth and then snapped it closed before throwing the only thing I had on me at him. He caught my panties, bringing them up to smell them before shoving them into his pocket.

"I don't work for you! You also don't get to dictate what I can do with my pussy. The bitch is starving, which means she will eat a dick!" I shouted, and several people near us paused, bursting out in gales of laughter until Kieran snarled, sending them all rushing away.

"Fuck me then," he offered, crossing his arms over his chest, watching me squirm as I fought to regain control of my temper and raging libido.

"Not happening," I snorted, glancing around us. "Is this your punishment? No orgasms? I mean, it is cruel," I admitted, stepping closer to him. "I can flick my own bean though, you know? I was self-sufficient when my ex didn't get my pussy off. I do have toys that appease my needs as well. I am very resourceful."

"You come when I say you can, woman," he shot back icily with a satisfied smile on his sensual mouth.

"How the fuck are you going to stop me from getting myself off?" I asked, laughing at the balls of the prick.

He raised an eyebrow, and pain sliced through my side. I crossed my legs, and a scream ripped from my throat before he grabbed me, yanking me against his massive frame as his lips skimmed over my forehead, soothing the ache he'd caused. Spinning us, he pushed me against the car, shielding me from prying eyes.

"Like that, Xariana."

I growled, digging my hands into his shirt until they twisted it up. Ripping it open, I pressed myself against him, smiling at the sound of his buttons scattering over the blacktop. It was petty, but also satisfying. He slid his hand around my throat, tilting my head back onto the car.

"If you need to come, ask me. I will make your body sing, woman. All you have to do is give me an answer first."

"An answer to what? I am not working for you. Not even if I never have another orgasm for the rest of my life. The answer is no. Hell no, to be exact. Have a nice night, asshole," I grunted, staring at him while he surveyed me. My reply would have been more badass if he hadn't been leaning against me, holding me in place.

"I bet all I would need to do is reach between those silky thighs, and slide my fingers against your swollen clit, and you'd weep all over me. Wouldn't you?"

"Most definitely," I hissed huskily, glaring up at him.

His jaw ticked, because we both knew it wasn't happening. The sound of cars pulling up all around us had him looking over his shoulder. My hunters piled out of their vehicles, strolling up to create a circle around us. If Kieran cared that weapons were trained on him, he didn't show it at all. Instead, he lowered his mouth against my ear, and tightened his hand on my throat.

"Let her go, asshole," Micah snapped, moving closer. "Now!"

"That's him, isn't it? The one that broke your heart?" Kieran asked, turning to smile coldly at Micah. "Is he the guy that couldn't get your pussy wet? Shall I show him how easily you would come for me? Right here, right fucking now? I should spin you around and make you scream, so he knows the difference between you faking an orgasm, and actually coming."

"That's none of your business," I whispered, shivering at the way his gaze slid through the hunters that had shown up in search of me. "Do not do that."

"Come on, just release her," Noah urged, his tone one of calm reasoning, even though I'd caught the edge in his words. "This doesn't have to end badly, man."

"Doesn't it?" Kieran asked, sliding that calculating stare back to me.

"Kieran," I whispered, licking my lips, and my heart began thundering at the look smoldering in his expression.

"Xariana." Kieran smiled, lowering his mouth to brush against mine.

I didn't fight him, realizing my team would attack if I did, and it wouldn't end well. Our lips touched, and I kissed him while using my hands to tell my team to wait, knowing they'd listen to me. His low chuckle vibrated against my mouth, and I felt my body heating for him, wetting with the need to take him deep inside of me.

"You have seventy-two hours before I break you," he whispered as he pulled back, staring at me with a cold look sparkling in his gaze. "Remember, I offered to make this painless, but you require evidence that you can't stop this from happening."

"Onyx, Micah, go to the club and get the information on the woman that just murdered the werewolf," Noah instructed, and I closed my eyes as I blew the air from my lungs, groaning the entire time.

"Cancel that order," I whispered sheepishly.

"We're here because some creature made a mush pile of some asshole in the storage room," Noah informed, nodding at the two hunters.

"Yup, that was me," I admitted, albeit hesitantly. "Kieran here cursed my—lady parts. I'm officially a fucking nun."

"Excuse me?" Noah asked, slowly sliding his gaze between us. "How would he have done anything to you—there?"

"Yeah, maybe you could explain that one, Xar?" Micah snapped coldly.

"Easily," Kieran bragged with a smug smile playing on his lips. "I plan to own that pussy. See you soon, pretty girl." He strolled off, leaving me with my jaw on the street. "Call me if I can be of assistance, or when you decide to change your mind regarding my offer."

"Did you make a deal?" Noah asked carefully.

"No." I watched the relief flash over his face.

I had a feeling that whatever Kieran planned to do

to me was going to hurt. He wasn't the sort of creature you turned down, and I had done so several times tonight. Axton thought Kieran wanted me dead, but I didn't think that was true anymore. He meant to play with me, which scared me more than him wanting my head removed from my shoulders.

Chapter Twenty-Four

Hours after my friends had thoroughly interrogated me, I sat inside my apartment, searching through the archives on the dark web. There wasn't any personal information about Kieran or the orphanage on my father's wall. It was as if the data had been completely wiped clean, and no fingerprints of it were left behind.

Sipping my chamomile tea, I stifled a yawn as a knock sounded on the front door. Gazing at the clock, I frowned at having a late-night visitor. Quickly shutting down the computer, I walked to the door, opening it just enough to peek through.

Micah stood with his head against the doorframe, peering into the room. His eyebrows pushed together, and he exhaled slowly.

"Can we talk, Xari?" he asked softly, dragging his gaze up to mine as he spoke.

"It's late, Micah," I pointed out, aware it wasn't a good idea to invite him inside. Something in his expression bothered me, though, and my stomach sank, realizing he wanted to talk about us. Not that there was an 'us' anymore.

I pulled the door open far enough for him to enter and exhaled the air from my lungs as I moved out of the way. Once he was through, I closed the door and went to the kitchen, reaching into the cupboard and pulling out a bottle of whisky and two tumblers.

"Make it a double," he stated, sliding into the chair that sat at the far end of the kitchen table.

Rolling my eyes, I turned away from Micah, opening the freezer. Grabbing ice, I added three pieces to the glasses before removing the cap and pouring two fingers of liquor into each of them. Silently moving back to the table, I placed a drink in front of him before taking a seat at the opposite end from him. He watched me, snorting at the gesture.

"I guess I deserve that, huh?" He wrapped his hands around his drink, holding my gaze, then he looked down and away from me.

"You don't deserve anything from me," I whispered thickly, fighting the emotions that threatened to swallow me whole.

Slowly nodding his head, he turned watery eyes on where I sat, drawing my finger over the moisture on the side of the glass. Neither of us spoke, both fine, sitting in the silence of the apartment as we had once done as a couple.

"I fucked up." He wiped his nose with the back of

his hand. "You didn't make being with you easy, Minx. It was a fight every day to be with you. Even when you were home, you weren't there with me."

My eyes lifted to his as a single tear slipped free. "I know I'm not faultless with what happened between us, Micah. But I never betrayed what you and I had. I would have ended us before ever doing that to you."

This conversation had been coming for some time, but I wasn't sure it would fix what he'd broken. He wanted back into my good graces, but he'd fucked me over so badly that I wasn't convinced we'd ever be that close again. I couldn't count on him not to hurt me, even as a friend. We could work together because I trusted him to have my back, and I'd have his. It was just who we were. In the gist of things, it was what we'd been to one another—a team, and the next step had seemed easy.

"I love you," he murmured, holding my stare. "I've always loved you, Xariana. From the moment I saw you, I knew you were meant for me. I figured I would eventually fuck it up, just like I did everything I wanted."

Placing my glass on the table, I looked away from him, hating the tears that swam in my eyes. I wouldn't return the sentiment, even though I still loved him. I wasn't in love with him, and that was the difference. I couldn't speak past the lump growing in my throat at his words.

"I didn't love Meredith," he admitted softly, shaking his head before he rose to grab the bottle from the counter. He held it up, and I nodded that he could drink more. "She let me in, though, and didn't hold shit back from me. You held me at arm's length, and she allowed me to see every part of her. That was the one thing you didn't allow. You never let me get close enough to give you all of me."

I snorted, holding his gaze while he challenged me to argue the truth. "I knew you'd ruin us, Micah. I realized it, but I didn't think you'd do what you did. Not to me. I deserved more than that from you."

"The first time I was with Meredith, it was unplanned. She was out with me on a hunt, and you were here waiting for me to come home. We had been drinking, and things got out of control, and we couldn't take it back. I was planning to tell you the truth, to let you know it had happened. But I came home, and you smiled at me, and I couldn't fucking come clean and say that I'd fucked up. You begged me to make a baby. I had never wanted anything more in my life than to have a child with you."

I lifted my glass, downing it before I sat back, remembering that day perfectly. That was an entire year before I'd caught them together. I'd almost died on that hunt, alone, because my father had assigned Micah to go on one with Meredith. I'd had an epiphany that day, and had decided that I wanted a family. I didn't wish to die without leaving something of myself in the world. It had been an insane idea, and unfair to any child left behind, but who said epiphanies needed to be reasonable?

"I took you that night, and afterward, I spent an hour in the bathroom throwing up, knowing I couldn't give you what you wanted. Not because I was unwilling, but because once you knew what I had done, you'd be destroyed. I couldn't knock you up knowing that I didn't deserve what you were offering me."

"No, you didn't," I whispered through the tears threatening to fall.

He groaned, lifting the glass to down it before setting it down, and leaning his arms against the table, watching me. "I went to the infirmary and had Bali give me the shot to prevent you from becoming pregnant. I wouldn't have done that to you."

Micah stood, then slid into the chair beside me. I didn't move away like I wanted to because I wasn't weak enough to fall into anything with him. I'd made peace with what had transpired, and while I hadn't forgiven him, I would never put myself in a position that he'd be able to do it to me again.

"The second time I slept with Meredith, you'd been gone for a few weeks out hunting with Noah. I got drunk, and she showed up at our place. I was lonely, and your dad forced me to take a few days off because I'd been sloppy out on my last assignment. He told me that if I couldn't get my shit together, he'd bench me. We were both sober the next time it happened. After that, I fucked her whenever I had the opportunity and could get her alone."

"You should go," I whispered, fighting the anger that rushed through me. "It's late."

"She and I created life, Xariana. And the entire time she was telling me she was pregnant, I sat there wishing it was you carrying my baby. I felt no joy hearing what she and I had made together. There was no rush of excitement or thrill in knowing Meredith carried my child. I wanted her to miscarry or end the pregnancy, but I never voiced that to her. I didn't want her to make that decision because of me. She asked me to be honest with you, and I told her I would walk down that aisle and marry the woman I loved."

Tears rolled from my eyes, and it took effort not to break the whisky bottle over his head. Instead, I moved my attention to his face, studying the pain that I felt reflected in his stare.

"The day you found us, I had tried to end it with her. She'd stripped down naked, showing me her stomach that cradled my babe within it. Meredith told me she planned to tell you what we'd been doing for the past year behind your back. She said you deserved to know, and that she was going to make sure you did. I couldn't handle the images her words conjured in my mind or your face when you saw how badly I'd fucked up. It ripped me apart and left me destroyed."

"So, instead, you fucked her on the island where I prepared your food? On the countertop that had the wedding cake we were supposed to taste that afternoon, together? You wouldn't have told me if I hadn't found out, would you?" I asked, wiping away the tears.

"No," he admitted, watching my face closely. "I didn't mean to molest you the other night. I promise. But when you whispered those words, something inside of me thought maybe we could fix this. I was hurting from the loss of my wife and child, but I also felt like perhaps I'd lost them so that we could have another shot at being together. I had come to check on you, to make sure you were okay. I knew what losing your father would do to you. You were vulnerable, and the moment you moaned and begged to be fucked, I couldn't walk away."

"I wasn't dreaming of you, Micah," I clarified, watching his dark head nod.

He laughed without breaking eye contact. A spark burned in his gaze, and he swallowed whatever emotion he felt. "I know it wasn't me. I knew when I heard your voice and watched you dreaming that you weren't calling out to me. You'd never sounded like that when we were together. Something in your tone was vulnerable. But when I started touching you, and you didn't push me away, I thought perhaps if you woke up, and we fucked, that you'd understand how sorry I was for breaking your heart. I regretted it instantly when I saw the look of disbelief and pain in your pretty eyes. Maybe even before that moment, but drunk me wanted the girl that he'd loved. The one that always made everything better with her smile," he admitted, standing to stare down at me. "For what it is worth, I fucking hate myself for what I did to you. You deserved better, and we both know it. I can't change the past, but I can try to win you back."

"It won't happen." I stood, leaning against the counter to put more space between us.

"You can't know that," he argued, slowly taking his seat once more.

I opened my mouth to inform him that I'd never be with him again when my phone chirped. Picking it up, I slid my finger across the screen, narrowing my gaze on the message.

Kieran Knight: Be ready by 6 p.m. I will send a car

to pick you up.

I stared at the name, frowning as I tried to figure out how he'd got his number into my contact list. Crinkling my nose, I looked at Micah, who was refilling his glass at the table.

Me: It's not happening.

Kieran Knight: Okay, then I'll kill them all.

Me: Who?

A picture of Noah, Onyx, and the sheriff came through, causing my stomach to flip-flop. Scanning the image, I glanced up at the clock before grabbing my drink to take a swig.

Kieran: Make it five, so we can go to dinner first. I find these galas tediously boring, but I promised to attend. I accepted your invitation as well, of course.

Me: You're insane. Noah is in bed, as are the girls. I respectfully decline.

Micah's phone rang, and he pulled it from his pocket before lifting his gaze to mine. "Noah, slow down. You guys found what?"

I swallowed before dropping my eyes to my phone as the dots slowly showed a message being typed.

"Yeah, we'll come down. Just give us a moment." Micah paused, watching me. "Yeah, we're together. I'll tell her to get dressed, and we'll be down in a few minutes."

Kieran: Mmm, the boy is calling you down, isn't he?

Me: WTF did you do?

Kieran: I invited a beautiful woman to dinner and a gala. I fail to see where the insult is in that?

Me: You threatened to kill people if I don't attend the gala with you.

Kieran: It wasn't a threat. I will kill them if you decline. However, I do like that you used respectfully in your reply.

Me: I'm coming down.

Kieran: I figured you would.

I grabbed a sweater, pulling it on while slipping on my shoes. Micah held the door open for me, staring at my phone before we started down the hallway.

"It doesn't sound promising, Minx. They discovered more bodies and babies."

"Who did?" I asked absently, watching the dots while waiting for a message to come through. We exited the building together, and Micah placed his hand behind my lower back as we moved to where my team stood with the sheriff. "Great."

Kieran: If that boy doesn't remove his hand, he dies, too.

Me: Excuse me? You don't own me.

Kieran: Yet.

Me: How did you even get your number into my phone? Stalker much?

Kieran: Ender did it while I was touching your surprisingly silky soft, very wet pussy. Which I can't seem to stop tasting or craving.

I blushed to my roots, stopping cold in my tracks. Micah paused, turning to look at me expectantly. I shook off the blush, moving toward the crew, who were looking at pictures on the patrol car's hood. When we reached the car, my gaze slid to the gates and then slowly around the courtyard. Sliding the messages back up to the photo, I looked at my team, and then my curious gaze went to where Kieran stood, smiling.

His dark head nodded before he slid into the shadows.

Kieran: So, tomorrow?

Me: I don't own a dress, let alone anything that could be worn to the gala. Find someone else.

"You didn't forget about tomorrow night, did you?" Jeffery asked, frowning, while the others examined the pictures of the women.

"Tomorrow?" The hopeful look in his eyes confused me.

"The annual gala," he stated, slowly exhaling. "I know you have quite a bit happening right now, but it's important that you attend. It raises a lot of money and helps us keep the kids out of trouble. Your father has always attended, never missing a year. It also prevents the feds and other agencies from being up my ass. Xavier makes a large donation every year, which keeps eyes off of this place. All the business owners come. All of them."

I deflated, knowing that Jeffery wasn't lying. My father wore a suit each year and went. I could remember being little, thinking he was handsome when he'd dressed up all fancy, yet he had never asked me to go with him.

Scowling, I exhaled before admitting defeat. "Of course I didn't forget. I even have a date," I stated, smiling awkwardly before sliding my stare toward the shadows. Slowly bringing my gaze back, I found my team frowning at me with surprised gazes. As if they didn't think I could manage to attend a stupid get together for the elite pricks of this town.

Kieran: I'm glad you respectfully changed your mind and saved the lives of your friends tonight. I will have a dress delivered tomorrow morning. I look forward to our date.

Me: It isn't a date, and I don't have any plans of doing anything with you, psychopath.

Kieran: It is a date. I already have someone picking out what I want you to wear.

Me: I hate you.

Kieran: It's probably best that you do. It makes the sex angrier when it happens. I enjoy hate fucking immensely. You should plan on us doing so often.

Me: That's not happening. What is wrong with you?

Kieran: Not yet. Goodnight, beautiful. I'll see you tomorrow evening.

Chapter Twenty-Five

The evening gown arrived before I'd even woken. Instead of opening the box or spending the day dreading wearing the damn thing, I went hunting. I spent hours tracking down a demon that openly fed on a woman who was clinging to life by the time she'd been discovered and taken to the hospital.

Entering the compound, I moved into the control room, watching Noah command the guild with ease. It really pissed me off how effortlessly he'd assumed and performed my duties. He didn't need assistance, and everyone seemed fine with him being in charge.

Exhaling, I left the main area and headed to the girls that were waiting for me. I'd ask Onyx and Kaderyn to help me tonight, realizing that I wasn't up to the task of preparing for the gala on my own. My father always had people to assist him, and I'd given him shit over it while secretly wishing he'd taken me with him.

The nervous energy of knowing I was going out with Kieran gnawed at my insides, leaving me mentally frazzled. When I entered my room, the girls turned, staring at me with mouths opened in shock.

"What?" I strolled deeper into the apartment to remove the bloodied jacket I'd been wearing.

"Shower and use a lot of soap. You have guts in your hair," Onyx frowned. "I placed the box that arrived for you in your bedroom. Don't change into the dress until we have your face and hair done."

Rolling my eyes, I fought past the nervousness that made everything seem more stressful than it should. This wasn't a date, or at least not one I'd willingly agreed to entertain. Instead of going straight into the bathroom, though, I went to the cupboard, grabbing the expensive whiskey to battle the nerves.

"We don't have time for you to drink, woman," Kaderyn said, plugging in curling irons.

Ignoring her look of disproval, I dispensed two fingers into a glass for her, and took the bottle with me into the bedroom. Setting the bottle down, I gazed toward the bathroom before sliding my attention to the fancy box with a red bow on it. Grabbing the whiskey from where I'd put it, I chugged, snorting loudly before going to the bathroom.

I took my time shaving every hair off my body, minus my head. I'd been to the salon not too long ago for a Brazilian wax, and it would have to do for tonight. Not that it mattered, since I had no intention of letting him touch me there, ever again. Stepping from the shower, I slipped into a robe and exited the room to find the girls smiling.

"You assholes are enjoying this, aren't you?" I complained, slowly going to the chair they patted, wanting me to sit.

"This is the first time you've dressed up," Kaderyn stated offhandedly. "You never even tried on your wedding dress. Everyone was excited to see you in it, all fancied up."

My shoulders slumped, and I pursed my lips as Onyx glared over my shoulder at where Kaderyn sat.

"She's got diarrhea of the mouth tonight." Onyx lifted a hand with primer on her middle finger. "Kaderyn just meant that you ought to dress up more often. You deserve a life away from the hunter guild, Xar. You spend all your extra time hunting, and the only thing you ever adorn yourself in is guts, entrails, and bruises."

"You think I should date?" I asked, slowly shifting my stare to Kaderyn, who shrugged. "I don't have the time to go out. What would you like me to do? Get on Tinder and see who wants to bump pelvises? And what? Am I supposed to cancel dates by saying, 'Sorry can't come out tonight. A demon ate a girl's face, so sorta busy?' I doubt that would go over well."

"You are being stubborn," Onyx argued, spraying a mist on my face and then blowing on it to help it dry.

"What are you doing?" I frowned at how she fanned me with her hand.

"It's a priming spray to make the concealer set

easier and not goop your pores," she explained, rolling her eyes before I could do so. "Hold still."

My hair was yanked every which way, but the right way, before Kaderyn clapped, announcing she was finished with the updo style she'd created. It felt like my face was being held back by my hair. Not to mention, Onyx was a master torturer with the makeup brushes and utensils she'd used to make me presentable.

Her gaze slid over her work, and then she smiled, saying she was done as well. "Go get dressed. You have fifteen minutes before Kieran gets here to take you to dinner."

"Is no one going to say what a horrible idea tonight is?" I snapped, turning to look at them. "This asshole wants to own me. As in putting a leash on me and walking me around like a poodle."

"You're Xariana Anderson. Are we worried that you're leaving here with Kieran? No. If he gets out of line, you'll eat his dick while you make him watch. You're one of the most efficient killers this place has raised, girl. We should be more concerned for him than you." Kaderyn placed her hands on her hips while she shook her tawny head. "Go open that box and put on that dress. We have been waiting all day to find out what he bought you."

Groaning, I went to my room and demolished the packaging that concealed my eveningwear. Opening the tissue paper and lifting the garment, I swallowed a gasp that tightened my throat. The gown was a soft, light brown color that shimmered in the light. It had spaghetti straps and was form-fitting, with a high slit that started at the waist, exposing the curve of my thigh.

The bodice had a thin layer of jewels that spanned the top, dipping into a plunging V that dropped to my belly button. The entire back was open, stopping just above the low waistline.

Kieran had also sent matching heels that wrapped around the calf and tied into a bow. Making sure he'd thought of every detail, two silver armbands with dangling diamonds were delicately placed in a black velvet pouch on top of a note. I grabbed the piece of velum from the bottom of the box, reading the message he'd left within it.

Wear no panties tonight. I can't wait to see you in this dress. ~K

Twisting my lips to the side, I sat down to put the heels on first, knowing that I wouldn't be able to get them on easily once I was dressed. Next, I slipped on the evening gown and went into the bathroom to stare at the stranger in the full-length mirror. Holy shit. Onyx and Kaderyn had done the impossible tonight. I looked like someone else entirely.

Putting on silver hoop earrings, I silently fought the desire to rip the dress off and undo the intricate hairdo that made me look pretty. Instead, I put the blasted armbands on and exited the bedroom. The gasp that echoed through the apartment had me itching to hide.

I peered at Onyx and Kaderyn from beneath my thick lashes as they slowly took in my appearance.

"It's too much, right?" I inquired through trembling lips.

"You're fucking hot," Onyx stated pointedly.

Kaderyn snapped a photo with her phone, and I groaned. "Seriously, who knew you could look like this? You're beautiful, Xariana. You're fucking gorgeous."

"What time is it?" I needed to get out from under the microscope.

"Time to go downstairs," Onyx announced, handing me the coat that I'd left on the bed, which was also from Kieran. She walked toward me, wrapping it over my shoulders, then smiled, shaking her head. "He is going to come in his pants when he gets a look at you, girl."

"I'd rather he not do that at all," I muttered, allowing them to drag me from the room. The walk to the lower level was brisk and did nothing to alleviate the nerves rushing through me. My butterflies had their own, which had babies that were goofing off inside my stomach.

We walked into the control room, and everyone turned around, gawking at me as I passed through it, the extravagant heels clicking over the tiles. Kieran had known my size, and everything had fit me perfectly. It also didn't help my level of uncomfortableness that I couldn't wear panties because the slit in the gown literally went to my waist, revealing my hipbone.

"Jesus," Noah whispered, his eyes huge and rounded as he looked me over.

"It's over the top, right?" I fidgeted with the diamonds that tickled my arms.

"You look ethereal, Xari. Absolutely beautiful," he said with something burning in his gaze. He stepped out of the way, and my eye slid to Micah, who swallowed hard, slowly dragging his eyes down my body.

"I have to go," I stated, walking to the exit. I felt everyone behind me and knew they were following me out of the gates.

I entered the cool evening air and fought the emotions churning in my stomach. Refusing to look at the gate, I paused, coming up with a million reasons why I shouldn't be leaving the compound. Everything inside of me said this was insane and that I'd end up right where I didn't want to be tonight if I went.

"Damn," Kieran's deeply dark timbre caused my eyes to lift, finding him a few feet from the door. He pushed off the black SUV, slowly moving away from it as his gaze slid unhurriedly over every inch of my body.

I started to complain about Kieran being allowed inside the compound, but he opened the car door, holding it open for me. It wasn't what I'd expected of him. Stepping carefully down the few stairs that led to the blacktop, I paused in front of him as his gaze searched my face. He smiled and looked over my head at the few people that had gathered behind us.

"I'll have her back before dawn, gentlemen."

"Return her the moment the gala is finished," Micah sneered icily.

"Afraid she'll be much later than that, little boy," Kieran said in a cold tone that screamed serial killer.

He didn't assist me into the vehicle right away, choosing to remove the shawl from around my shoulders. Once he'd set it on the console and collected my purse to add with it, he held his hand out for mine, helping me up into the SUV and closing the door. In three long strides, he appeared at the driver's side, sliding into his seat.

"You're stunning, Xariana," he said softly, smiling wickedly before he turned the engine over and began backing up.

I glanced at the crew that watched us exiting the compound, my heartbeat pounding a thousand beats a minute, sending the blood racing to my ears, deafeningly so. Once we were beyond the gates, he started us toward downtown.

Kieran wore a black suit with a bowtie that was still untied. I felt his gaze on me, forcing me to peer in his direction. He smiled, his attention moving to the leg that had slipped out of the fabric when I'd sat down.

"I'm glad you changed your mind about going tonight," he murmured.

"You didn't give me much choice in the matter," I returned, examining the way his eyes danced with mischief.

"You saved lives. You should be celebrating that you stayed my hand. Your friends have been allowed to live another night. Have you considered my proposal?"

I stared at him with my mouth hanging open. "I believe your terms were that you want to own me. I fail to see where there was a proposal in that statement, sir."

"You will get my protection, and I will get you. It's a good offer, little hunter. I was right. You're very delicate without weapons and your silly vests covering your—assets. You really are an exquisite creature."

"Thank you." He barely looked at the road while barreling down it at an ungodly speed. Turning my attention away from him, I noted at least twelve similar SUVs behind us. "You brought security? Are you afraid you'll be attacked tonight?" I couldn't keep the hopeful tone out of my question.

"On the contrary. They're here to ensure I don't murder anyone who looks at you too long or inappropriately. I tend to be very possessive of my things."

I blinked slowly, chewing my lip while working out an argument about how I didn't belong to him inside my head. The moment I was about to object, he pushed a button on the steering wheel and turned on the radio. You Shook Me All Night Long by AC/DC started, and my gaze slipped to him, watching his lips move as he sang the lyrics.

So I did what came naturally. I silently sang along. It's just what you did when you heard Malcolm Young. His music was contagious and stirred the need to sing the familiar song. After several minutes, Kieran exited the freeway and into a posh part of town. We pulled up next to a tall building, and I glanced at it quickly before narrowing my stare at him as he smiled.

"There was a minimum three-month waitlist at this restaurant," I stated cautiously. "They won't permit us in here without having reservations." Instead of answering me, Kieran exited and appeared at my door before I'd had time to open it.

"Allow me, gorgeous," he murmured, holding out

his hand to help me from the SUV.

I eyed him suspiciously while allowing him to help me out. He smirked, tilting his head as if I was the one acting off. Once he closed the door, he reached over me, forcing my body back as his lips brushed my ear.

"You look good enough to devour, woman. I'm anxious to know how the dress looks off of you tonight," he purred, backing up with my shawl and purse in his hand.

"That's not happening, Kieran," I whispered breathlessly.

"It's not happening—yet," he said offhandedly, winking at me before he turned, staring at the shadows. "Ender, ensure no one touches Xariana. I'm sorry, but you'll need to excuse me for a moment, beautiful. I have something that needs my attention."

I watched him tie his bowtie as he walked away to the darkened alley, where the woman that had used me for target practice stood, glaring at me. If looks were lethal, I'd be dead. Striding away from the vehicle, I looked back to find the guard that had been in attendance for my lackluster quickie that had ended in murder.

He didn't speak, merely stared at me expectantly. I frowned, glancing at the building where a man stood, smoking a thick cigar. Approaching him, I heard the valet close the car door and drive off, and I smiled demurely while he raked his gaze over my body hungrily.

"Do you have a spare?" I asked, and the man grinned with the cigar still between his teeth. Producing one from his jacket pocket, he snipped off the end and held it out for me. Accepting it, I wrapped my lips around the tip, uncaring that the armed guards left to babysit me were watching my every move. The man produced a match, covering it from the wind as I lowered to the flame, hollowing my cheeks as I pulled on it, lighting it.

"Friends of yours?" he asked, nodding at the men around us as we puffed the delicious tasting cigars together.

"I wouldn't call them friends. More like hostile, unwilling babysitters," I admitted, watching Ender's lips twitch with the reference.

"Stunning woman like you, I can see why they're surrounding you protectively," he stated, beaming at me with piercing blue eyes that had me smiling in response to the infectious curve of his mouth. "Little thing like you could end up hurt or easily stolen."

"It wouldn't be as easy as you think." I shrugged, puffing smoke from my lips while I waited for Kieran to return. "I'm a hellcat with one hell of a punch when needed."

A woman walked up to us, frowning at me while she slipped her arm through the man's, claiming her turf. I merely winked at her, watching as Kieran strolled up, glaring at the man next to me. The moment he was close enough for the man to recognize, he paled and quickly strode away with the woman being dragged behind him, leaving me smoking alone.

Kieran watched me, his eyes solely on my lips, which were wrapped around the cigar. I exhaled slowly, making the shape of an 'O' with my mouth, producing rings of smoke while he stared. Before I could take another drag, he grabbed the cigar and smelled it before tossing it on the pavement.

"Later, I will let you sample a Gurkha Black Dragon cigar. They are very rare and exquisite, just like you, Xariana."

"Have you finished your business?" I was curious, but I wasn't an idiot. I'd walked away from them to observe their conversation. They'd both been talking about me, looking at me the entire time.

"Indeed, I have. Sorry about that, but occasionally things come up that cannot be ignored. I hope you weren't put out by waiting a few moments," Kieran stated, offering me his elbow.

I smiled at his choice of words as he escorted me to the door. Once we reached it, the owner himself yanked it open. My eyes widened, and I started to speak, but he gushed all over Kieran.

"Mr. Knight, your table is waiting for you as requested. A bottle of your preferred whiskey is chilled and has been on ice since last night. We've made your favorite dishes and the few you asked to be cooked as well. If you'll follow me, I will escort you upstairs to ensure that everything is how you wanted it tonight," he said in a thick accent that had my brows hiking up my forehead.

We walked through the restaurant, causing heads to turn in our direction, and the upper class whispered as we passed. Entering a wide, mirror-covered elevator, we shot up to the top floor. My hand on Kieran's arm tightened, hating the fluttering it caused inside of my stomach. He leaned closer, brushing lips against my ear that sent a jittering sensation through me before it turned into something darker.

"Someone doesn't like heights, does she?" he questioned softly, nipping my ear as I closed my eyes. His arm shifted, sliding behind my back to touch against my bare skin. "I won't let you fall."

Opening my eyes, I suppressed the urge to tell him I wouldn't have to worry about falling if we weren't heading to the top of the building. Words were lost to me as the cityscape came into view. The whole floor was empty of guests. Staff waited in a line against the wall, with curious looks cast in our direction.

Exiting the elevator, I glanced at the ceiling, where a large, elegant chandelier sent colors and rainbow prisms dancing over every surface. My heels were the only sound inside the room, clicking over what looked like marble floors.

The moment we approached the table, Kieran pulled out a chair for me, and I narrowed my eyes at the action. Taking my seat, his gaze lowered to my bare leg, revealed once more from sitting. Rounding the table, he sat, staring across to where I waited, uncertain what to do next.

"Leave," he stated firmly, shifting his focus on the owner that stepped back, nodding vigorously before signaling the staff, who all rushed out of the room. Kieran stared at me, smiling wickedly as he reached forward, grabbing the expensive bottle of whiskey. "You seem to be shell-shocked, Xariana. You can relax. I don't intend to eat you, at least not until dessert has been served."

I chewed my lip, studying how his fingers held the glass he filled, offering it to me. I took it, inhaling the amber liquid as I glanced around the windowed walls surrounding us. Plants and other such things covered the lower portion of them, and some were huge orchids dyed blue, drawing my focus to them.

"What are you thinking right now?" he asked, studying me as if he couldn't quite figure me out.

"That I don't belong here. I don't fit into this crowd, Kieran. I'm also uncertain of how to proceed since I have never even been on a date," I admitted, fidgeting. He narrowed his eyes as if I'd just spoken to him in a foreign language.

"You've never been on a date? You were to be married, Xari."

I snorted, sliding my focus back to him. "That wasn't like this. Micah didn't date me. We grew up together and hunted as a team. There wasn't a lot of romance happening between us. It was just expected. Hunters are a family unit, and we try to find a match within the guild. We know not to expect too much from one another and never take what we have for granted. Tomorrow I may go on a hunt, and by midnight, they could be salting my remains to ensure my corpse isn't reanimated by something wanting to use it for nefarious reasons."

"So you have never seen anyone outside of the—"

"I've never gone out with anyone. I've only had one relationship, and that was with Micah," I interrupted, stopping the conversation in its tracks.

"But you've been with other men," he returned, watching me.

"I have had emotionless sex," I elaborated. "I found pleasure where I could, and then I made sure never to return to the area again. I would go to a new place and find someone else to scratch that itch when it arose. It was easier than looking for something that would, in turn—"

"Hurt you."

"Exactly."

"Eat, and enjoy the meal," he urged, sitting back to stare at me with an expression in his eyes I didn't wish to see.

Chapter Twenty-Six

Kieran wasn't anything like what I'd expected him to be. He could carry on a conversation and wasn't sharp or angry when the reply was personal. However, I did think he was feeding me false information rather than the truth about himself.

"Why do you want to own me? You could have anyone you wanted. So why me, Kieran?" I asked, once the dishes from the most delicious meal I'd ever tasted were cleared. I had to refrain from licking my plate clean. I'd almost done it just to make sure I got every morsel he'd paid for when the bill arrived.

His violet gaze lowered to my mouth before slowly returning to hold my stare prisoner. "I want you because you would hate it," he replied honestly. "You are in my way, and the only alternative I have to ensure you don't interfere with my interests is to make you mine."

"Why not just kill me then?" I asked, hating that

the meal was turning sour in my stomach.

"Death is too fucking easy, isn't it?" He smiled, and his focus slid to the wall of glass. "Pain is much more pleasurable than delivering death to someone. Don't you agree?" He returned his attention to me and grinned. "There's an art to inflicting anguish on your enemies, a simple joy in watching everything they love destroyed. They have no recourse and no way to escape, realizing all they have and everyone they've ever loved is slowly being rendered to ashes. The feeling of having no control over what is happening, witnessing it unfold with no power to prevent or stop it, is one that reduces them to nothing more than a broken soul. It's more gratifying to watch it happen, knowing that I am the one responsible."

"You're a fucking psychopath," I murmured as my stomach dropped to the bottom story of the restaurant.

He grinned as if I'd given him a compliment. "Maybe." He pondered what I'd said for a moment. "I learned early on that there was little satisfaction in murdering my enemies outright. I found more pleasure from their eternal torment, knowing they had to live forever without the things they cherished most. I make no excuses for what I am or what I do to people. I provide them with a solution to a problem, and in return, they offer me a blood debt. It ensures that they never come for me, and if they do, I simply call it in and enforce its terms to be paid in full."

"So, you can't kill me because Enzo called in a favor."

"Exactly, and by doing so, he left me only one option."

"To own me," I hissed, and he nodded his head as if this wasn't the most insane conversation I'd ever had. "And how did that make you feel? Being denied the right to kill me?"

"Like I want to fucking murder you," he stated coldly, smiling. I swallowed audibly, fidgeting nervously with the napkin in my lap. "But I cannot do that because I am a man of my word. So here we are, trying to decide what to do with you, Xariana. You are truly beautiful, and I find the options are unlimited for the plans I have for you."

"You're insane, but you know that already." I zeroed in on the way he looked at me like he wanted to taste me carnally.

"Am I? Because you're the one who came to dinner with a man who has repeatedly stated that he wants to own you."

"You threatened to murder my friends."

He shrugged. "Friends come and go. You have left me in a strange position that I don't like. I want you, and I have never wanted anyone I wished to murder. You're beautiful, sharp-witted, and a murderous little creature that entices me. I can't look away from you tonight. I'm wondering if I bent you over and feed this hunger you created within me, if this need for you would dissipate."

"And this is why I don't date," I uttered, placing the napkin beside my glass, glaring at him from across the table. He smirked, nodding as he stood and came around to pull my chair out. Standing, he grabbed my arm, turning me to face him. My breath caught in my lungs, stuck there while he stared at me through narrowed eyes.

"You prefer I had lied to you?" he asked carefully.

I laughed at the absurdity of his question. He pulled me closer, studying me as he leaned over, whispering into my ear.

"Your beauty saved you. It wasn't only Enzo's request that stayed my hand from murdering you that night. There is something about you that calls to me, and it pisses me off. If I had really wanted you dead, you would be. There are a million ways to escape making a deal, but I chose not to do so with you," he admitted, slowly lowering his mouth to my throat, kissing his way up my jawline.

"I will not be owned, Kieran. Kill me if you must, but you will never own me," I murmured, holding onto his jacket as I felt his lips curve into a smile. He licked the wildly beating pulse, nipping it between his teeth before he chuckled. The sound of that laugh was chilling, and yet my thighs clenched together with need.

"We're late for the gala," he informed, changing gears so quickly and rapidly that it left me teetering on my feet until his hand touched my lower back, guiding me to the elevator. "I now know why you were so surprised by the simple gestures I made. You've never been courted or known a gentleman's touch. You merely experienced a boy pretending to be a man."

"There's not much of a distinction," I informed.

"It's the difference between being cherished and treated properly and being fucked up beside the wall in a warehouse. I assure you, the two are not the same.

One leads to disappointment and a quick fuck, the other to being treasured for hours until you plead for mercy. I will show you the difference, Xariana."

"I don't think I want to know. You're only interested in getting me out of your system. Not expecting anything other than dissatisfaction keeps me free of expectations."

We got on the elevator, and he turned, staring at me with something churning behind his eyes. "You hold yourself away from people. It's not because you think you're unworthy of their love. It's because you fear being hurt by them. You've watched others fall in love and die. You've seen the results of that loss. Your lifestyle has taught you that one day, you will know that pain. So you strive never to feel it, ever. You're not broken. You're brilliant in deciding not to have that weakness in your life. That's why you settled for Micah. You'd hurt when he died, but you wouldn't ever be distraught because of it, correct?"

I blinked, hating that Kieran had figured that out when I'd just discovered it myself. I shook my head, trying to argue that he wasn't right, but I couldn't. Licking my lips, I peered away from him, pondering how I hadn't deduced that myself before now.

"Your mother died in childbirth, and your father raised you. It left you—wounded. You watched other mothers with their children, knowing you had killed yours when you came into this world."

"Jesus. Are you fucking dissecting me?" I snapped, fighting the urge to step away from him. He wasn't gentle about precarious subjects, using all the finesse of a wrecking ball to talk about them.

"I'm learning you, but I don't have to guess that you make it difficult for anyone to know you. You're exquisite. Your anger shines in your eyes and comes from deep within you. I bet you fuck like a wounded beast."

Frowning, I reminded myself that he was a psychopath and that trying to reason with his words would be hopeless. He smiled, slowly closing the distance between us, then cupping my face. I stepped back as his mouth lowered, claiming mine in a kiss that left me breathless.

His tongue danced against mine, dominating it in a way that only he had ever achieved. His hand slid to my thigh, lifting it as he drew back, staring down at me. Kieran created a wealth of emotions within me, and I wasn't certain how to handle them.

"What is it about you that I can't ignore, little beauty?" he asked, sliding his finger to my naked pussy, leisurely rubbing his fingertip over my clit. The elevator stopped moving, and he reached over, pressing the button to keep the doors closed. "You are different from anyone else I have come across," he continued, slowly working a circle against my clit.

"We should get off," I whispered huskily.

"One of us should," he chuckled, watching as my eyes rolled back in my head.

He shielded me from the doors, and yet he didn't stop driving me toward the precipice I was teetering.

I parted my lips, and his hand lifted, smothering the cry that burst from me as I exploded. My entire body shook with the force of the orgasm shooting from my belly into my pussy. It felt like the world was shaking around me, and before I could argue that we shouldn't be doing this here, he dropped to his knees, pushing the dress away as he licked me there.

The noises he made against my sex were indecent. He pushed his finger into the heat of my core, creating a pained sound while I clenched down, sucking it deeper into my tight channel. Another orgasm started blossoming, and I slipped my hands through his hair as all coherent thoughts left my mind, and pure desire took control.

Kieran licked and fucked me with his finger until my legs threatened to give out, not carrying my weight. Repositioning me, he lifted my leg over his shoulder, continuing to kiss, suck, and devour my pussy until I was crying out his name as another orgasm swallowed me whole. He pulled back, his mouth covered with my pleasure, and he smiled at me, slowly pushing two fingers into me as I floated back to earth.

"Good girl, Xariana," he purred huskily.

Gradually, my mind returned as he stood, licking his lips while watching me struggle through the aftershocks of the orgasms he'd given me. He withdrew from my body, studying the way I breathed and fought to regain control of myself.

"I'm not even disappointed we skipped dessert now. You are more delicious than any sugary dish could ever be," he whispered, leaning closer to capture my bottom lip between his teeth, pulling on it. I tasted myself on his mouth, and I chuckled at the craziness of the entire night. "In five seconds, I'm going to open the doors, and you and I will walk out of here like you didn't just get that pussy eaten. Five, four, three, two, one…" the elevator opened, and he slipped his hand behind my back, steering me through the busy dining room, nodding in thanks to the owner, and then cold air washed over my face as we exited the restaurant.

Kieran produced a cigar, holding it with his mouth before gripping it with his teeth, striking a match, and pulling air into his lungs to light it. Then, smiling wickedly, he held it out for me. Still quaking, I accepted it, slowly taking a few pulls.

Unlike the previous cigar I tried, this one tasted divine. I puffed out ringlets, knowing he watched the way my mouth worked. Turning with my head leaning against the outside wall, I passed the cigar back to him, and he took several quick puffs before licking his lips, then closing his eyes to exhale.

"You know, these Gurkha Black Dragons are $1,500 each, and I've always thought they were exquisite. But now I think I prefer the taste of you on my lips, running down my throat," he whispered, glancing at me.

I blushed at his words, uncertain how to respond. I'd met no one as crazy or sexy as Kieran in my entire life. There was a darkness inside of him that spoke to me on a primal level. He wouldn't ever cringe at me wanting him to do bad things to me. He would never judge me when he learned I liked it rough, and that pain got me off.

"What are you thinking about right now?" he asked, offering me the cigar.

"I'm thinking that you're insane," I whispered,

and his eyes narrowed to slits as if he didn't like my response. "But also that you're unlike anyone I've ever met before. It's refreshing in a twisted sort of way. I may be high on the orgasms you just gave me, though. If you ask me the same thing tomorrow, my answer will probably change back to you being a fucking psychopath."

He smiled, and it took my breath away. It wasn't a cocky half-smile. Instead, this one lit up his violet eyes, stealing the air from my lungs at my first unguarded look at Kieran Knight. He was serious trouble because there was something about him that appealed to me on a deep level. Kieran was like me, wounded so profoundly that you had to pretend you were untouchable. You had to show the world another version of yourself, one that looked unshakeable.

He grasped my arm, slipping his beneath it while walking toward the SUV coming up the drive. We were running late for the gala, and I was very aware he'd planned it that way so that everyone would be there to watch us enter.

Kieran was making it known that we were out on a date. He was pleased that people were seeing me with him, which felt strange. No one ever wanted to be seen with me, but in all fairness, it normally meant they'd given information on someone. All things considered, I was enjoying the night, right until we entered the gala to find Rhys, Cole, Enzo, Ezekiel, and the other heads of houses gathered at the bottom of the steps, witnessing Kieran and I entering the party—together.

Chapter Twenty-Seven

Kieran procured drinks, slowly feeding me alcohol while he stood guard, observing all the people that milled around us. I could feel the weight of the curious stares, but he didn't seem to care about them in the slightest.

I was still high on the releases he'd given me, and I found myself wanting to be near him tonight. He guided me with a simple touch behind my back, his fingers rubbing against my skin. He wasn't insecure about who or what he was, and it showed.

"You are smiling," he stated after twirling me around the dancefloor.

Smirking, I sucked my bottom lip between my teeth before releasing it to study how he looked at me. "You're a very good dancer."

His eyebrows lifted at the compliment, and he

nodded. "In my world, knowing how to blend in comes in handy."

I laughed, shaking my head while ignoring the music playing in the room. "I doubt you blend in anywhere easily."

He frowned absently, skimming over the party-goers in the ballroom. "And why would you think I don't blend in?" He acted as if he was offended by my observation.

"Because you're disturbingly beautiful," I admitted, blushing as his gaze returned to mine, heating at my words. "When women see you, they stop to look at you. Men, on the other hand, tend to give you a wide berth. They sense you're a killer. Like dogs entering a park, sniffing out which male would be the alpha of the pack."

"And you think I'm the alpha?" he asked with a wolfish grin.

"No." I watched his smile falter. "You would be a sigma male."

He turned it over in his mind and was about to argue, but I stopped him in his tracks by placing my finger on his lips.

"You don't give a shit about social protocol or hierarchy. You wouldn't need a pack to lead because people are naturally drawn to your side. Your silent authority and personality allows men who don't fit into normal packs the chance to join yours. You don't command the room when you enter it, either. You walk in quietly and control it through your silence. Alpha men demand to be noticed. You don't do that, which in turn, makes folks more inclined to do so. You're an introvert, one who prefers to be in his own presence but will come out when needed. You don't conform to social structures because you couldn't care less how others see you."

"And what else causes you to believe I am a sigma male?" He handed me a drink from a passing tray, and I accepted it with a smile, studying him as I took a long sip from the bubbly champagne flute.

"You're a loner, Kieran. People surround us, and yet your posture is telling them to hold their distance. You don't hate being around others, but you do prefer them to approach you on your terms. Where alphas and betas need strict and rigid schedules and rules, you are adaptable to most situations and easily handle changes. You lead without exerting command. You act, and they follow because they recognize you're an excellent leader. You also don't change who you are, ever. You show them who they're dealing with and don't care if they disapprove. You also don't seek validation or attention, and alphas thrive off being given those things, be it male or female, as long as they get what they crave." Kieran stared off at something in the distance, turning over everything I said inside his mind.

"I enjoy dominating you with my presence," he admitted, and pink rushed to my cheeks.

"Yes, but if I chose to throw you down and ride your cock, you wouldn't be afraid of me assuming control. You would watch me and allow me to do so. You wouldn't feel the need to toss me on the floor and force me to submit. You would enjoy my dominance." I glance at him briefly, noting the way he caught his lower lip, biting it to hide the smile curving his mouth. "But if I never submitted, you'd be okay with continuing to try for it. Therein lies the difference between a sigma and an alpha. One needs submission, the other desires it, but if they get off, they wouldn't care. You'd slowly chisel my willpower down, piece by piece, until you got what you wanted. Conrad wouldn't do that. He'd fight me to get me to give in to him." Kieran's eyes zeroed in on the male I'd just named.

"You'd enjoy it, though, right?" He pulled me with him through the open door onto the veranda. "You would let me chip away at your defenses and learn everything about you if I touched you like this," he whispered, slowly dragging his nose over the curve of my shoulder. "You would permit me to devour you again, wouldn't you?"

The cool evening air ruffled my hair, and the heat of his breath sent a shudder of desire rushing through me. Kieran was aware of what he was doing, and every touch was calculated, meant to seduce my body so that my mind would follow.

"Kieran," I whimpered through the desire he created.

He turned me toward the cityscape, settling behind me as he slid his magical fingers past the slit of the dress. The other hand slid up around my throat as he kissed an inferno of heat on the back of my neck. He didn't force his fingers into my body, but slowly drifted the tips over the inside of my sensitive thighs.

"This city is going to break your heart, Xariana," he whispered against my neck. "You need to be more careful who you allow close to you."

"Like you?" I returned, hearing the silky huskiness of his laughter like music to my ears.

"Those we love most can hurt us the deepest. We never see it coming until we're bleeding out, and they're holding the knife that cut us open."

I blinked at what he'd said, uncertain of how to reply. I was still pondering a response when he stepped back, pulling me by the hand toward the party. Eryx was leaning against the balcony, watching us with a worried look in his expressive gaze. I stiffened when I noticed him studying us.

Eryx lifted his drink, twisting his lips into a bitter smile while Kieran paused, nodding to where he stood. Enzo and Ezekiel were also staring, blocking our path into the fundraiser.

"Interesting company you're keeping tonight, Xariana," Enzo snorted, stepping up as Kieran smiled coldly. "I doubt your father would approve of him."

"He also probably wouldn't have approved of her coming on my lips earlier either, but he isn't here right now. Is he?" Kieran asked, without showing a shred of fear while facing off against one alpha and two demons. "Xariana is exquisite, isn't she? I'm surprised none of you have tried to taste her delicious pussy yet. Scared of daddy? Or do you still think she's too fucking young? I assure you, she is all women."

"It's called respect," Rhys Van Helsing stated, and my attention swung to him.

I hadn't even noticed him until he'd spoken. My brow furrowed at the reminder that they'd all thought I was too young and unworthy of holding my position at the guild. I tugged on Kieran's hand, but he merely tightened his grip on my fingers.

"Xariana is young compared to the rest of us," Cole grumbled, stepping up beside his brother. "That doesn't mean we don't respect her or Xavier. She's one of us, Kieran. Do try to keep your cock out of where it doesn't belong, yeah? Xari is nursing a broken heart, don't add to it, asshole." With that, they all turned, leaving Kieran and me to walk as one into the ballroom. My stomach somersaulted while I pondered what they'd said. They embarrassed me. Each had vocalized their feelings about my position, and none had stood up for me that night. Every time I closed my eyes, I've heard their words echoing inside my head.

"They never showed any interest in you?" Kieran asked, spinning me to face him as his hands slipped down my back.

"No," I admitted. "We hunt together and fight against the same enemies. Nothing more has ever happened between us. My father wouldn't have liked the idea of me taking one of his friends to my bed, and I don't believe that would be a wise move to make. Even if it were a fleeting fling, it would cause hunting trips to be awkward."

"Mmm," he stated, lowering his forehead against mine. "You would be opposed to me murdering them all, wouldn't you?" he chuckled, and I tensed beneath him. "I'm bringing you home with me tonight."

"I don't think so," I snorted, pulling back to peer into his violet eyes that sparkled with a thousand diamonds trapped within their depths.

"Oh, but I assure you I am. I crave to see how you look with me buried in that tight body of yours," he admitted with an intensity that caused the air to become thick around us.

"Xariana Anderson!" Missy, the sheriff's wife, called out with a broad, friendly smile on her pink lips. Wide, cornflower blue eyes looked from Kieran to me and then over to Kieran once more. "You look amazing tonight, child. You're all grown up into a beautiful woman. Your mother would have been proud," she stated, hugging me into her bosom.

Kieran allowed it, stepping back to watch the display of affection. I'd known Missy since before I could remember. She was the sweetest woman I'd ever met and was always quick with a friendly smile and a refreshing, no-nonsense attitude.

"Thank you," I supplied, hiding the pang of regret that her words drilled into my heart. "You look beautiful, Missy." I silently took in her sapphire-colored dress that hugged her lithe, slender frame. "Where is that husband of yours tonight?"

"He's mingling with the suits," she snorted, waving her hand around the room before grabbing a drink from a server that passed by us. "And you would be?" she asked in a curious tone laced with steel.

"Kieran Knight, My Lady," he stated, grasping her hand to place a gentle, chaste kiss on the back of it.

Missy's eyes grew large and owl-like, and she mouthed 'wow' before he righted himself. Her eyes sparkled with wonder, and the hand not holding the drink fanned her face. Kieran stepped back into place at my side, slipping his hand around my waist.

"Xariana has told me much about you, Missy," Kieran lied, and it was smooth. There was no hesitancy in his voice or hint that he was lying through his teeth. "It is a pleasure to meet a woman as beautiful as you."

"Oh, stop it," she said playfully. "Where did you find this one, child? He's a keeper."

"Personally, I reserve the right to argue that theory," I muttered, watching her eating out of his palm.

"There you are, wife," the sheriff stated, his color pale and flushed, alerting me that something wasn't right. "We need to head into the office for a moment," he continued, staring at me.

I didn't ask him what was wrong. Missy didn't know that we existed, and since she'd seen me growing up as a small child, she assumed I was human. I turned, looking out over the crowd as Missy grabbed her stomach, drawing my attention back toward her with worry.

All three of us watched her, and I was the first to realize the problem. The thick scent of copper filled the air, and a soft cry of pain slid from her lips. She shuddered, shaking her head.

"I think the alcohol has gone straight to my head," she announced.

"Are you okay?" I asked, watching the sclera's of her eyes turning crimson. Then, I focused on Jeffery and saw him holding his hand over his mouth before he coughed, splattering blood everywhere. "Something is wrong." I lifted my gaze to Kieran, who watched them with a look of boredom.

"It would seem they have been poisoned," he returned in an irritated tone. His keen eyes surveyed the crowd as more and more people dropped to the ground throughout the gathering. "It would appear someone miscalculated their target."

Blinking, I peered at the party-goers once more, noticing a group of men that stood off to the side, glaring openly at Kieran. His guards slid in around us, and one helped the sheriff and his wife to their feet, taking them toward the balcony. I shivered, noting several more beings were sending waves of hostile energy directly at Kieran.

"You were the target?" I asked, incredulous that someone would be stupid enough to openly attack Kieran Knight.

"Indeed, I am," he chuckled, as if these men hadn't just poisoned an entire party to get to him. "Be a good girl and close your eyes for me."

I was pissed off on his behalf! These assholes had come into my town and tried to murder my date. Anger shivered through me, and he smirked, sensing my emotions. Ender, the man he had babysitting me before, stepped up beside me, taking Kieran's place as he walked away.

Power filled the room; ancient, raw energy that caused everything within me to snap to attention as it shot through me. Kieran glanced over at me, grinning, and I really looked at him. He'd changed into a taller, more terrifying being. His features sharpened and pointed ears poked through his hair. He removed the suit jacket, revealing the bronzed skin of his forearms, and smiled, exposing long canines that made my blood leave my face to pool in my expensive heels.

"You're fae," I whispered through trembling lips.

"Of course I am." He said it like I should have understood that before now. "I own the shadows, the same ones that played with you in the forest, and my office, Xariana. Now, close those pretty eyes." I did as he'd asked, right until I realized I didn't have to, and I needed to see him.

Kieran strode through the throngs of people on the floor, spewing blood from their lips. He slowly dissolved into shadows that branched off to slither past the crowd. He divided into dark wispy particles that rushed forward toward his victims, responsible for his attempted assassination. The moment he reached them, he entered through their mouths, noses, and eyes. Seconds later, they imploded. Blood and gore splattered through the room, covering those closest in the carnage of his strength.

My breathing became labored, unable to get my heart to stop battering my ribcage with what my eyes told my brain was happening. The ballroom was held in a pregnant silence as the humans tried to figure out what they'd just witnessed, unable to compute it in their minds. My chest rose and fell with the realization of what this meant and with whom I'd had indecent touches.

Kieran appeared before me, cupping my face between his hands while I struggled to calm my reaction to him. Finally, he smiled and lowered his head, brushing his mouth against mine.

"You were peeking," he growled, nipping my bottom lip with his teeth. "Naughty girl," he uttered huskily.

"So punish me, Kieran." I chased his lips as he backed up.

"I'd love to take you up on that offer, beautiful. Unfortunately, I have enemies to murder for trying to kill me."

"You're going to hurt them. Aren't you?" I asked, uncertain why that fact made my thighs clench with need.

"Worse," he chuckled, slowly dropping his gaze to my legs as if he sensed I was getting hot and bothered knowing he was planning to murder the people who had ruined my night out. "I'm going to end every last fucking one of them."

I smirked, chewing my lip to stop from smiling. Kieran's eyes grew heavy with lust, and he stepped closer, forcing my chin to tip as his mouth found mine. He kissed me with a fire that created a burning need inside of me. His hand slid up my spine, twisting through my hair as he devoured me. A soft moan escaped my lungs, only to be swallowed by his hungry mouth. When he broke the kiss, he stared down into my hooded eyes, smiling.

He cradled my jaw, applying enough pressure until pain warred with pleasure. "Bloodthirsty little bitch, you're making me want to take you home and feel you from the inside. My shadows want that, too, Xariana. But, unfortunately, this party looks—dead, and I need to get you to the guild safely." He didn't release me right away, and that was fine by me.

I had never faced another being like me, not in this capacity. It explained the magnetic impulse to have him. Kieran was fae, which meant he could probably sense that I was, too, even if he didn't comprehend the truth of it yet.

Kieran's bitch had shot me with iron. He was testing me to see if I was like him. Now, it seemed perfectly logical knowing he'd been sensing me in the same capacity that fae beings met and danced. I was an unmated female, and he was something I could claim and mate. But my needs were suppressed, tethered by magic and spells that prevented another being from knowing what I was.

I'd never seen Kieran with my father, and he wasn't there when he was taken. That meant he'd come here to find or discover what it was my dad had stolen. Did I trust him? Absolutely not. Did there need to be trust for me to fuck him? Nope. I had needs, and I knew he would soothe my ache unlike anyone else before him. I'd felt more alive in that few moments inside that elevator with his head buried between my thighs than I ever had before.

"Come, little savage hunter, I'll escort you home," he whispered huskily.

His words were like a glass of ice water poured over my head. My desire for blood was in the red zone. I needed to make these assholes pay for what they'd intended to do to him. The need to hurt them was driving through me, awakening the monster that slumbered inside of me. My fae half wanted revenge for the slight done here, proving it wasn't as dormant as my father had assumed it was.

"You better kill every last mother fucker responsible for what happened tonight, Kieran," I hissed, watching his lips jerk up into a blinding smile.

"You bet your pretty ass I will, Xariana," he chuckled, yanking me against his powerful frame that caused my pussy to flutter with his intoxicating scent of raw, masculine energy.

He kissed me quickly, and then pulled away. I scanned the room, thankful that the heads of houses and other immortals were helping the humans by administering antidotes while steering clear of us. They sensed the desire between Kieran and me just as surely as we felt their heavy stares on us while we exited the venue to the awaiting SUVs.

It was a quiet drive back to the compound, and Kieran made a quick escape after dropping me off at the guild. My head spun from the events of the night as I floated into the main building with a wealth of information I'd learned. Since Kieran was fae, that meant he wasn't really here to own me. He was here to get what my father took from them, and I was in his way.

Chapter Twenty-Eight

I hadn't heard from Kieran since he'd dropped me off outside the compound and sped away to murder those responsible for the events that had happened. Apparently no one had died from the iron being put into the food or drinks served at the event. Unfortunately, a large majority of them were in the hospital this morning.

Brodie, our medical examiner had summoned me to the morgue. Apparently, sheriff Jeffery had told him to get in touch with us about some of the findings he'd discovered. The entire morgue was filled with corpses, most of them being female.

"Hey," Brodie said, coming into the cold, creepy as hell room filled of dead bodies. "That was fast."

"I was in the area," I muttered, having been stalking Kieran's house for anything to use against him. "You said you found something?"

My attention moved from the motionless bodies to his heavily tattooed one. Brodie was an incubus demon, one that specialized in the dead. He had been hired by my father to keep otherworld beings out of the eye of the human's, and in doing so, had been hired by the city as the medical examiner for the sheriff's office.

He had the prettiest blue eyes I'd ever seen, with short spiky black hair that barely covered the tattoos that flowed up his back into his hairline. At six foot five, he was on the shorter side for a demon, and a lot scrawnier than most I'd met. The blue scrubs he wore hugged a well-defined chest, which tapered off to the traditional drool worthy V-line, with one hell of a package that delivered a first class orgasm.

"You want to go into the freezer?" he offered, smiling until he peered over my shoulder to find Onyx leaning against the wall. "I'm down for a threesome."

Snorting, I shook my head slowly. This was exactly why I'd only been with him once, and that had been quick, but effective for what I'd needed from him.

"Sheriff said you'd found something?" I repeated, watching the smile playing on his lips before he exhaled, nodding.

"Yeah, I did. So just to clarify, threesome isn't in the cards today?" he asked, sliding his sinful gaze slowly over Onyx's body. "Damn, momma. You look good enough to eat today."

"Brodie, do focus," Onyx stated in a clipped tone, having also experienced him more than once. She was a frequent flyer in his bedroom, but a lot of girls were.

Brodie made a strangled sound, slowly shooting

a regretful look at the tight dress she wore today. He nodded toward the body that was covered by a white sheet, and we followed him toward where it was placed on a slab.

"As you are already aware of, we've had some weird shit coming in lately. Last night we had more bodies discovered, but unlike the others, these ones didn't have the babe left beside them," he explained, pulling back to the sheet to reveal a heavily pregnant corpse. "These ones hadn't delivered. We assumed the others hadn't given birth because the knots in the pelvis that occur from pregnancy weren't present."

"Yeah, which made no sense," I agreed, fighting the anger that tore to the surface at the needless loss of life. "Get to why these ones didn't deliver."

"You planning to skip right to the twisted shit?" he snorted, shaking his head before he pulled open a locker, and pulled out another body. "This is one that had an infant left beside her. There's no sign that she was ever pregnant on the surface. However, when I ran the metabolic labs, she did have elevated hormones. She had human chorionic gonadotropin hormones, which are only present during pregnancy. It's the hormone that gives you a positive pregnancy test. They all have it, but the ones with physical signs of pregnancy, don't. There are also no fetuses in their wombs. Merely expanded uteruses, without a fetus present inside of it."

Blinking slowly, I slid my gaze over the woman's protruding stomach, frowning. "You're saying that the women that we found, with no physical signs of pregnancy were pregnant, but the ones that look pregnant, weren't in fact, pregnant?"

"Fucking crazy, right?" he continued, nodding toward one of the bodies. "Then there's this," he pointed out, moving the hair away from the woman's ear.

Swallowing, I stared at the line of studded surgical steel earrings that covered her upper earlobe. I had the same thing done with mine, which prevented the pointed ears I was born with from being noticed. Next, he moved to the teeth, holding her upper lip open to reveal that sharp canine teeth.

"She's fae by origins. I'm guessing at least ninety percent by birth. The other women, the ones with the elevated hormones are half-breeds. The babes aren't present, so I can't test them to see what genetic level, or species they are," he informed, slowly lowering the sheet to expose the belly of the woman on the slab. "There's also this," he continued, showing me the intricate swirling pattern of ink on her stomach. "That's a fae marking, one that says she's been claimed by a male." Where the mark on my side was black, and wispy, hers was silver and gold.

"Are the half-breeds marked as well?" I questioned, fighting the urge to vomit.

"A few of them had markings, but they're not in the same location. They're on their genitalia, and beneath their ribcages. The males that came in are human. They're not otherworld species. I can't make sense of it, Xariana. In all my time working in this hovel, I have never come across something I couldn't figure out. This one though, it's freaky."

"The woman with the hormones present, do they show any signs of postpartum?"

"No, that's another thing. They don't have the oxytocin levels that should be present once birth has occurred, either. They also don't have the relaxation in their joints needed for giving birth. Their hips never spread, and there's no physical or visual sign that they ever gave birth to those babies that were left with the corpses."

"Do you think it is possible that they were merely used for the hormones? Fae women cannot have children, right? They lost the ability to become pregnant. But half-breeds didn't because our world isn't missing what theirs is. Is it possible that it was an experiment gone sideways?"

"That's a theory. It doesn't explain why there are fae women being left murdered inside out world, however. If you look closer, you can see that each one had their bodies pumped full of iron. See the silver coloring here," he stated, opening one of the women's eyes.

The veins in her eyes were silver, which meant someone had pumped her full of poison. He held out her forearm, showing me bruises that had occurred before death. Someone had purposely pushed iron intravenously into her system.

"They were murdered," I whispered, fighting the saliva building in the back of my throat. "They were brought here, experimented on, and murdered?"

"Yeah, and the half-breeds died of natural causes. There's no sign of foul play in any of the corpses. We assumed there was because they'd been disposed of, and left to the elements. The blood that covered their corpses wasn't theirs. It wasn't even blood. It was a mixture of iodine, and something else I'm running test on to discern what it is. I have the pictures of the men up on the dark web already. No hits for missing persons, or criminal records yet. My guess is, if it is an experiment, we have not seen the last of mass body dumps. There will be more."

Nodding at his forewarning, I chewed my lip, peering down at the fae woman. "The alternative is that they're so fucking desperate to create children that they're willing to die for them. It's sad and disturbing."

"Xari," Onyx whispered, staring down at one of the half-breeds that she'd been examining. "It's Jenna."

Moving closer to the body, I peered down at one of the seven women taken days ago from our compound. Jenna had been among the first women taken in the assault that had ended up with my father vanishing.

"You know her?" Brodie asked, peering down at the woman. "She was among the bodies, but she had only a trace of hormones in her blood. Not anything like the other women had. According the sheriff, there was no child sat beside her, either."

"She's only been missing for a couple days," I informed, watching his eyebrows pushing together before they shot up on his forehead.

"She was taken when your father was?" he clarified, moving to more of the women, uncovering them for us to see.

The blood left my face as I slowly slid my gaze

over the familiar faces. How had we missed it?

"When did these ones come in?" I asked, watching the way he frowned before answering the question.

"Last night," he confirmed, nodding toward the bodies that appeared pregnant. "With them. None of these fresh ones had hormones though. They were just deceased, and left with them."

"Do they have injection marks?" I countered feeling my stomach churning with unease.

"Bruises that indicated they were restrained and tearing around their vaginal area. They appear to have been raped, and then death occurred. I haven't concluded my autopsy report on them yet." He lowered the sheet, revealing wide bruises on their legs and wrists. They also had bruises covering their nether regions, and bruises that looked like handprints. "They do appear to be severely dehydrated, and malnutrition might have played a role in their deaths. But if they've only been missing for a few days, that doesn't add up."

"It does if the fae tried to breed them without the help of artificial assistance. A few years back we came across a case that was sickening. It appeared a half-breed woman had been put into a cabin, and used to breed a child for a fae couple. She was skeletal like, and when we touched her, she evaporated into dust particles. A week later, we found an entire laboratory of women that were similar to her. But where she'd become nothing more than dust, the remains were more like husks of dried tissue."

"You think they're breeding half-breed women? That would only give them heirs, that would end up be like the ones they condemned for not being pure enough," Onyx snorted, tossing her hair over her shoulder.

"If you wanted a child, and you couldn't make one yourself, what would be the next best thing?" I pondered, twisting my mouth to the side, staring down at the hunters that had suffered because I hadn't been able to save them.

"You'd take what you got, and accept that it couldn't be what you wanted it to be," Brodie stated softly, exhaling. "I assumed this job would be easier than dealing with trafficked women, and here we are, with victims that were sexually tortured by monsters."

"They're not monsters," I grunted, hating that my father was unintentionally responsible for this mess. He'd taken the one thing that would allow them to breed away from them, and in turn, they were looking for a way around it. "They are designed to create life. Each couple has one thing that adds to their realm. If you take away the elements, the world becomes unstable. It isn't the child they're working to create. They're trying to stabilize their world, because the elemental wheel is broken. He fucking broke it, and knew what would happen. He had to know what would happen to them," I whispered, fighting the pang of regret that rushed through me.

"Who knew?" Onyx asked carefully.

My phone chirped, and I peered down at the message.

Kieran: You have a situation developing. I'm bored waiting on your decision. Time to play, woman. Are you ready for me? I did something bad, but it felt so good.

Me: What the hell did you do now, psychopath?

Kieran: Come play with me. I miss that taste of your pussy dripping down my face, Sunshine.

Me: Stop that. It isn't happening again. You're insane. Mistakes were made that night.

Kieran: Is that a no? I don't like being told no, Sunshine. Besides, you'll change your mind soon. Very soon.

Me: Get used to being disappointed.

My phone rang, and I snorted, peering at the number before swiping it, answering Noah's call.

"Hey, what's up?" I asked.

"We have a situation. I'll send you the address," he stated, hanging up before I could get another word out. My phone chirped and I scanned the address, nodding at Onyx.

"We have to go now," I stated, watching as Brodie covered up the bodies before turning toward where I watched. "If you find anything else, call me. Once you've finished with the autopsies, let me know. I'll arrange transport to get them to the estate to give them final rites."

It was becoming the new normal to have more questions than answers. I hadn't even blinked at the wrongness of the entire situation. I needed to figure out what was happening with the infants, and where they were being taken. If there were fae children being created, they needed to be found immediately before they ended up in the wrong hands.

Chapter Twenty-Nine

I pulled up to the address Noah provided, slipping from the Jeep to scan the thick forest surrounding the rickety home. It had taken me longer than usual to find the place, but it was deep in the country's backwoods. The terrain had been a bitch to maneuver, but we'd managed.

Exiting the vehicle, I glanced around the area, taking in the high rock walls that made it difficult to see the property from the road. A rock quarry had once owned it, but they sold it several years ago to a private investor. The quarry on this property had closed after the sale. So there was no reason for someone to come out this far or this deep into the abandoned mines.

Noah appeared on the large wrap-around porch of the old shack, his face downtrodden as if he felt sick from whatever he'd discovered in the home. Frowning, I mentally prepared myself for what I would find inside the deserted, boarded-up house.

"Jesus Christ," Micah said, coming out with a pasty complexion. "Sick fucking bastards."

Onyx and I made our way to the porch, and I caught the scent of rot and excretion drifting from the structure. I pressed my arm over my mouth and fought the urge to throw up what little I'd held down today. Both men turned, staring at us with slumped shoulders and a sad expression on their faces.

"What is it?" I asked, not moving my arm from my nose.

"Use this," Bali announced, exiting the house to hand us a cream. "Put it beneath your nose. It will help some, but it won't take away the stench of what is inside that horror show of a fucking mess."

My eyebrows shot up, but I schooled my features and did as he'd instructed. The menthol ointment made my nose run and my eyes water, but it did aid in masking the putrid smell that had been unleashed.

Someone inside was opening windows as I glanced over at Noah and Micah. Both men looked ill over whatever they'd discovered, and I waited for one or the other to explain what we were about to walk into, but they seemed to be having trouble speaking.

"You need to prepare yourself for what you're about to see, Xariana," Noah stated, causing the skin on my nape to rise. I glanced between him and Micah, finding them both watching me with a weary look in their gazes. "Brodie called me, and I agreed to let you handle the situation at the morgue while I followed up on what had happened here. I wanted to make sure it was him. I didn't want you to be the first one to find your father like this."

The blood left my face, draining as my heart shattered. I shook my head, knowing they had to be wrong. This wasn't happening. It couldn't be. It had to be a mistake. Nausea burned the back of my throat, and both men wiped at their eyes.

"I'm so sorry, Minx," Micah whispered thickly.

"This is where the captives were being held," Noah continued, fighting to remain in control of his emotions. "In the basement is what we believe to be a breeding program. Incubators and medical beds line the walls, and half-breed remains are secured to each bed with chains. We're still investigating this as an active scene, but you deserve to know what happened here, Xariana."

I nodded slowly, fighting to make words leave my lips, but nothing came out. Noah pulled me close, holding me tightly against his massive frame. Micah watched solemnly while Onyx wiped at the tears running down her cheeks. Kaderyn exited the front door, observing us before she turned away, tossing up the contents of her stomach over the porch railing.

After a few moments had passed, Noah grabbed my hand, pulling me inside behind him. It looked like teenagers had used this place as a party house. There were broken beer bottles littered on the floor with used condoms and trash everywhere.

Noah directed me to the stairs that led to the lower level, his hand tightening on mine as we descended to where the staunch scent of death was rising. It was a startling change from the main floor. The walls were covered with medical-grade plastic, and they had divided the basement into rooms, using the same thick material.

Micah held a sheet of plastic back, and I fought the bile threatening to come up my throat. On the first bed was what appeared to be a fae woman, and beside her, with a chain on her wrist, was a half-breed. Both were in different stages of decay, and an empty incubator sat near the bed with more high-end medical equipment.

I slowly removed my hand from Noah's, using my foot to push the half-fae woman over to reveal her stomach. It was rounded as if she'd been pregnant. An incision from her chest to her pelvic bone indicated someone had performed a cesarean section on her. Turning to the woman on the bed, I narrowed my eyes on her abdomen, which had also been cut open.

"They tried to transplant the fetus into the fae mother," I pointed out, and Noah and Micah nodded in silent agreement. "The women Brodie showed me didn't have any incisions that would indicate they had been opened up."

"No," Noah stated. "They were in the early stages of the program. There are beds down the hall with women chained in a manner that forced their legs apart. We think they were being raped until conception. After they'd become pregnant, they moved them here to have the fetus transplanted into their fae mates. It explains why none of the victims had the notches to indicate they'd ever birthed a child. They never made it to that stage of their pregnancy."

"The women in the morgue didn't have a fetus in their wombs, though. They merely appeared as if they had a baby within their bellies," Onyx pointed out, gagging as the smell grew thicker.

"Because they'd already given birth," Micah snorted. "They found a way around their infertility issues. They used these women as test subjects, uncaring if they suffered or perished during the process. These fae women weren't the ones wanting children. They were the unlucky victims used to make sure the procedures worked."

"It's a lab," I swallowed past the saliva forming in my mouth, needing to excrete the bile growing within my stomach. "The fae women were here voluntarily to ensure their realm doesn't die. They are desperate to create the elements their world lost, and these women gave their lives for the cause. You'll notice they're not chained to the beds," I said, motioning to a corpse. "They came willingly."

"Yeah, we guessed that when we found the chamber further below. Unfortunately for them, they chose the one home surrounded by iron that would slowly poison them to death. I believe that's why none of them showed signs of what killed them. An iron mine is less than a mile up the road, and they failed to detect it until it was too late. My guess is that they had someone here helping them, and they didn't investigate what was in the area," Noah stated, nodding toward an opening at the back wall. "Xavier is in there, Xariana. You don't have to see him like this. We can take care of the body and bring him outside."

I shook my head, slowly peering into the space that had been secured with large locks on the door. Everything within me screamed to run, not to enter the room, and to pretend he wasn't gone. But my father had raised me better than that. He'd taught me never to believe something was dead unless you'd looked into its soulless eyes and verified the truth for yourself.

Trembling, I crept toward the darkened area that sat off to the side of the plastic breeding chambers. I touched the door, closing my eyes with regret. There would be two versions of me now—one before my world was shattered, and one after. I wanted to tuck my tail between my legs and run away. I knew if I did, no one would judge me. No one but me, and I couldn't escape myself.

Pushing the door open, I peeked inside. Dried blood caked the walls, and on a dirty mattress, with half his head missing, was my father. I choked down a scream that was building in my chest as everything inside of me rebelled. A thousand words of denial shot through me as my surroundings spun. My dad had been torn apart, as if he'd fought for his life.

His hands were shredded, with parts of them gone, and his torso had been ripped open, leaving his guts spilling out of his abdomen. There were machetes and other wicked-looking blades discarded around his body, as if several beings had taken part in his torture, enjoying the slaughter of my dad.

Turning away from the sight, I ran from the room blindly, exiting the scene before my stomach lost the fight, and I threw up everything within me onto the earth. Hands touched my back, and a bottle of water was handed to me, which I accepted and drank greedily, only to throw it up, too.

"I'm very sorry, Xari," Noah murmured, kneeling

beside me when my legs gave out, and I went to the ground, hard.

"This can't be happening," I whispered past the quivering of my lips.

"We will bring Xavier to the estate so that he can be buried with your mother," Micah said softly, touching my hair to comfort me.

How had he gone from helping the fae attack us to being dead? Had he been an unwilling accomplice? Had they crossed him somehow? I couldn't put the pieces together. Nothing about any of these deaths made sense. Micah helped me up and directed me toward a dark SUV. My head swam with denial, and my emotions were too much to handle.

Tears endlessly rushed down my cheeks, and I wanted to scream and refuse to believe that it had been my father inside that room. They'd butchered him like an animal to the slaughter. A strangled sob slipped free, filling the car as Onyx and Kaderyn crawled into the backseat. They both held my sobbing, trembling form.

Nothing would ever be good again. I wouldn't be okay until I found those responsible and showed them what true savagery looked like as they took their last breath. The vehicle started forward, and my mind switched from a grieving daughter to a ruthless hunter. I blinked slowly, wiping away the tears, staring at the startling beautiful sky as it gave way to clouds, threatening to unleash the storm I felt churning within me.

Chapter Thirty

They say when you suppress grief, that you deny the truth to keep your soul from breaking. I had never believed that could be true because I hadn't experienced it before. I'd seen hunters mourning their loved ones, and I'd felt the loss with them. It was different, though, when death sought those you cared about, destroying you in the process.

That kind of pain numbed everything around you, muting your emotions and thoughts. I was living in a fog. Nodding and agreeing to plans about the service for my father and those we'd lost in the attack. I made a few suggestions and pointed out things he'd have liked as his dutiful daughter. I looked composed from the outside, but my insides were broken.

When I'd learned that my birth had caused my mother's death, I'd been wounded. I had to live with the knowledge that if she hadn't had me, she would still be alive. It couldn't be changed, and I could do nothing about it. That was a sad fact. My mom had died so that I could live. It was the ultimate sacrifice, and her first and last act of love as my mother.

My dad lived his life protecting those who couldn't do it themselves. He'd chosen to live by the sword, and he'd died by it, too. As hunters, we knew it would happen, eventually. One hunt went wrong, or a bullet stuck in the changer could mean the difference between life and death. But what had been done to him was on a different level. It had been a personal kill.

The retrieval team had placed his corpse and the pieces they could find into a body bag. Bali had tried to sew everything back together, but at my request, he'd stopped. It didn't matter how he was buried, as long as he was honored, and given his last rites.

I'd left the compound earlier in the day, needing to escape the events surrounding me. I was exhausted hearing the hunters express their regrets and condolences. There was only so much that could be said before you wanted to throw down and knock their teeth from their mouths. Saying sorry didn't take away the visceral pain of the loss. It didn't make those left behind feel any better or keep you from remembering that your loved ones were never coming back.

I peered around me, staring absently at where I'd ended up. Kieran's estate loomed before me, calling to me. Slowly, I walked toward the gates, pushing the buzzer. After a moment, a guard answered by opening the fence, glaring at me with a look of intrigue.

"He wasn't expecting you." He didn't bother to ask why I'd shown up here.

I felt like laughing at the absurdity of me coming to the home of this psychopathic playboy. In the last twenty-four hours, he'd called my phone a hundred times. I'd ignored every one of the calls. Kieran had sent me text messages, one after another, asking what was going on, and then all at once, he'd stopped. Why? Because he'd figured out what had happened and had probably decided that I was dysfunctional. Kieran most likely had anticipated that I would come here, and knew I didn't need his encouragement to show up today.

Entering the large courtyard, I retraced my steps from my first visit to his office. Once inside, the door was closed, and I silently looked around, wondering why I had shown up to see him. Why run to the one being that was insane, even if he called to me? Kieran wouldn't tell me he was sorry. That much was a given. He wouldn't pretend to care that his people had brutalized Xavier.

I knew why they had murdered my dad. He was protecting his secret, and in doing so, he kept me hidden from the fae. Xavier died so I could be free from the treachery that surrounded their kind. They were a savage breed that enjoyed destroying anything that threatened them. Half-breeds had been a blemish to their race, an ugly secret they'd enjoyed creating, but hadn't wanted us to tarnish their bloodlines.

We were the result of their lust skulking out of the Otherworld and flowing into this one. The results of them fucking humans and making what they considered to be impure bastards. Now we were the one thing that could save them, and they no longer needed the elemental my father had stolen. In the long run, he'd still paid the price for infringing upon them.

The office door opened, but I didn't turn around. I could smell the enticing scent uniquely belonging to Kieran. His dark undertones of masculinity called to the monster within me as he entered the room.

Kieran's lips brushed my neck, and his hands grabbed mine, placing them on the desk where I'd rested. He didn't speak, but then I wasn't here for words. I needed to forget the pain consuming me. I wanted to feel him instead of the debilitating emotions ripping me apart.

His fingertips danced over my shoulder, slowly pulling the spaghetti straps of my blouse over it. His heated kiss teased my skin, and his teeth nipped the curve as he cupped my throat, pushing his other hand through my hair, moving it away from my neck.

Kieran pulled against the thin camisole, freeing my heavy breasts to slide his fingertips over the jeweled nipple. A soft whimper escaped my lips as he twisted the barbell. Then, gently, he turned me around, peering at the tears that slowly trailed down my face. His jaw flexed, and something akin to regret danced in his pretty, dark, violet gaze.

He lifted me, sitting me on top of the desk as he settled between my thighs. Softly, his lips touched mine, brushing them teasingly. He raised his hand, wiping my tears from my cheeks before kissing the trail they'd taken.

"Given everything that has happened, I didn't think you would come to me," he whispered huskily, slowly dragging his mouth over my collarbone.

"I want the pain to go away, if only for a moment," I admitted softly, my voice thick with emotion. His forehead rested on my shoulder, and then he pulled back, searching my gaze.

"Fuck it," he snorted, grabbing my jaw roughly before his mouth collided violently with mine.

Kieran kissed me like I was his last meal, devouring me with hunger. His tongue tangled with my own, capturing and fighting me for the dominance he craved to hold over me. His free hand slid up my spine, twisting his fingers in my hair before yanking my head back, hard. Then, exposing my neck, he traced his heated mouth over my delicate skin, sucking against the rapidly beating pulse he discovered there.

Slipping my hand into his waistband, I wrapped my fingers around his silken length, and the growl that escaped him was rough and guttural. Tightening my grip, I started working him over as he stared down where one hand caressed him while the other skimmed over his abs. His stomach tensed, and his breathing grew labored, matching mine.

Kieran released my hair but continued his grip on my jaw. His hand moved to my skirt, sliding between my legs, and I moaned loudly at the slight contact against the inside of my thighs. He drove his fingers beneath my panties, gliding them through the seam of my sex teasingly.

"Gods damn, you're soaking wet for me, aren't you? This pussy wants me to fuck it hard, doesn't it?" he groaned, his dirty mouth causing a moan to escape my lips.

He thrust two fingers into me, and I immediately clamped down around them. Kieran made a strangled sound and buried his head in my shoulder. He wasn't gentle, but then I hadn't come here for him to treat me with kid gloves. He moved his thumb, leisurely stroking my clit as if he were painting a picture.

I moved my hand faster, caressing the silky head of his cock. My thumb slid through the pre-come, rubbing it over the thickly rounded tip. The sound Kieran made was pained, and it made me crave to be on my knees, with him buried in my throat.

He continued pushing into me, slowly withdrawing while he teased me closer to the edge. My entire body was in a highly intoxicated state from his fingers alone. I almost feared what it would feel like with him inside me, destroying me.

Kieran knew how to render a woman to mush. He was built for seduction, bathed in hard, sinewy muscles that pulsed and tensed, driving me insane. I removed my hands from his sex, ripping open his shirt and hearing buttons scattering over the marble floor, echoing through the room.

"Impatient little savage, are we?" he growled, pinching my nipple before twisting it. His mouth captured mine, and his hand slid beneath my ass, lifting me as his other pulled my panties off, exposing my sleek heat. His fingertips pushed through my wetness, until I felt them against my opening. "You're soaked for me, Xariana, aren't you?"

"Yes," I groaned, wiggling my hips until he smirked, but it wasn't friendly. It was terrifyingly beautiful, like the smile a wolf gives you right before he rips out your throat.

Kieran removed his fingers, replacing them with his thick tip. He slowly tortured my core, sliding it against my pussy until the silkiness touched my clit, sending me teetering on the edge of bliss. He slid past my opening, gradually fed me an inch, and then he paused, tilting his head, and cocking to the side.

"Fuck," he grunted, closing his eyes.

I whimpered, lifting to rub against him. My feet landed on the desktop, fully intending to use him if he didn't give me what I needed and craved. Someone opened the door, and I tensed as Kieran turned his head, shielding me from whoever had entered his office.

"That better not be my fucking daughter, Knight." My father's angry tone slithered through me, forcing my mind to churn as I leaned past Kieran's protective body, staring at my very alive father.

My entire world spun off its axis, and all I could do was blink while my core clenched tightly around Kieran's thick cock. Tears burned my eyes while no one moved from their positions.

"You motherfucker," my dad hissed, murder lacing his words.

"You may want to step outside of my office, unless you intend to see a lot more of your pretty little princess than you wished, Xavier," Kieran chuckled, shooting my dad a pointed look over his shoulder.

"Get your ass dressed now, Xari!" my dad demanded, slamming the door, shaking the bookshelves and art on the walls.

"What the fuck just happened?" I whispered, uncertain I believed my eyes and ears.

"That asshole couldn't fucking wait until we were done," Kieran growled, peering between us before he slid in deeper inside me.

"What the hell?" I demanded, but Kieran shook his dark head, withdrawing from the cradle of my body, and I blinked to clear the fog in my brain, unable to do anything more.

Kieran grabbed my legs, lifting them as he descended on my naked pussy. His tongue glided from one end to the other, and then latched onto my clit, his fingers entering me once more.

Stars exploded in my vision, and everything started shaking around me. My spine arched off of the desk, chasing his hungry mouth as he sucked and licked my pussy while holding me in an endless, earth-shattering orgasm.

He pulled away, watching my body convulse before stepping back to stare at my naked sex with regret.

"That fucking heartless, selfish prick," he snorted. "I seriously want to murder Xavier for not letting us finish first. You wouldn't mind him returning to the grave, would you?"

"Kieran!" I hissed, sitting up, uncaring that aftershocks rushed through me.

"Is this going to complicate things between us? I really hope not," he stated, continuing to stare at my swollen sex.

"Tell me that wasn't my father, asshole," I spat between my teeth. Pounding sounded at the door, and I turned, shaking at the prospect that Xavier could be alive. "That was my dad," I whispered, hope flaring within me.

Kieran nodded his head, pulling his pants over his erect cock. Exhaling slowly, he brushed his fingers through his hair, lifting his turbulent eyes to mine.

"Your entire world is about to be destroyed. I advise you to take a moment and enjoy this time," he offered softly, retrieving his shirt off the floor where we'd tossed it in our rush to fuck.

"Did you know he was alive?" I asked carefully, my tone turning angry while he pulled his shirt on and stared at me. "Of course you knew." I swallowed past the lump growing in my throat.

"That's his story to tell you, Sunshine. Not mine," he muttered. "I do hope you forgive me soon. I crave the feel of you against me, woman. I'm not a patient man." Kieran walked into the hallway and paused before closing the door. "Try to keep an open mind about what is happening here. Join us in the common rooms when you're—ready." I shook my head, uncertain what was taking place.

My father wasn't dead. But I'd seen his body! I saw him in the courtyard, in full fae form! How could he be here, in this psychopath's home? I blinked past the emotion, wiping my tears as I looked around for my panties. Grabbing them from the floor, I pulled them on and opened the door. Ender waited for me, his eyes lowering to my blouse.

"I suggest you cover that sparkly titty before proceeding to the den, Xariana," he teased, forcing my attention to where my camisole was still pushed down.

I tugged the top up, righting the shoulder straps, as I headed to the sounds of raised voices in a heated argument. Stepping forward, I paused the moment I entered the doorway.

"You were supposed to fucking watch my daughter from a distance! Nowhere in this agreement were you to fuck her, Knight! I said to keep her fucking safe and make sure she didn't do anything stupid. I asked you to monitor Xariana so that she stayed out of the way of what we were trying to accomplish. You had one fucking job!"

"You failed to consider the fact that we're both fae, and she's primal, Anderson. I didn't start this shit. She did. Your daughter projected her image into my fucking house. Do you think I didn't try to ignore her? Xariana is beautiful and all woman."

"What the fuck?" I whispered brokenly, glaring at the man who'd raised me. He turned to me, his soft blue gaze meeting mine, swallowing before he pushed his hands into his pockets. "I saw your dead body."

"It wasn't me, Xari. What you saw was my twin brother. His recent appearance in this world made it easy to replace me in the eyes of our enemies." He searched my face as the color drained from it. "You should sit down, Kid. A lot is happening that you don't know about."

"I planned your last rites ceremony," I cried. "I arranged for your fucking funeral!"

"Pocket it, Kid," he ordered, watching the tears stream down my cheeks. "Get your shit together, Anderson. Now!" he demanded in a firm tone.

I blinked slowly at the ludicrousness of his statement. My father didn't die, which meant that his twin was the fae that had attacked us, and I hadn't even realized it. Of course, I'd never met my father's brother, since Xavier had stolen his wife, my mother, from him. I felt like the earth was shifting around me, and I didn't know how to stop it from moving.

Chapter Thirty-One

I stood inside Kieran's den, gradually fighting through the emotions of wanting to beat the shit out of my father and hug him for not being dead. He had refused to tell me anything until Noah, Micah, and the others in our small group were present. While I called, asking them to meet me at Kieran's estate, my dad sent a quick message on his phone, then informed me that a few hunters he had hand-picked to aid him with his secret plan, would also be joining the meeting. My dad depended on these individuals to blend into the background to help run the guild from the sidelines. When my team entered the room and saw who was in attendance, their shock and expressions mirrored my initial reaction.

"Those of you that had no knowledge of the events unfolding should at least take a seat before I begin," he demanded, holding my stare. "Xariana, sit down."

"I don't want to sit. I need to know what the hell was so important that you let your only child assume you were fucking dead. I have been searching for you. I mourned your death, and you've been here, at Kieran's estate this entire time?"

"Yes, and no," he stated carefully. "The murders started a year ago, and I have been working the case with only those I chose to be in the loop regarding recent events." His admission caused my stomach to churn from the mistrust I heard in his voice.

"And you didn't trust me?" I countered, rethinking my need to sit on the couch. Instead, I crept toward him, fixated on his stare.

I slipped my hand from my pocket and tossed salt into his face, causing him to swear. Withdrawing my other hand, I squeezed a tiny bottle of holy water on him. Then, reaching into my bag, I pulled out some sage, lighting it and placing it under his nose while he glared murderously at me.

"Satisfied?" he snapped crossly, tilting his head.

I wasn't because I knew he was full fae, which meant I couldn't test him with iron. He'd fail. Instead, I brought the sage to my lips, blowing on the smudge stick Talia had given me. Embers touched his skin, and he growled as he put them out.

"No, you taught me better than that. I learned never to trust my eyes or my infallible heart. Unfortunately, the only conclusion I can come up with is that you didn't have confidence in me."

"Stick a pin in it, Xariana. Join the others on the sofa or leave the room. Make a decision, now!" he ordered.

I blinked, popping my jaw before I turned on my heel to join Micah and Noah, who waited impatiently, trying to figure out what was happening. It burned that my dad had called all these people to Kieran's house before explaining the situation to me. He clearly had no intention of filling me in until everyone was present. I stepped up beside Noah, searching his eyes while he did the same to me.

"How?" he whispered, grabbing my hand.

"I don't know," I replied, squeezing his in return.

I looked at Kieran, who was studying me closely. His lip twisted, but the cold, lethal glare I sent in his direction made it vanish. My father moved to the front of the room, commanding our attention as he stood before an opulent stone fireplace.

"As you are all aware, our mission is to stop the trafficking of humans and Otherworld beings. What you don't know is that I began this battle long before starting the guild. As a boy living in the Otherworld, I witnessed the death of my oldest brother, who was the keeper of the sun element. When he died, the fae were plunged into darkness, remaining that way until the sun chose a new host. Our world was unbalanced, creating a void that prevented my people from bearing offspring. Without the means to procreate, the sun element could not be reborn. We lived with little hope for nearly a hundred years until a soothsayer came to visit the Day Court. She read a prophecy to my father, the king, telling of an heir that would be born into our kingdom in the spring, restoring the sun." My dad glanced at Kieran and then at Noah and me before continuing.

"During this time, I watched men savagely take unwilling women, trying to force nature to provide children. Kings attacked their courtiers and subjects, craving an heir to hold their title, because, without one, a king could be challenged for his throne. When their mates failed to become pregnant, they took other women to their beds, enslaving them, raping them as they begged to be freed. My brother, Xaven, was born five minutes before me, and was declared the heir to the Day Court. Try as he may with his bride and the women he held captive, Xaven couldn't produce an heir to ensure his kingdom was safe from challengers." He paused, exhaling as he stared at me, and I noticed a flicker of unease in his expression.

"My wife was one of those women. Xaven had forcibly taken Nyla from her family, marrying her in hopes of birthing a royal heir. She approached me during one of my trips, asking me to take her away from him, and I brought her here to escape Xaven's cruelty and insanity. I went back to free others and soon found that I had nowhere to hide that many women and young girls. So, I sought the one being that had already slipped from his kingdom, choosing to leave his throne in the hands of his mad uncle instead. Kieran is the rightful King of the Shadow Court. He had all the connections I needed to build my operation, becoming an unexpected ally. He agreed that the events taking place in the Otherworld were wrong and couldn't be allowed to continue."

I swallowed past the shock of his admission. Xavier stole my mother from his twin? I hadn't known that, but then I had no reason to ask until now. He'd always seemed standoffish when I brought her up, so

I gave up at a young age, deciding I would rather be oblivious than to have him relive painful memories.

"We removed hundreds of women, full-blood and half-breeds alike, but the one I claimed as my wife, my fated mate, she had a secret. When I discovered Nyla was pregnant, she told me she was a Princess of the Spring Court, and it was then that I realized why Xaven had taken Nyla from her family, and that our child was destined to be special. Three months into her pregnancy, Nyla began getting sick, and we didn't have healers or know how to find or fix what was wrong with her. The center wasn't finished, and we still lived inside the mansion. Every day, I watched her waste away to nothing. Then the day came that she gave birth, and with the new life we'd created, hers expired."

I fought the tears that pricked my eyes and the emotions closing off my throat, while my father studied me as if waiting for me to curse him, or worse. A sinking feeling entered my stomach the longer he stared at me. Sliding my gaze to Kieran, he shuffled his feet, looking at anything but me as if wanting to be anywhere but here right now.

"What aren't you telling us?" I asked carefully, hating the emotional sensation threatening to make me cry like a bitch.

"Nyla didn't give birth naturally. We had to remove my son from her body and breathe life back into his premature lungs," Xavier stated, and I tilted my head, frowning.

"You mean daughter. I don't have a dick. I better not have a dick."

"I can vouch that you don't, Xar," Micah snorted, but the comment didn't ease any of the tension in the room.

In fact, it was smothering with the intensity that hung thick in the air. My dad swallowed audibly, tearing his gaze from me. My stomach churned, and my palms began to sweat when he failed to correct his statement.

"Your mother was my mistress, Xariana. Noah is the son that Nyla gave to me." He lowered his eyes to the floor before pulling them back to where I stood. I waited for him to say he was joking or that this was a sick, twisted prank, but the words were never spoken.

"Excuse me?" I asked, slowly fighting to control the confusion that burned through my mind as I tried to fit the puzzle pieces together.

"What the fuck? You're telling me that my whole life has been a lie?" Noah sneered.

"Xari's mother was a half-breed servant that I'd rescued, and we had a brief affair before I met Nyla, my true mate. She was among the first group of women I brought to this world." Xavier's attention swung between Noah and me. His expression was firm, but his eyes looked sad.

"Sandra was a gentle soul, and she understood the cost of what I'd created with the guild. Sacrifices had to be made. Until you were both born, we didn't know at the time that only a full-blooded fae child could carry the missing element. We couldn't let the fae know that Nyla and I had produced a son. If they had discovered that Noah existed, especially since the sun element chose him as its host, they'd have attacked endlessly. The fae would have come for Noah, and once they had him, they could invade this world on a level, unlike anything we've ever seen before."

"Xariana is my sister?" Noah dropped my hand and took a step back.

"Yes, half-sister," Xavier clarified, glancing at me.

"I'm going to be sick." Noah covered his mouth, turning to stare at me with wide eyes. "Fuck."

Blinking slowly, I saw him go pale. His posture went stiff, and Micah snorted, laughing coldly.

"She doesn't know, asshole." Micah's tone was filled with mirth, and I turned to look at him. "Noah is in love with you, Xariana. He's always been in love with you."

"Shut up," I stated, barely able to grapple with the fact that the man that raised me had been lying to me since the day I was born. My attention moved back to Noah, trying to find the similarities between us, but his horrified expression caused my hackles to rise. "Fuck. I saw you naked!" I blurted, and his face heated with embarrassment. "Oh—that's fucked up." It came out so low that I wasn't certain anyone else had heard it until Kieran snorted.

"That was why I had Micah spelled and placed with you." Micah's laughter ended abruptly, and he glared at my dad as if seeing him for the first time. Xavier looked at him unapologetically and then turned back to me. "Micah was a diversion meant to keep you and Noah separated so that situations like this—," he waved his hand between Noah and me, "wouldn't happen." As he said the words, something inside me slid into place. I held his gaze as tears filled my eyes.

"Noah and I were born only days apart. His birthday is one week after mine. You raised us together, but only I carry the marks that make it clear to anyone paying attention that I am fae."

Xavier nodded, flinching when he noticed the tears roll down my face. He didn't look away, but the pain in his expression ripped me apart.

"Sandra agreed not to claim you so that we could use you to shield Noah from the fae. No one other than Nyla knew Sandra carried my child. Noah had to be protected at all costs. You weren't royalty. You were just the offspring of a girl I used one night to slake my eternal hunger. We concluded that you would be the child I openly claimed, while raising Noah as an orphan beside you. Since you were only three-quarters fae, you still carried a lot of the traits and outward appearance of a full-blooded fae, and what you lacked, we altered to make it look like we were trying to hide your heritage. The same witch that spelled Micah, placed a strong glamour on Noah, making him appear as if he were part hellhound and incubus demon. I'm the only one that can remove it."

"I was bait." I could barely look at him, fighting against the turmoil churning through me, eating me alive.

"I'm sorry, Xariana. It made sense to use you. We only had two fae babes born that year. I didn't have a choice." His tone pleaded for me to understand their logic.

"So, if the fae came looking, they would have taken me, thereby keeping your son safe and sound. You never hid me from view. In fact, you fucking paraded me around, showing me off. In reality, you didn't want or care about me. You hoped the fae would take me instead of Noah, because I am nothing to you."

"Noah is the heir to the Day Court and holds the element of the sun." We all looked at Noah, who was sitting silently, dumbfounded.

"And I am your fucking daughter," I spat, barely squeezing the words past my emotions, choking them off. "One only good enough to be thrown away, apparently?"

"It didn't end up like that, Kid."

"Don't call me that, asshole," I hissed through the bile burning my throat. "Were my ears naturally pointed?" I asked, seeing the truth of it in his eyes.

"It had to look real to the fae watching us," he stated, shoving his hands into his pockets.

"You fucking tortured me three times a year so that they could watch? You cut the ends of my fucking ears off and filed my teeth. I was a child that was held down and put through fucking hell because of you. Who the fuck are you? I don't even know you."

"You know me, Xariana. I raised you to be strong. I made certain you could withstand the tests the fae would put you through. I couldn't undo what I'd started, once I'd announced a female heir had been born to the Day Court, but I made damn sure you were trained and immune to iron. You weren't supposed to steal my heart, Kid. I looked into your eyes, and I hated myself for what I was about to do, but if I didn't, and they took your brother, they would have sent armies to this world, and they wouldn't stop until everything was destroyed."

"Ask me if I care, Xavier." I stepped back, and Micah cleared his throat.

"You spelled me to love your daughter?" he asked, causing my father's gaze to slide to him.

I'd been raised believing I'd killed my mother, when, in fact, she'd thrown me away. I'd allowed the body modifications to be done, thinking it was hiding me from the fae. But actually, I didn't need them at all.

I wished the floor would swallow me whole. I wanted to run and never see any of these assholes ever again. The hunters leaning against the wall hadn't blinked when they'd heard Xavier's confession. Only my team had, which meant the others always knew the truth.

"I removed the spell two weeks before you and Xariana were to be married," Xavier admitted, and I looked to Micah, who glared at me like I'd been part of it. "It wasn't her fault. I didn't want Noah falling in love with his sister, and I couldn't tell any of you the truth with my brother hunting my heir to retrieve what I'd taken from the Otherworld."

"Meredith?" he asked. "What about the attack on the guild? People are fucking dead. My wife and child died, Xavier."

"The attack was real, but the fae that grabbed me did so to protect me. I was brought here to Kieran. Xaven wanted my attention, and life means nothing to him, especially not a half-breed."

"That's all? That's all you have to say about it?" Micah demanded, causing a pang of regret to flood my chest.

"I will speak to you after we've concluded here," my dad promised.

"If there's more, I may throw up with Noah." I was unwilling to look at my father again. I couldn't. If I did, I'd have to face the fact that he wasn't the man I'd thought he was. He hadn't hung the moon at all. He'd simply slipped a leash around my throat, holding it out for the fae to take.

Chapter Thirty-Two

My father insisted I tell him about my visit to the morgue, so I purposely turned my back to him and faced the others in the room, methodically explaining what I'd seen, pointing out the similarities to the corpses found at the farmhouse. Noah filled my dad in on events surrounding the guild and its daily operations. I listened, but didn't add to his report. I had a hard time talking past the pain swallowing me after the mental shit show that had been laid before us.

"We haven't discovered how the fae have been able to procreate without the sun element, but they found a way." Xavier nodded at Kieran, who unrolled a scrap of leather, lifting his gaze to mine, as I looked away. "They've figured out how to use changelings to bring babes into the Otherworld. Any female with a shred of the fae mutation can breed an embryo, which is then placed into a fae mother's womb, and carried to term. The one thing stopping the fae from invading this world is that they're afraid of Kieran and what his shadows can do to them. They are also leery of the guild because they don't know our numbers or strength. I've built an army from the unwanted, impure bastards they created when the first invasion occurred, hundreds of years ago."

"Why don't they stay?" Noah asked, finally over his issue with me, even if he wouldn't make eye contact.

"Iron." Xavier studied Noah's face. "This world is filled with it, making it impossible for the fae to remain here permanently. Kieran found a way to block the effects of iron, and he passed that knowledge on to me. As a result, you and Xari have been receiving supplements in your food for years, making you virtually immune."

"That's why I had you shot, Xariana," Kieran admitted. I felt the heat of his stare on my face, but I wasn't willing to lift my gaze. "The fae were watching, which is why we set the scene as we did. You used your power in front of them, making me deviate from my original plan to murder them, opting instead to shoot you within plain view of their scouts."

Everyone in the room waited, but when I refused to reply, my dad moved forward, leaning in to touch me, and I jerked back, glaring with the same murderous expression I'd inherited from him.

"Do not fucking touch me," I hissed, slowly stepping to the side and away from the eyes, watching me.

"I requested Kieran cut you off from the others.

You were too damn close to figuring things out, forcing me to intervene. Rhys, Cole, Eryx, Ezekiel, and Enzo were recently told that I was alive. I asked them to trust me and to keep you at arm's length." I remained in place, holding his gaze with a deadened stare. "You stepped down from your duties, and I wish to know why you showed weakness, appointing Noah as your successor."

"Because I saw your face in our courtyard, and it was on the opposing side of the fight. If you had betrayed us, I couldn't lead the guild. So I removed myself from the equation, since it clearly created a conflict of interest." I snorted, shaking my head as I continued. "You taught me that the guild always comes first, and that if I was ever in a position that made the other leaders question me or my loyalty, I was to step back. Guild before pride and hunters before honor." He nodded, turning to look at Noah.

"I am proud that you stepped up, son. You did an amazing job given the mess Xariana left for you to clean up." Xavier slid his angry glare over me, and I cocked a brow in annoyance. "Maybe next time she'll keep her knees closed and think only with her brain."

"Fuck you!" I laughed coldly. "I'm not the asshole who knocked up two bitches, and then used one of those children as bait for the monsters. That would be you. I put the guild ahead of my worry and fear. I did everything I was taught to do. I followed the trail, which apparently, you thought I would be too damn stupid to find, and I worked our sources until you cut me off. I never strayed, not until Kieran threatened to murder my team. You weren't the priority because, once again, the guild comes first. We continued hunting and were seen in public, even if it was the last thing I wanted to do. I didn't stop until I stood over what I thought was your dead fucking body and felt my soul ripped apart. And yeah, after I spent an entire day planning your fake-ass funeral, I came here to ask Kieran to take that bone-deep, earth-shattering grief away from me so that I could stand before the heads of the immortal houses and all the guild leaders to send you off to the Otherworld."

"You're still going to perform the ceremony," he informed coolly, his eyes losing their sharpness once he'd spoken to Noah with praise.

"No, I am not. I am not standing in the presence of our people, weeping for you, Xavier."

"This isn't over. It's barely begun. The fae are inside the guild, and we need to know who and where they are. I require your help to finish this, Xari. If they figure out how to get a purebred fae from the halflings, we're fucked."

"What's my position? Bait? Maybe you can tie me up like a sacrificial fucking goat and slit my throat. Nah, too dramatic," I snorted, slowly shaking my head at the truth.

"You are more than that, Xariana Sunshine Anderson."

I flinched, inhaling sharply. "Gods damn, it's even right there in my name. I'm surprised you didn't just hand me to them when I was born. It would have been a lot easier, but without me, you wouldn't have had an excuse to get close to Noah, would you? He was my dearest friend, the one beside me through thick or thin. But then, you'd made sure of that, didn't you? Is there any part of me that hasn't been coerced or dictated? My best friend, my fiancé, my job leading the team at your direction? Anything I'm missing here? Oh, that's right. I forgot my torture to ensure I was the spitting image of an Otherworld being pretending to be human."

He frowned, placing his hands on his hips before lifting his head to stare at me. "You think I wanted this for you? I didn't have a fucking choice. I had to decide the fate of two children. One was my heir, and born of my true mate. The other was the serving girl's bastard, which would never be anything more than what I made her to be. I only had one option when they first attacked, looking for my son. It doesn't change who you are or what you became. You've always been this bright light in a dull fucking world. You ignited and accelerated when you began training. I expected you to fail, because your genetic makeup wasn't half of what Noah has. You outranked him on every test and skill. You showed up to show off since the day you were born. Noah was sickly, but you were this healthy babe that never cried, and just watched him from your crib inside my office."

"I had to be extra diligent, training day and night because everyone whispered about me. They figured you were playing favorites, and that I was nothing but a spoiled little bitch. I was your daughter, which meant I had to be better and go hard at everything I did. It turns out that it wasn't me you were going easy on the entire time. It was your precious prince, and I was just thrown to the wolves. And now, I am aware of it all."

"We need to figure out how to move on from here, Kid."

I ground my jaw together, watching as his cheek jumped at the sound. Power erupted behind the door, and Eryx, Rhys, Cole, Ezekiel, and Enzo came into the den, sliding curious gazes to where Xavier stood in front of me.

"Rhys, have you or your team found any more unwanted babies in the woods?" Xavier asked.

"You planning to use them as bait, too?" I smiled coldly, and the immortals that had just entered the room went stiff, turning guilt-ridden eyes in my direction.

"No, but they're not surviving long enough for that purpose, hunter. Put a fucking pin in it, or go home and cool off." I turned, bumping into Rhys and Cole as I tried to leave. "Sit the fuck down, now. You're needed for this conversation. Not as bait, but because you work through problems with a skill that no one else can achieve."

"What's the matter? Underestimate my willingness to leave here and never look back?" I countered, crossing my arms to lean against the exit. So what if the immortals thought I was being more childish than they already believed?

My entire world had just been ripped apart in less than an hour. Today was officially the worst Monday of my life.

Rhys studied me briefly, then turned his dark, midnight stare back to my father, who'd moved to the center of the room. I looked to the unguarded doorway, but something slithered along my leg, and I peered down at the wispy tendrils of black smoke that had wrapped around it. My attention shifted to Kieran, and he frowned with what appeared to be genuine regret.

Fuck him too. I didn't need a damn babysitter.

"There were no children or infants that we could find. Conrad sent his pack out, and if anyone were out there, he'd have found them. We haven't discovered any more corpses, but Bali and Brodie have people looking for anything inside the states that would trigger alarm bells. Kieran ordered more E.V.I.E. agents in the area to be on hand if needed. They'll appear to be here for the service. We have hundreds of people coming in, each using your untimely demise as their cover. Saint is en route as well." Rhys completed his report and turned to Cole, who was watching me with an unguarded look. "Cole has ears to the ground, and has been monitoring the traffickers while we direct our skills elsewhere."

"Did you convince Remington to create more ammo and weapons?" Xavier asked, frowning as Rhys shook his head. "I didn't think that would work. She's rather peeved that you kicked her out while she's pregnant."

"It isn't something I'm willing to talk about here, Xavier," Rhys's tone was filled with anger. "That woman has turned everything upside down."

Xavier nodded. "So, what are the fae missing from their process? Why are their changelings dying soon after birth?"

"You got me," Rhys snorted.

"Maybe they lack a genetic marker," Enzo offered, leaning against the wall beside Kieran. He shifted, staring at the male before snorting and moving further away from him. "When demons are born, we have certain safeguards that we have to hold within us, or we'd die before breathing air into our lungs. They may be missing something needed to sustain life when the babies are transplanted into the host," he pointed out.

"Maybe, but half-breeds can birth fae babes. Xariana's mother was a good example. She was only one-third fae, and she delivered Xari at full term, and she was healthy. Noah's mother wasn't, and he was born early and sickly."

The immortals looked at me before sliding their attention back to Xavier, confused. I turned it over in my mind, tilting my head slightly before my father's words interrupted my thought process.

"What is it, Xari?" he asked, knowing my brain enjoyed solving puzzles.

"I almost fucked the King of the Shadow Court." I snorted, watching the anger enter his eyes, and he lowered his stare to where the tendrils of shadows held my leg. It felt good to piss him off, but that wasn't helping the problem we were facing. "None of this makes sense, but then neither does implanting a growing fetus into another body. They'd have to inseminate pregnancy to have the womb there to accept the embryo. You can't just shove a fetus into someone and expect it to grow. It doesn't work like that. They've figured that out, but why reject the babes once they are born? Maybe they're only abandoning the weak ones. We counted the number of children the sheriff found, comparing them to the women in the morgue and the ones in the house where your fucking corpse—your brother was. We had more adult females than we had babies, and those had given birth, albeit violently."

"I calculated also, but discovered the same amount of bodies as infants." My father rubbed his chin, leaning over the desk before he stood. "The first group, though, they were off."

"No shit? Gees, I didn't think about that," I snorted. "Are we done? I want to be pretty much anywhere you're not right now."

"Go and get your shit together. You need to handle your emotions."

"Me? I just had everything I thought I knew about myself torn apart. But yeah, I can stick a pin in the fucking grenade. What is it that I can do for you, father?" I asked, but the coldness in my tone said I couldn't care less if he needed me or not.

"I want you at the mansion," he ordered. "I need you stable and with your emotions under control for the funeral. We're being watched."

"Good, let them fucking come for me. It's what I'm here for, right?" I laughed, bordering on hysterics, before I exited the door.

"Micah, let's you and I speak outside, alone." My father's tone caught my attention, but I wasn't staying to hear their conversation.

I would handle my business because that was who I was. Afterward though? I wasn't sticking around to be fodder for the fae. I hadn't asked to be born or used as bait. I had spent my life assuming my father loved me, when he'd simply needed me to protect the child that meant the world to him. Fuck them all and everything they expected from me.

Chapter Thirty-Three

I arrived at the mansion and went into the large family room, where I heard the others speaking, staring at the pictures that adorned the wall with fresh eyes. In each photo, Sandra had worn baggy clothes and was never near my father. He'd always had eyes for my—Noah's mother. I didn't hold Xavier's love against him because I knew what it was and how it should feel. What I held against him were all the lies he'd told me throughout my life.

It was embarrassing, and it hurt me on a level so deep that I realized I hadn't scratched the surface of the emotions stirring within me. How does one come back from that, from learning things about your life that you'd never imagined could be true? I wasn't even fully able to breathe.

My attention shifted to the bar, where Noah was speaking to my father and the others. The plan they had decided on was morbid. Xavier would use a spell to appear as someone else to the people at the funeral. Anyone privy enough to know he'd returned from the grave wouldn't see him as anything other than his new appearance.

Frowning, while tearing my stare from them, I turned my focus back to the pictures, studying Sandra. I wasn't calling her mother. Titles were earned, and neither of my parents deserved the familial term. I'd been a shield and nothing more to them when I was born.

I left the downstairs, heading to the room, still decorated in baby shit. My father had suggested I use it, like a sitting duck waiting for a hunter to perfect his aim. Once inside, I slid to the bed where I'd hidden my things. Dropping the bag of identification cards and petty cash, I slipped into the dress I'd borrowed for the funeral service this evening.

The outfit wasn't anything fancy. The top had wispy shoulder straps tied into bows adorning my shoulders, dipping into an A-Line, which opened on the sides to leave a slip of skin exposed. The skirt was mid-thigh, with a small ruffle on the bottom. I'd chosen a pair of black, clunky heels that wouldn't sink into the green earth of the courtyard.

Leaning against the railing of the balcony, I silently watched cars full of visitors pulling up for the service. It would be hours before they left, but that was normal when one of our own died. The wind rustled my loose hair, and I closed my eyes, allowing a moment of silence for the girl I was yesterday, preparing myself for who I was becoming.

I wasn't that same girl. Where before, I'd been merely broken from something I'd done by mistake, now I was shattered. I was the pieces left from the lie that was my life, and this version of me was darker. This one wanted to hurt the people who hurt me. I wouldn't, though, because no matter what had happened, Xavier hadn't treated me badly. Minus the body alterations and the whole show he allowed to happen for the benefit of the fae. That stung the hardest.

"Don't do that," Kieran's silky, dark voice whispered from the shadows. "Don't let that pain control who you are, Xariana."

"Do you need something? I don't require a babysitter tonight," I returned without looking at him.

"I wanted to make sure you're not planning to run after the service is over." He slowly settled beside me, peering at the people milling about. "I didn't initiate this thing between us, Xariana. You did that when you projected your image to me and entered my space. In our world, it's considered a challenge to find prey taunting a predator. You came to me, and I wasn't leaving it at that. One taste, and I had to have you. What happened between us wasn't me watching you, Little Savage. That was me hunting for what I craved."

"Hunt someone else, psychopath. I've had enough of everything and everyone." I turned to move away, but he grabbed my arm and pulled me up against him. "Let me go," I demanded coldly.

"You're mine, Xariana. I marked you, and that isn't something I will take back, ever. I get it, your entire world was just fucked sideways, and you didn't see any of it coming. You weren't supposed to, though. Your father made a split-minute decision, one he had to show up for and own, or everything we did would have been for nothing. No woman would be safe from the fae or their need to eradicate this world by breeding out what they didn't like. So suck it up and look at it from where he was standing. Xavier had two fae infants. One was a royal prince who would become king, housing an element. Then he had his mistress's bastard daughter, who he never intended to love. He does, nevertheless. He loves you more than he ever intended."

"Is that supposed to make me feel better? How do you know what he feels? I don't recognize that man down there. I thought I knew him, but I severely misjudged him."

"You misjudged what? That he'd do anything needed to protect his family? That he poisoned you with iron so that if the fae tested you, they would find you impure, and leave you inside this world? That he raised you to be this savage little murderous thing that no one ever sees coming until your teeth are stuck in their fucking carotid artery, bleeding out? You survived iron arrows in front of three fae princes, Xariana. Had he not taken those precautions, the third that witnessed your magic, vanishing before I could stop him, would have returned to the Otherworld with a story of Xavier's daughter wielding fae powers. They'd have never stopped hunting you."

"Good thing you were a great babysitter then." I yanked my arm away from him to reenter the room.

"I know you're angry. Don't make any stupid decisions while you're in this blind rage, thinking that running is the only way to stop the pain. Leaving won't stop that pain you're itching to remove from your soul. It's just a part of you now, Savage."

"My name isn't Savage."

"I've known your name longer than you have, Xariana. I was here when your father decided your path. He made a deal for you to be protected one month after he'd chosen to claim you to keep his son safe. I saw the regret plaguing him. I watched him pick you up and hold you in this very room. He promised to do everything he could to get out of our bargain, and I did whatever it took to ensure nothing could ever break it. Not on the fae aspect, anyway. You looked like trouble, and I wasn't willing to spend my days keeping you from getting scratches."

My blood turned to ice in my veins as I turned, staring back at him. "What did you ask for in this deal with my dad?"

Kieran was the fucking King of Shadows. He was whispered about in the light, because saying his name in the dark would conjure him. Or so they feared. He hadn't lied about what he enjoyed doing to people. I'd seen the truth of that madness burning in his stare as he spoke of it.

"I asked him for you," he chuckled. "He isn't willing to fulfill that agreement, though, which should tell you everything you need to know about how he feels about you. He's the good guy. I'm the bad guy, but you don't want to turn me into your villain. Your father owes me your hand by the stroke of midnight, on your twenty-fourth birthday. The day your fae genes will be cemented, and you'll be of breeding age." I glared at him, panic wrapping around my throat at what he was saying.

Digesting the information, I cocked my head before narrowing my gaze at him. "Why would he agree to that? If he loved me, why give me to the bogeyman?" I challenged.

"Because no one fucks with the bogeyman, my little savage." He crept closer and trailed his fingers over my cheek. "I didn't think I wanted you, Xariana. I thought I'd look after you, please your father, and then simply hold my claim over his head. I was wrong. You're an exquisite, murderous little creature. Plus, I promised to protect Noah, because he's the sun, and darkness doesn't thrive without the sun to cast its shadows. I knew you weren't the princess he said you were, but I didn't care. I wasn't looking for a beauty to become my queen. I needed someone whose madness could see mine and not look away. It also helps that you aren't afraid of me. You've never been fearful of me, because you were born into the darkness of this world, and you still grew like the most beautiful rose with no assistance from the sun. Only the rarest flowers grow without light, Xariana."

"You're insane, Kieran." I started to argue, but the door to my room opened, and Xavier and Eryx entered, eyeing us before he slid his gaze to the pack on the bed.

Silently, I saw my father remove the identification cards, credit cards, credentials, money, and anything else he could find that would help me escape this nightmare. I snorted, glaring at him before folding my arms over my chest.

"What the hell are you doing?" I demanded frostily.

"Making sure you don't flee after the funeral ends," he said tiredly. "I know you. Remember? You're my daughter."

"I'm uncertain that is the truth anymore." His eyes shot to mine, locking with them in silent challenge.

"You are, Xariana. Even if you weren't my blood, you'd still be my daughter. I raised you, trained you. I ensured you were protected at all times, by any means necessary," he snapped, moving closer to me with my things in his hands.

"Including selling my soul to Kieran, apparently," I returned, snorting at the look of worry etching over his features.

"You couldn't fucking wait until shit calmed down to tell her, could you?" he growled, staring murderously at Kieran.

"She intends to bolt," he hissed back, smiling wickedly. "She needed to know why that wasn't a good idea, Xavier. I don't plan to start our relationship with even more deception lies than I was already forced to keep."

"We don't have a relationship, psycho! There's no you and me, or us. And you," I said, pointing at my dad. "You don't get to dictate my life anymore. You lost that ability when you lied to me about everything. Don't you understand? You had no intention of ever accepting me, did you? You meant for Sandra to give birth to your child in a safe space, and what was the plan once I was born? Ditch us? Your mate was pregnant, and you loved her. I know that to be true. You wanted Noah, but me? I was an inconvenience until the moment I could benefit you. No child deserves to be done that way. But you went beyond that, which is why you broke the spell on Micah. He couldn't have me, because you'd already struck a deal with Kieran for me to belong to him. So not only did you wreck what could have been for me in the past, but you stole my future too, by giving me to Kieran. You've taken enough from me, father." I stepped back, shaking my head as I sidestepped the men to exit the room.

Xavier thought he could stop me by stealing my shit? The master of deception had taught me himself. I had a backup plan. I also had more options if any of those fell through. I had over three hundred ID cards and credentials stashed around the continent. I'd hidden money in offshore accounts and buried some beneath rocks in the woods across America. I made friends with many people not associated with the hunters' guild, just for this purpose.

I didn't need my dad or the things he'd taken. If I wanted out, nothing would stop me. As hunters, we often had to hide for weeks or months in the forest. I knew every vacant cabin, hut, and hunter's perch within 1,000 miles. I had been dropped deep inside 100,000 thickly wooded acres at twelve, forced to survive with nothing but a knife and the world around me. If he thought stealing a few items from me would halt my exit strategy, he was sorely mistaken. All three men were watching me with wary looks on their faces.

"Your funeral will begin shortly. I suggest you put on whatever face it is you intend to wear tonight. The guests have taken their seats already, and the fires should be lit within ten minutes. I'll meet you downstairs. What is it I call you now?"

"Your father, Xariana," he growled.

"Oh my, haven't you heard? He's dead. Wouldn't want to confuse the attendees, now would we?" I asked, sliding my gaze to Kieran, who watched me carefully. "Unless, of course, you've changed your mind about tonight?"

"We're going to get through this, Kid."

"No, you are. Me? I'll survive because it is embedded in my fucking DNA. That doesn't mean I intend to get through anything. Now, stick a pin in it, and prepare for another shit show that's about to go down. I need a fucking drink, or ten."

Chapter Thirty-Four

My fingers slid over the rim of my glass, uncaring that tears rolled down my cheeks. It was my father's funeral, after all. Tonight would be the only time I allowed myself the weakness, needing to give the funeral-goers a show. The sound of feet moving through the hallway forced me to wipe my face, and I lifted the glass, taking a sip, and closing my eyes as the liquid burned its way down my throat. Pouring another drink, I downed it before a hand reached out, grabbing the bottle away from me.

"You need to be sober in case anything happens," my dad ordered.

I slid my stare over his face, turning to look in the mirror at his reflection. Micah's image watched me, and I swallowed down the irony that my father chose to assume the identity of my ex-fiancé, whom he'd personally fucked over, to attend his funeral.

Dropping my eyes to my hands, I narrowed my gaze before darting it to his. "Where is Micah?"

"He's been reassigned," he informed smoothly, as if he hadn't just stated he'd relocated one of my team members and oldest friends without letting me know first.

"Excuse me?" I asked, blinking slowly while he filled a glass for himself to the rim with the whiskey.

"Micah wasn't willing to come to terms with what had happened here. He chose to leave and be stationed someplace else. If you make it through tonight, I may even tell you where he is. It was his choice, Kid."

"And he chose not to say goodbye?" I asked, sensing all the people in the room watching us with worry exuding from their pores.

My dad and I had never fought, ever. I didn't argue with his orders or second guess them until now. But things had changed, and I wasn't able to give him that trust because he'd broken it. In our world, trusting the person at your back meant everything. If you couldn't depend on them to guard you or to watch it, you had nothing.

"Micah didn't want to make a scene," he replied, slowly lifting his glass. "Try to use his example, Xariana. Once we've finished here, you can take a few days in your apartment to rediscover yourself and accept what has happened. I cannot undo it, and I can't stand here and say I would, either. What was done is done. Get over it, and move on."

"As you wish, Xavier," I said firmly, squaring my shoulders as I marched toward the doors that Ezekiel and Enzo prepared to open into the backyard, where the ceremony was beginning.

"No theatrics, Kid. Keep to the plan, and just do as you'd intended to do before you knew I wasn't dead. I went through the plans you made, and if I had died, I'd have been proud of you. No hunter could want more from his child," he admitted, causing my stomach to churn and bile to burn the back of my throat.

You Should Be Here, by Cole Swindell, played outside the door, and I blinked away the prickling of tears. Straightening my shoulders once more, and shaking off his hand, I spun, smiling coldly.

"I'm glad you approve," I lied. The smile on my father's lips thinned as the doors was opened.

Exiting the house, I walked tall. I didn't balk at the glances or the pitying stares that turned my way. I ignored them, heading to the makeshift podium. The heavy weight of those watching me was smothering, and the grief and sadness within the yard only made it more so.

Standing on the small wooden stage, I stared at the crowd, focusing my attention on the front row, where my father sat, wearing Micah's face. Looking away, I waited for the song to end before I swallowed and exhaled to calm myself.

"Today marks the end of an era. My—Xavier Anderson was one of a kind," I stated, fumbling over the title that littered the paper I was reading. "They say you don't get the parents you want. You get the ones you need. Xavier was that to all of us. Each and every one of us that was abandoned and left to rot because of our differences. He created something here. It's bigger than we could have ever prayed to find." I glanced at the words, watching them blur with the denial and anger that shot through me. Wadding up what I'd written before finding out he wasn't dead, I tossed the paper from the stage, listening to the murmurs running through the crowd as my father rose, fully intending to intervene. "I'm not going to stand up here and read some pre-written shit that came from the heart. That isn't us. We accept death as part of this job. We know one day it will come for us. Those blessed with immortality can succumb to it, and sooner or later, you die. It's part of living. We live by the sword, and we understand we will eventually die by it, too." I slipped my gaze to the next page, nodding as I found the hunter's poem.

"Every life is a light, and when it's extinguished, this world becomes a little darker. Xavier was a bright light that shone in even the darkest of places. It was as if the sun came into the room on his shoulders, kissing the flesh of those around him. You could always say the sun was close to him, but as hunters, we don't know that element well."

Xavier's eyes flashed in silent warning, and I slowly blew the air out of my lungs. The crowd echoed their agreement, and I waited for them to calm down once more. I scanned their faces, noting each one that wasn't paying attention to the eulogy.

"When the road ends, and my hunt is finished, do not grieve for me. Let me go. When the sun sets and the moon rises, think of me, but do not mourn as I am finally free. This earthly body and useless flesh wasn't enough to house the soul set free. I neither need nor want any funeral rites in a gloomy field. Why would you be sad or grieve for a soul that has been released? You may miss me and cherish the time you had with me, but do not drink for me with your head bowed. Lift it instead for the memories we made. Hunters know that our time is short, and that life is fleeting. We understand death is a journey we must walk alone, a final hunt that no one else can take with us. When you remember me, go to a friend, and find solace in the living, for the dead do not weep. Laugh at the things we did together, but do so with pride." I tampered down the emotion, sliding my eyes back to my dad. "For I am gone, and this isn't me. I am not this weakness that you feel, nor this desolate despair that clouds the air. I am a hunter, and I am strong. I know that life doesn't end here, because I will always go on through you and the others that will come after me. I am infinite. I am the song you will play and hear while you recall a moment shared. I am the air that floods your lungs when you run after prey and make this world a better place. I am not shrouded upon the pyre, for this flesh does not house me any longer. Salt my bones, and burn it to ash, for fire brings new beginnings and cleanses the world of lost souls."

I stepped back, staring off into the sea of vehicles spread out in the field beyond the gates of the estate. James Blunt's Monsters started through the speakers, and I shifted, moving toward one of the fires, grabbing a handful of salt and a smudge stick of sage. Talia's eyes caught mine, and I nodded, standing ready to burn the body of my father's twin brother the moment she'd finished blessing it to return to the earth.

Silently, I watched her and the witches placing flowers and herbs over his corpse. Ironically, it was a full blessing for the monster that had hurt others. It had to be perfect, though, because most of the creatures present tonight would know if one thing was done incorrectly. Xavier had even changed the setting, removing the covering from the head to ensure they saw his face and thought him dead.

Once the witches finished their part of the ceremony, I stepped forward, holding the salt in my hand. Xaven looked exactly the same as Xavier. There wasn't a single thing I could find that would signal to anyone else that he wasn't the man that had raised me. A hand touched my shoulder, and I turned, peering at Micah—my dad, before I jerked my arm away and tossed the salt onto his brother.

"And with this salt, I return your spirit from whence it came. May you find peace and solace in death, Xavier," I whispered, lighting the smudge stick from the flame beside the body, tossing it on the deceased. I moved as the flames rose, rendering Xaven to ashes and embers that lifted into the darkening sky, catching the wind.

It would be really ironic if we ended up causing a forest fire from a mock funeral. Turning from the dead, I walked to the spot where we had planned for me to accept condolences, but instead of remaining there, I walked to the podium.

"Drink, and find peace tonight. Tomorrow we return to hunting," I stated firmly. "Noah will lead us into the next prayer, but I find that I need a moment for myself. I will change my clothes, and then we'll all drink to the memories of Xavier Anderson, the founding father of this establishment."

My dad narrowed his eyes on me, but the crowd seemed appeased by my need for some time alone. Plus, I wanted out of the outfit. I entered the house the way we'd come, feeling eyes on my spine while I made my way up the staircase and to the baby's room.

No sooner had I slipped out of the dress, than a knock sounded on my door. I opened it a sliver, peeking through the crack to find my father staring through it, lowering his gaze to my exposed side.

"Did you need something? Maybe send in my babysitter if you don't trust me to get changed and return to the party, Xavier," I offered, watching his eyes close before he nodded.

"Make it fast, Kid. Noah is floundering out there," he muttered.

"It isn't my job to save his ass. It was to become a sacrificial lamb to protect his life. Nothing else," I snorted, waiting for him to reply with something. Anything would have been better than the pain-filled stare that locked with mine before he stepped back, allowing me to close the door.

Shoving away my emotions, I put on a pair of pants, a snug tank top, and boots. As soon as I was clothed, I went to the bathroom, staring down at the needle-nose pliers. Ignoring them for the moment, I pulled my hair into a tight ponytail and then grabbed them. I slipped into the bedroom and walked out onto the balcony, arranging my clothes on it.

Steeling my strength, I used the pliers to remove my back tooth, where the tracking device was implanted. Smothering the scream of pain, I spat out the blood before dropping the molar on the pile of discarded clothing.

Peering at my watch, I jumped on the railing and leaped down, landing on my feet. I hit the ground running, pumping my legs as hard as they would go. When my hands gripped the fence, I projected my body over it, never slowing down until I rounded the rock formation just beyond the property line.

I skidded to a halt as a dark figure stepped from the shadows, grabbing me and teleporting me a mile away, snatching my hand to slice through it. My blood dripped onto the ground, and I smiled coldly, darting around the male to run the next leg of the Journey.

Another male grabbed me, and then another, moving space and time to put distance between myself and the estate I was leaving. Stopping suddenly on a cliff, I snatched the climbing gear, shimmying into it before I propelled down the sheer cliffside, ensuring my blood was covering the rope. Once my feet were back on land, I allowed the next man to transport me to the waiting car.

A smile twisted my lips as I approached the Bugatti that had been taken from outside the funeral, right beneath Kieran's nose. Sliding into the driver's seat, I started the sleek beast up, inhaling the owner's enticing scent deeply. The engine revved to life, and I had a moment of regret about what I was going to do.

Starting forward, I pushed my foot against the gas pedal, smiling while it raced ahead. Rounding the curve at the end of the straightaway, I stopped, opening the door to exit the car as one of my accomplices turned, grinning at me. He hefted a corpse that matched my body mass, size, and bone structure into the seat and maneuvered it toward the canyon's edge.

"Such a waste." I actually felt bad for sending Kieran's sleek, expensive thirteen million-dollar car into the canyon. But only a little. He deserved it for his part in my pain.

The man pushed it from behind, and it toppled over the cliffs of the canyon. He grabbed my healed hand, and we appeared in a room bathed in light. Axton smirked, sliding his gaze down my frame before he spoke.

"You're certain you wish to do this?" he asked, his stare searching mine with understanding, then he nodded. "You know he will hunt you down. Kieran won't give up if he claimed you, Xariana."

"I'm just Ana now, Axton. There's no part of that girl left in this body. My father named me, and that life isn't mine anymore. As of today, I am Ana Hunter." I smiled, which was the first real one I'd given in days. Exhaling, I spun as Onyx and Kaderyn entered the room, staring at me.

Chapter Thirty-Five

I stared at Onyx and Kaderyn, waiting for them to speak. Kaderyn moved closer, smiling with a swollen cheek, presumably from removing her tracker. I'd instructed them through the dark web about what to do and where to meet me before I'd sensed Kieran slinking outside my room. Xavier had pocketed my phone, but I'd had one hidden on my person. No one knew about it other than Noah, my closest friends, and Axton, who had been implemented into my escape plan since before my dad had gone missing.

If nothing else, he had instilled the need to survive in me, no matter what I had to do to achieve it. He'd taught me to blend in to avoid detection. He had done that right, and I intended to use every single tool he'd handed me to run from him and this town tonight.

"You both removed the trackers?" I needed to ensure everything was unfolding as planned.

"Of course," Onyx stated, flipping her hair. "Not an amateur."

"Are you going to tell us what is happening?" Kaderyn asked, noting how my expression crumpled. "It's bad, isn't it?"

"From where I see it, yes. You guys aren't required to come with me. I need you both to know that. I can do this on my own."

"Is it about who murdered your father?" she continued, scrubbing her hand over her face. "Don't answer that," she amended, sliding her attention to Axton, who hiked a dark brow at her as if he was offended.

"I'll explain it all once we are safe and away from this town. I promise you I didn't decide on this course of action easily or without the right mindset to begin an escape strategy. We can only use it once, though, and if it fails, the backup plan will include the sewers."

"We weren't noticed leaving, and the alerts went off when our trackers went dead. They'll think we died or left willingly. We've now entered dangerous territory. They're searching for us, and we are in the center of town," Onyx pointed out, narrowing her eyes at the tears pooling in mine.

"Yeah, we're borrowing Axton's car, and they'll be following us until we reach the border. They expect us to be in the woods, on foot. My jeep is in the compound, still damaged from the initial attack, so they'll assume we're without transportation. No vehicles from the hunters' guild are missing. The Bugatti is at the bottom of the canyon, which they'll trace back to me by the amount of blood I left inside. The trackers sent to find us will count on it. Noah is buying us time. He will have the pack of hellhounds he's been running with alerted to the blood trail. The guild will need their assistance to get the car and body out of the ravine."

"Body?" Kaderyn asked, flinching as I snorted.

"I had one on ice that I killed a year ago. Once a year, I pick a hunt where the perpetrator has a similar bone structure to me and could pass as a sibling. It will take them time to confirm that it's not me inside that car, dead from crashing into the ravine. I plan to drive right by them. They're expecting us to do what our training has taught us, which is to go into the thick forest. If they don't buy the body theory, they will think we're running into the mountains. We're doing the last thing they'd anticipate. We are leaving town while they watch us. I believe the convoy that Micah was sent out in should only be a few hours ahead of us. Axton's Humvee holds enough gas that we can catch up to them before needing to refuel. He's also agreed to be the distraction, helping us to appear as a bunch of bimbos he's taking home to bang."

Both women snorted, rolling their eyes at Axton, who smirked. We all knew he was an insufferable playboy and horribly vain. That was one of the reasons I liked him, along with his unapologetic attitude toward the world.

"It's been a pleasure, Ana. But I suggest we get moving. The morning is coming, and with it, more chances of your plan going awry. I already placed the belonging you stored here into the car. Shall we?" he asked, and I slowly approached him, peering up into his amber eyes.

"Thank you for not being the bad guy," I whispered.

"I'm not the good guy either," he countered, forcing me to smile.

"Sometimes it isn't the good guy we need. It's the right guy at the right time," I returned, as his eyes sparkled with amusement.

"Kieran will probably kill me for this, and I don't even get a kiss?" He lowered his mouth to mine, and I spun away at the last moment. "Had to try, right?"

"You're incorrigible." I pulled back to push him away playfully. "You have the light ready?" I asked, knowing that Kieran would know where to find me when I stepped into the shadows.

One of Axton's men came forward, producing a high wattage light that he turned on, forcing all of us to shield our eyes from it. I'd spent time with Talia tonight, learning what her people had discovered about Kieran and the King of Shadows. He had limitations, but not many. Artificial light and daylight kept his shadows from being able to travel, making it harder for him to find anything he was hunting. That meant that I would spend a lot of time sunbathing.

Talia had supplied herbal bags and remedies that would keep us from being detected. She had also given me the names of witches I could trust when my supplies dwindled. Axton opened the door, and his guard stepped out into the alleyway. An army of SUVs sat in the front and back of us. He seldom, if ever, traveled without his guards.

The only time I'd seen him alone, outside his club, was in front of the guild when he spoke to me. I scanned the cars, walking with the light until Axton slid into the Humvee and turned on the interior lights. Of course, he had a vehicle decked out with lights, a sound system, and plush leather. I settled into the passenger seat, exhaling the stress before Onyx, Kaderyn, and I popped the corks off the potions that would alter our appearances. It was the same one Xavier had used to attend his funeral, but only those in the car and the one guard would be able to see our real face.

Herbs protected my scent and ensured that no one caught a whiff on our way past the accident scene. I scanned the floor, finding the hex bags to keep shadows out, which wouldn't seem off to Kieran since Axton normally included them within his territory when he wanted privacy.

"Once we are a few miles from town, the Humvee is all yours," Axton stated. "You can't go on foot because they're moving quickly. Noah was forced to call in reinforcements from the funeral at the behest of Micah, to find you before you did something in your grief-stricken state. I'll take you to the state line, and you can move through Idaho easily. They won't think you made it that far. Do you have places there to hide?" he asked, watching me as engines started up all around us.

"I'll be fine. It's best you don't know the plan from there. Kieran might come to you for answers once the herb-enhanced scents end. Not to mention, you're giving up this beast, and he will notice that. I think it's better that you give us one of the SUVs instead. I may not like you all the time, but I also don't want you dead."

"Aw, you like me," he grinned, shaking his head. "This is the only car that has lights installed, I'm afraid. As you're aware, it isn't unheard of for me to go missing for days. Once I emerge from this drunken orgy, I will learn that three inebriated beauties have stolen my baby. A reward will be offered, but you will have found the cash in the back and abandoned it to purchase a new vehicle by then. Or so I assume. Being a playboy known for having disastrous shit befall him often has its perks. There's also the potion I will drink, removing all memories of tonight from my mind, thanks to a saucy witch."

"Thank her for me."

"I won't remember to, but she said to tell you that you're welcome," he muttered, putting on his seatbelt. "They tend to have a keen knowledge of the future."

"She's intuitive," I stated, knowing exactly who had made certain no one would be hurt by my exit strategy being activated when I'd walked out of Kieran's house as my world had fallen apart.

"It's fucking creepy no matter how you sugarcoat it," he muttered, starting forward as the line of SUVs filed in around us. "If the hunters stop us, one of you better be on my lap, groping me. Not Xar. If Kieran claimed her, he would feel her when she's touched."

"Trade me places, Kaderyn."

I climbed into the back, frowning as we drove through the backstreets of town. It was silent, but I knew there were hunters within it, watching the major arterial streets. Of course, Noah would have had to order it, and if he hadn't, my father would have known he was allowing holes to be opened for me to slip through. I hated leaving Noah behind, but he needed to stay where he would be safe and protected if he were truly being hunted. Out in the world, nothing could prevent the fae from taking him, not even me.

We hit the highway that led out of town, and it took only a few moments for us to reach the first roadblock. The sheriff shined his flashlight in the car, scanning each of our faces, oblivious to the fact we were the ones they were trying to find. A pang of regret tightened my chest, but Onyx patted my leg, smiling tightly at me as one hunter watched her.

"Where you heading, Axton?" Jeffery inquired, still shining the bright light on Axton's face.

"Home to get fucked. Where the hell do you think I'm going?" he asked, sliding his golden gaze to the passenger seat, where Kaderyn was giggling, rubbing up against him. "Can we go? Or do you wish to check all the cars? You can, but it will be a waste of time."

Jeffery didn't comment to Axton, but the hunter beside the sheriff did. "Search them all and any space large enough to fit a body. Be quick about it."

Axton shrugged, pulling a squealing Kaderyn onto his lap. He cupped her behind the neck, bringing her mouth flush against his. The hunter's lips peeled back, and his eyes rolled at what he was being forced to watch. It took a while for them to search every crevice, but eventually, we were allowed through the blockade and on our way again.

Kaderyn didn't climb off of Axton's lap, however. I had been about to comment on it when I caught the hunters off the road watching the cars passing their locations. Snorting, I had to admit that Axton was insightful about how to escape, but it also raised the question of how much shit he'd gotten away with over the years.

He looked at me over Kaderyn's head, as if he was sensing what I was thinking. His eyes crinkled with a smile, and he returned to nuzzling her throat while she mimicked doing the same to his. Flashing blue and red lights became visible through the darkness of night, and I forced my mind to clear and my emotions not to give us away.

Xavier stood beside the road near Noah, while Kieran stared at his destroyed sports car. I fought the urge to groan at seeing the Bugatti rendered to nothing more than charred, bent metal. Hunters stopped the convoy and asked questions while I peered at the trio.

Noah was staring at the body being cut from the car. My dad had tears swimming in his eyes, no doubt feeling the pain I'd felt at finding his corpse. It didn't bring me any joy, though. I'd thought it might, but watching his grief mar his expression only made me need to fight harder to hide my emotions.

Someone said something, and Xavier dropped to his knees, and a sob ripped from his throat. Kieran stared at the burned remains with a strange look on his face before sliding it to where we sat, observing the scene. Pain wasn't a good look churning in his violet, diamond-speckled depths.

Abandoning the Bugatti, he slowly walked toward

the line of vehicles that had been stopped, lifting his nose into the air. He placed his hands on the window, indicating for Axton to lower it. Kieran pushed his head inside the car the moment it was down, slowly searching each of us before he turned to Axton.

"What the fuck happened to your car?" Axton asked, his tone giving nothing away.

"Fuck off, asshole," Kieran hissed, but the emotion in his voice wasn't sadness. It was fury, undiluted, pent-up rage. "Xariana was in it, apparently."

"When it went over the fucking cliff?" Axton countered.

"She isn't that fucking stupid. I'm guessing she placed a body inside and is somewhere watching this unfolding with amusement. She's my fucking savage, psychopathic mate. She's perfect for me, don't you agree?"

I ignored the way Axton tensed when Kieran had said the word mate. I studied Kieran, ignoring how Onyx slowly teased my thigh, which drew Kieran's eyes to it with laser focus. Her hand moved, and his head tilted, taking everything within me to keep my heartbeat steady and even.

"She is rather rabid and savage. I guess if I were playing matchmaker, you'd be the one male who could tame that murderous little vixen."

Kieran smiled, and I had to control myself for an entirely different reason. "What are you fucking up to, Axton?" he asked smoothly, searching my face before he focused on the male in the front seat.

"Trying to get fucked," he returned. "What if it isn't a body she planted? What happens if that is her?" Kaderyn's eyes moved to mine, her face hidden against Axton's neck, where she made sexy sounds.

"I'm not even going to entertain that fucking thought. Let's just say I'd destroy everything if she left me. Everything and everyone," he clarified adamantly, causing a shudder to rush down my spine. "If she believed I was a psychopath before, she hasn't seen anything yet."

Axton shivered, and I clamped down on the one that tried to shoot through me. Kieran's eyes slid to mine, narrowing on them, making me squirm. Tilting my head, I grinned coyly at him, patting the seat beside me.

"How about you join us?" I asked in a sultry tone that wasn't my own, and his glare narrowed to slits.

I watched him push off the car, but before it started rolling down the road, he turned and smiled in a way that made my blood curdle.

"If I find out you helped her escape me, I will murder you. I'll do it so slowly that you won't die anytime soon, but you'll beg me to fucking end it. Unfortunately, you don't have anyone left to torture, but that won't save you from me. I will bathe in your blood and make you watch as I cut each organ from your body and feed it to my dogs. Remember that, and consider if it's smart to cross me, Axton. I am aware of who you are and from where you've come. I know which kingdom to bring to its fucking knees. Fuck with me, and I will fuck you harder. I don't use lube either, asshole." He strode away from the Humvee, and I slid my attention to my dad, who had yet to stand. Instead, Noah had sat beside him, awkwardly patting him on the back.

Axton's gaze met mine as I adjusted in the seat. The girls were both staring out at Micah's form, and the looks on their faces threatened to reveal us. The cars started forward, and I shifted slightly, glancing at Kieran, who watched us slowly drive away from the accident site.

"Kieran knows that you're his mate. Which means he won't ever stop searching for you," Axton whispered, barely above a breath of sound. "He will rip apart this world until you're back here, where he can protect you." His voice was shaken by what Kieran had promised to do to him. I didn't doubt he'd do it, either. The man was a psychopathic asshole who got off on scaring the shit out of everyone. It was sexy and disturbing. "Are you turned on right now?" Axton demanded, his eyes growing wide at the way I fidgeted.

"Some people like prince charming. Apparently, I'm into psychopaths," I muttered, smiling as he snorted, shaking his head.

We drove toward the border between Washington and Idaho, where we would part ways. I didn't have a plan past escaping this town, but I knew my worth and that I needed space. Time could heal wounds, but it wouldn't change what had created the damage.

When we reached Idaho, Axton exited the vehicle, unfolded his ungodly tall frame from the driver's seat, and leaned against the door. I settled beside him, taking in the beauty of the rising sun over the mountain range.

"I realize you can't tell me where you're going or what you intend to do, Xariana. Whatever it is, I hope you survive this journey and that you find what you're looking to discover. Come home when you have the answers," Axton said, exhaling as we watched the sunrise.

"I'm not sure what I'm doing yet," I admitted, chewing my bottom lip before blowing the air from my lungs. "I do have to get Micah back. I owe him that much. His life was fucked up because of me. I have no intention of letting Xavier send him off to someplace that he'll never be heard from again. I'll vanish for a little while and remain hidden until I want them to find me. You know me, I always come back."

"This time is different, though. Isn't it? You're not running from some guy that cheated on you. You're leaving behind the people that betrayed you. That changes shit. Your father was what brought you back here, and your friends came in second to him. What he did to you, that sort of shit will fuck with you forever. It can't be healed, Xari. It is a part of you, and you need to understand that. It's what created you and why you're here. Refuse to sink and stand tall instead. Don't let it change you, though, not too much anyway."

"Words of wisdom, or something you lived through?" I questioned, turning to take in his side profile.

"Both," he snorted, pushing off the vehicle. "Don't beat my beast up too badly. I do like her, and she's custom-made."

"Axton," I moved toward him, wrapping my arms around his neck, hugging him tightly. "Thank you. I can't pay you back, because what you're doing for me is huge. I can, however, make sure that Kieran doesn't torture you. If you get into trouble, use this if you need to reach me." I handed him a small, decorative skull that looked more like a charm than an emergency alert. "You tap the button three times, wait a full sixty seconds, and repeat the three clicks. It will set off the alarm I have on my phone, and I'll know it's you." Pulling off his necklace, he attached it, giving me a crooked smile.

"What can you do against that psychopath? If he really wants me dead, Xari, I'm dead."

"I have something he wants more than you. I have me, Axton. He won't kill you. The torture part, though—" I made a face, wincing when he laughed nervously. "We're all going to be fine. We'll be okay."

I watched him as he slipped into the waiting SUV and headed back the way we'd come. I looked at the girls and snorted.

"Guess we should catch us a convoy and free my ex," I chuckled, sliding my ass onto the seat Axton had abandoned. I adjusted the seat and mirror before looking at Kaderyn, who studied me from the seat beside mine. "My father is alive, and he used a potion to look like Micah, which I'm sure you picked up on. Noah is my brother," I admitted, waiting as they grasped the gravity of what that meant. "I was used all these years as a shield to protect Xavier's son." I explained the gist of it, skipping over minor details. "In short, I was fucking bait. Now, do you choose to continue with me or do you want to remain here?"

"I'm with you, Xar," she stated, eyeing Onyx, who

hadn't spoken through the entire conversation.

"Of course I'm with you," she grunted, rolling her eyes. "That's fucked up."

"Yeah, well, this next part is where you may freak out a bit. I intend to build a hunting party of our own, and figure out how to get into the Otherworld. Once we're there, we will find a way to end this war before it even begins. First, we should gather supplies and lie low until they end their search for us. My father painted a target on my back, and then he regretted it. Kieran showed the fae I was immune to iron. But that won't be enough for them to stop searching for Noah. I won't let him die or allow them to reach him, either. I want to give myself time to figure out how to return with this fracture that Xavier drove between us. We'll need them for this plan to work, but not until all the pieces are in place."

I had mapped out a direction, but how to implement it remained a mystery. In no world would I allow the fae to get Noah. Finding out he was my brother had been a low blow, but I'd never really thought of him as anything else. He had always been a brother to me, at least in my eyes.

Turning the ignition over, I started us down the empty freeway. It didn't matter what happened, because, in the end, we'd be okay. We were trained to survive, and that was embedded within us, taught from birth.

I had been driving for hours before a group of cars that were pulled off of the highway caught my attention. "Bingo. That's got to be the team escorting Micah to his new location." I declared, grinning as the unmoving, standard-issued guild vehicles sat silently on the side of the road.

I smiled, turning to the girls that were digging through their bags for weapons. My gaze settled on the motionless cars, and the blood drained from my face. The mutilated remains of hunters came into view, and my world spun around me. Cop sirens blared behind us, and while I slowed as we rolled past the wreckage, we didn't stop.

"What could have done that much fucking damage?" Onyx asked, peering out the back window. "I count five bodies within sight, and none of them are Micah. There's a vehicle missing, too. Look at the tire tracks at the front of the caravan. Someone wanted away from it in a hurry."

"Well, we aren't leaving Idaho quite yet, ladies," I muttered, as the cop exited a car, emptying his stomach onto the ground beside the dismembered corpses. "I guess we're going hunting for whatever, or whoever, did that to our people. We'll need to stay low profile, because we're not far enough away from the guild. There's a cabin a few miles off the main road that I used to frequent with Micah when we wanted to be alone. Get your weapons out and prepare for the unexpected. Something tore through every car of the convoy easily, which means we're not safe yet. We're also in Lycan territory. That will complicate things a bit."

I hadn't expected to hunt this close to the guild, but I wasn't going to abandon Micah. His life had been destroyed because of me. I owed it to him to make this right.

I needed to heal, but that would take a while. I'd lost everything. My identity was gone, and that meant I had to settle into my new one as Ana Hunter. I had to rediscover who I was and who I wanted to be now. I had to figure myself out because I had to be the warrior they would need me to be when I returned.

I was planning to go against the fae, to end the slaughter of our women. They were stealing our wombs, using our genetics to create their children. If the fae believed they could get away with that, they were dead wrong. I may not have been the princess I thought I was, but I would become the beast they would fear.

Kieran was insane, but he had the right idea. You didn't have to be a hero to win. You just had to run out of fucks to give them, and I had. My basket was empty. My entire world had been flipped upside down, but I would choose how that changed me. I don't want to be the good guy anymore. Being the better person is exhausting. I am tired of playing by the rules and sticking pins into the grenade of my emotions.

The pin was out.

My new identity is beginning to form.

With it, they wouldn't recognize the monster they made or the beast they were unleashing.

I'm returning, and when I do, I will show them why you don't break people, because they learn how to live with those tattered pieces. They're scarier and more resilient because it was the only thing they had left. They were tougher because surviving what destroyed them made them choose between giving up or coming out stronger and more independent. I won't lie down and die, nor would I give up. I am not weak. I am a powerful woman, and they are about to hear me fucking roar.

The end, for now

Other series by Amelia Hutchins

Legacy of the Nine Realms

Aria and her sisters return to the Human Realm of Haven Falls to find one of their own that's gone missing. They soon discover things have changed in the Human Realm and that nothing is what it seems, including Knox, the egotistical, self-centered, frustratingly gorgeous man who declared himself King during their absence.

Sparks fly when the two enter a fiery battle of wills as Aria learns she is more than just a witch in the Hecate bloodline; she is much, much more.

Will Aria embrace her savage side to find her sister and save her family, or will she burn to ashes from his heated kisses and burning hot embrace?

Knox has ulterior motives for being in Haven Falls and never expected the little witch to show up and brazenly challenge his rule.

It was supposed to be easy; get in and get out. Move pieces into place and set the stage for the war he's been planning for over five hundred years. Aria is his sworn enemy but something within her calls to him and he hates himself for craving the fiery kisses that have reignited his cold, dead heart. One taste and he thought he could get her out of his system. He was wrong.

Will Knox let go of the memories of the past, driving his need for revenge that will destroy the pretty little witch he craves, or will he push the boundaries to fight for and claim what is his by right? Either way, war is inevitable. And nothing will stop him from reaching for what is his.

Epic Fantasy with heavy love-hate situations with adult situations.

Bulletproof Damsel Urban Fantasy Series

One sassy female weapons master...who doesn't get out much.

One alpha-hole who lays claim to her the moment he sets eyes on her.

She's a weapon in the hands of her enemies, and Rhys intends to use her.

An ancient family feud between the legendary Van Helsing's and Silversmith's who once made their legendary weapons...

What can possibly go wrong?

When Remington comes face to face with Rhys Van Helsing, the world will never be the same again.

For Remington Silversmith? Apparently everything.

The Fae Chronicles – Paranormal Romance

Finished series

Have you ever heard of the old Celtic legends of the Fae, beautiful, magical, deadly and a love of messing with humans just for kicks and giggles?

Welcome to my world.

What started out as a strange assignment, leads to one of the most gruesome murder mysteries of our times and my friends and I are set and determined to find out who is killing off Fae and Witches alike.

Couple of problems in the way. I hate the Fae and the Prince of the Dark Fae is bound and determined that I work for him. He's a rude, overbearing egotistical ass with a compulsive need to possess, dominate and control me. Oh, did I mention that he is absolutely sex-on-a-stick gorgeous and he makes me feel things that I never ever wanted to feel for a Fae…every time he touches me or looks at me with those golden eyes seems to pull me further in under his spell, despite my better judgment.

My friends and I can't trust anyone and nothing is as it seems on the surface. Not even me.

Monster series Dark Fantasy Romance

My coven has remained hidden in the shadows for centuries.

We've avoided the 'real world' altogether; hiding from monsters

and other creatures we share this planet with.

We found protection in the Colville National Forest, nestled in a town protected by magical barriers.

Our powers are locked by an ancient curse, one meant to protect us from being found.

Until now.

The past has a way of repeating itself. A new game is beginning. No one is safe.

He's coming for me.

He's hunting.

The monster we've run from for centuries has found us.

How far will this deadly game go?

How far will I be able to take it, or will he destroy me and everything I care about?

Will the one thing I can't live without, be the key to destroying and undoing the past?

Or will the past destroy me before I can save the people I love from what I've done.

Moon-Kissed High Fantasy

Alexandria Helios is on a mission to find her brother. Landon disappeared on his quest to find the Sacred Library that holds the cure to the moon sickness affecting their people. There is one problem. Her journey will take her through the Kingdom of Night and directly into Torrin's path as the head of the Night King's army. He's egotistical, sexy, sin incarnate, and everything she knows she shouldn't want, but his whispered promise of dark desires awakens something deep within her that makes him hard to resist.

Torrin didn't expect the lead assassin of the Moon Clan to walk into his trap. Alexandria has ignited something within him he thought was gone, and he knows he shouldn't crave her, but he does. She's a fire in a world of ice, bathed in blood and moonlight that calls to the darkness within him.

Secrets are unraveling as both are tossed into a ploy that neither is destined to survive. Can they find common ground and work together to defeat the darkness? Or will the world come crashing down around them as they tear each other apart?

Made in United States
Orlando, FL
16 January 2022

13547724R00221